Readers Love *Oathsworn*

"…it shows what a real relationship is all about. The good, the bad and the ugly. And for that, it made me appreciate this story so much more."
—Love Bytes Reviews

"…I was drawn in by the puzzle of being magically ensnared and a non-magic person learning of this whole new world."
—Paranormal Romance Guild

By SEBASTIAN BLACK

CHARMD SAGA
Oathsworn
Wishborne
Soulspawn

Published by DREAMSPINNER PRESS
www.dreamspinnerpress.com

Wishborne

Sebastian Black

Published by
DREAMSPINNER PRESS

5032 Capital Circle SW, Suite 2, PMB# 279, Tallahassee, FL 32305-7886 USA
www.dreamspinnerpress.com

Trade Paperback ISBN: 978-1-64108-668-4
Digital ISBN: 978-1-64108-667-7
Trade Paperaback published September 2023
v. 1.0

Printed in the United States of America
∞
This paper meets the requirements of
ANSI/NISO Z39.48-1992 (Permanence of Paper).

ACKNOWLEDGMENTS

Firstly, I would like to offer my thanks to each member of the Dreamspinner team who was involved in the production of this book. When it comes to cultivating queer fiction, they really know their stuff, and I'm incredibly grateful to have a place on their shelves.

Special thanks are also due to Kris Norris for producing such fabulous cover art for this series. You absolutely nailed it.

And finally, I must express my appreciation to my loving partner, Zac. Thank you for being a continuous sounding board as well as a constant source of sage advice.

CHAPTER ONE

AIRPORTS WERE always something of a pain in the ass, and JFK was no exception. Whether that was down to runway delays, the ever-looming security presence, or the endless capacity of people to display last-minute forgetfulness, Blayze couldn't remember a time when the ordeal was anything less than an eye-watering snorefest. And that was without the events of the last seventy-two hours, when the shit had really hit the fan. Now? Now there seemed to be as many people leaving the country as arriving.

He held his spot in line and danced between each foot on the squeaky marbled floor. The latest family of five finally finished sticker-tagging their fourteen bags, and when it was his turn to step up to the check-in desk, he pasted on a smile, plowed ahead, and prayed to sail through.

"Good morning, sir," chirped the clerk, whose nametag read Monica. She radiated sophistication in a burgundy blazer, and despite being in her early thirties with an oval face and tied-back platinum hair, she'd look for all the world like a beauty blogger if it weren't for the bags under her eyes. "Where are you flying to this afternoon?"

"London," Blayze said, almost asked. He hoped he sounded confident enough not to raise any alarm bells. Though it was extremely unlikely given the time frame, he couldn't be sure if airports had integrated any extra security protocols. He'd soon find out when he passed over his ID.

"Oh, fantastic," Monica chirped, seeming to show genuine interest as she scanned the QR code on his smartphone. "Always wanted to go myself but never found the time. What do you plan to get up to on your trip, and how long will you be staying for?"

Blayze scrunched his brow and wondered for a second if she might be hitting on him. Then he remembered the questioning was mandatory. What was a suitable answer? Telling her he was fleeing the madness of the country because a bunch of his kind had been publicly outed by an independent news press was off the table. And it was probably inappropriate to say he was sick and tired of New York since he'd taken a turn with almost every guy in the city and had recently begun the shameful process of unblocking people. And he *definitely* couldn't confess that when he bussed tables at the Plaza a few years ago, his colleagues bragged about how great the famous London gay scene was, and Blayze had visions of being a kid in a candy store with all the hunky guys to choose from.

Even if all those things were true, he had to think of something else.

"I'm going away to, uhh, see some sights, and I'll be there for exactly one month."

"Lovely." Monica tapped something onto a screen, then held her hand out for his passport. "Only one bag for a whole month? Do you normally pack so light?"

"Yeah," Blayze lied. His pride wouldn't let him tell Monica he didn't want to pay for extra luggage, and though he'd dearly miss an extra five pairs of Levi's, he was sure the hotel would have adequate laundry service. He'd manage with only a week's worth of boxer shorts. With any luck, he'd be spending more time out of his clothes than in them. "It's funny. I'm coming to realize material things aren't all that important in these crazy times, huh?"

Ugh. Why did he have to go and mention it? By the pained look on her face, she probably hadn't planned on addressing the issue, and she also probably didn't want to weigh in her opinion when everything was so up in the air. She was simply doing her job; he was just being paranoid. He sternly told himself to get a grip and keep smiling. There was no way anyone here knew about him or what he could do, and he'd be fine as long as his heart rate chilled the fuck out and his palms stopped sweating.

"Gosh," said Blayze. "I'm so starved I can't wait to get to the food court. Are we close to being done?"

When Monica glanced up at him for a very well-measured two seconds, he swore his life flashed before him. He imagined her jaw dropping to the floor and her finger pointing accusingly as she called over the guards to drag him away to a dusty custom-built prison cell until the world worked out what to do with him. But when she handed back his ID, she switched the smile back on. "We sure are. Have a great trip over the pond, won't you?"

Blayze's shoulders slumped in relief, and he tipped his head by way of thanks, then kicked his bag into position so he could wheel it across the marbled floor. Things were better now that there was a clear path ahead, and with a flutter in his chest, he beelined for the cologne stands. The staff he passed were more than ready to launch into their sales pitches, but he bustled to his tried-and-true, one and only brand—Dior. His holy grail never let him down when it came to hookups, and, eager to be reunited with the ooh-ah-ah sensation, Blayze grabbed two of their largest bottles and the cashier rang them up while he contemplated a third.

"Screw it," he said, grinning at the clerk, who seemed more than welcome to rack up another easy sale. Blayze tapped his gold AmEx credit card and tried not to imagine yet more negative zeroes—that was a problem for future Blayze. Before they so much as touched the bottom of the canvas tote, he couldn't help tearing open a carton and dousing himself in amber nectar.

Leaving duty-free was slightly bittersweet, mostly because it gave a full view of the anarchy that was the airport. Weaving his way up to the departures board with his suitcase in tow, Blayze wondered how many of his brethren were hiding among the normal folk and, more specifically, how they were handling all the ambiguity. He knew of a certain app that could provide a pretty straightforward way to find out... and yet the adrenaline comedown of check-in had given him a sizeable appetite. So he shoved his baying thoughts to the back of his mind and finally entered vacation mode. The first task on the agenda was to sniff out the Golden Arches to see what iteration of burger would befit his much-needed getaway.

HAVING FLOWN to Australia a handful of times, Blayze didn't bat an eyelid at a six-hour haul. Once the safety demo was done, the plane taxied down the runway and soared into the air without a hitch. Tucked away in the back corner next to a window, he tried to get the burned-in images out of his head, but in a short space of time, they had turned into one of those earworm pop songs you can't seem to shake no matter how much you distract yourself. Just in case he'd missed anything, he whipped out his cell again to revisit the world's currently most-watched video.

In the frame, a lithe figure clad in shadowy robes was at the foreground of a cheerfully lit Ferris wheel in Atlantic City. It was night and the footage was maddeningly shaky, but when he raised a hand into the air, it was very plain to see that a dumbass with Electrokinesis had called down a giant bolt of lightning from the sky. It struck the ground and instantly scorched the concrete below him. The brightness of the bolt was quick to wash out the exposure levels on the smartphone camera. There was a loud screech, and then it cut out—no context, no motive, no follow-up post to shed any light on whether it was the real deal or if it was a photoshopped hoax.

Scenes like that took talent to fake, and the account that uploaded it was an everyday homemaker from Cincinnati who had a modest amount of followers, and her personal feed consisted mostly of reblogged crotchet videos with the occasional vegan lasagna how-to thrown in. Maybe she was using a digital alias for personal protection, but even if she were an undercover mage gunning for insurrection, it still begged the question— why post something like that now?

An amateur video was easy enough to discredit, but things got too close for comfort when *The Daily Scoop* followed up with an extensive exposé. They claimed to have eyewitnesses at the source, and even if their slam post was largely based on speculation, that was what every human in the world was doing right now. Speculating. They based most of their arguments on opinions that were a laughable reach, but the world had noticed, people were actively paying attention, and it was disconcerting to watch everyone's eyes as they were glued to news feeds that replayed the same video over and over and over.

No. In his heart of hearts, Blayze knew the truth. The video was no more fake than his Gucci wallet, and because it had always been collective priority number one since birth to conceal mage nature at all costs, it felt like a punch to the gut when it took all of twelve seconds for Joe Bloggs the Stormcaller to toss that notion into the trash. Though he definitely didn't run in the same circles, Blayze couldn't fathom what had compelled the man to do such a thing. There had to be a very, very good reason. Maybe he had been coerced or was under the influence of someone or something. Maybe he'd been defending the planet from a sudden scourge of aliens. Whatever the case, it was hard not to feel a pinch of resentment at the thought of being forcibly outed, and he sure as shit didn't envy what the Magical Regulation Force had in store for him. They would not take this lightly. But it had been years since he worked for them, and it was no longer his issue.

Blayze shoved his phone in his pocket. Even if he was opinionated enough for about three people, he didn't often get political or project many of his world views far beyond his own head. But this was different. This wasn't something he could sit back and watch from a distance or stroll down to the polling station and cast a cheeky little vote on if the occasion suited him. This was his livelihood, his place in the world, his very existence. Something big was bubbling under the surface, and whether it was ultimately resolved with drastic measures or something preferably much more amiable and peaceful, he wondered whether trotting off halfway around the world and letting everyone else deal with the fallout was the best idea.

But he hoped he was doing the right thing by leaving. Only time would tell.

"Good evening again, ladies and gentlemen," cooed a distant voice over the intercom, breaking Blayze free from a deep sleep he hadn't realized he'd fallen into. "We've landed ahead of schedule at Heathrow terminal in London. The temperature outside is a brisk four degrees Celsius, and the local time is 7:17 p.m., exactly five hours ahead of NYC. We hope you enjoy your visit, and it will be our pleasure to accommodate you again soon."

Blayze nodded to himself as he fetched his bag. Vacation time. No more toiling over things he couldn't change. Setting himself a plan, navigating the terminal, and locating a cab for the half-hour drive should take him to around 11:00 p.m.—just enough time to catch a glimpse of some landmarks and dump his bag at the hotel before he swung by a bar.

The British airport was no less confusing than the one back home, though it was mercifully less busy. Electronic passport control gave him another mild panic attack, but Blayze smirked as a horde of passengers sped off to baggage claim while he zipped through arrivals and eventually Nothing to Declare.

Beyond a travelator and a set of rotating doors, the crisp winter air socked him in the face. Bright lights dominated his vison, both in the gloriously moody cityscape and in the clusterfuck of vehicles. He scanned the line of cabs for a vacant one as he zipped up his sweater and pretended to be bothered by the cold. Only once in his life had winter ever bothered him, and if by a very slim chance it did present a concern, he could simply create a toasty campfire between his hands.

Probably best not to do that in public.

"Hey, bud," Blayze greeted a gruff-looking driver with his window down. "You free?"

"Nah, but I am cheap." He chuckled heartily and tapped at his Bluetooth earpiece. Then he paused as if waiting for Blayze to join in on the joke. When he didn't, the driver jerked his head sideways and set his mouth back to a grim line. "Nuffin in this life come free. You'll learn that soon enuff, lad. Jump in already, yeah? Ain't payin' to heat the streets."

Smiling awkwardly, Blayze climbed into the back and shoved his bag to the side. They began to cruise out of the airport before he'd even told the guy the location, and despite the car being roomy, the pine air freshener swaying with every turn didn't quite manage to mask the unmistakable scent of cigarettes that clung to the leather seats.

Blayze eyed the meter and wondered how many pounds he'd already racked up. Was it by time or distance? It seemed uncouth to ask.

"Heading to the Savoy, please."

"Sure thing, Mr. Fancy Pants." The driver whistled through his teeth and then adjusted his shoulders and put both hands on the wheel. The air seemed to change in the vehicle, and it had nothing to do with the air con.

"So, pal, you got any idea woss goin' on back your way?"

"Do you mean that video?"

When he gave Blayze a look of *What else would I mean?* he nodded slowly.

"Not sure what to make of it, to be honest," Blayze fibbed. "All seems so wild and out there."

"Wouldn't worry much, mate. It's all bollocks," claimed the driver. "Don't believe everything you see on the telly, lad. There's 'bout as much chance of those Yanks havin' superpowers as getting me cataracts fixed."

While he appreciated the sentiment in a roundabout way because it meant there were solid seeds of doubt already in people's minds, hearing about the driver's vision impairment wasn't exactly what he wanted when Blayze had entrusted him with his safety.

"Maybe it's some kind of prank?" Blayze offered as they wove through cars at questionable speed.

"Yeh, too right. Probably more of those some stupid teens tryin' to go viral on TokTik."

Though Blayze had heard many stories about the tragedy that was London driving, the journey was surprisingly short and uneventful. He had glimpsed plenty of glittering billboards and boutique stores, mostly as he scrolled listlessly on his cell. He expected everything would look better on foot than out of a grubby window.

When they pulled into a parking bay, Blayze was relieved to see the door attendants busy with a pack of legitimate highfliers. Before they could get the chance to earn a tip, he jumped out of the car, dug into his wallet, and forked over a few of those slippery plastic notes he'd had changed up. The driver had an expectant sort of look written on his face, probably hoping for some generous display of gratuity, but Blayze had heard all about the nonmandatory tipping in this country, and he planned to take full advantage of it.

"Well, you be sure to have a nice night." He waved a hand, palmed his luggage, and headed to the polished steps.

"Sir, please allow me," said a gorgeous blond in a three-piece.

When the twinkish concierge reached out for his luggage, Blayze was so startled that he very nearly let go. Hidden fees on personal services didn't bear thinking about, and once he came to his senses, he jerked a totally awkward sidestep to maintain his hold on his possessions, if not his dignity. "Ah, I'm honestly fine, thank you. Could you, uhh, maybe point me in the direction of reception?"

"Certainly, sir." The boy leaned in, and Blayze welcomed the breach of etiquette when he put a hand on the small of his back and breathed softly, "It's right over there to your left, sir."

Anyone with eyes could've spotted it, and yet something about the way he kept saying *sir* in that British accent was unspeakably alluring, and Blayze found himself wanting to find reasons to keep him talking.

"Ah, yes," Blayze said, absently putting on his classy voice. "There it is. How silly of me."

Now that they were both staring in the direction of reception, he was confident enough to glance at the lines of the concierge's chiseled face and perfectly coiffed hair.

"Thanks a bunch."

"Not a bother, sir. If there's anything you need from me, please do let me know."

Shivering all over, Blayze wondered whether the hotel's customer service accommodation policy covered a night between the sheets. Before the growing bulge in his pants became too much of an issue, he composed himself enough to dart through the revolving doors.

The hotel was exquisite. Everything his eyes touched had some element of gold, whether it was the ornate picture frames, the opulent art-nouveau overhead lighting, or the antique furnishings that looked perilously delicate yet serviceably cozy.

As he headed across the polished black-and-white-checkered marble floor, Blayze spotted another gorgeous specimen standing behind the desk, and he giggled like a teenager. Man, screw the ethics and logistics of a potential mage uprising. He was already so damn horny, and at this rate, if there were any other scorching-hot studs parading about the place, he'd probably bust in his pants before he reached his room.

CHECK-IN WAS a breeze. Arthur, the desk manager who so kindly swiped his credit card for a month in advance—yet another problem for future Blayze—also gave him concise directions to the nearest LGBT+ bar. He was so full of excitement that he barely got the chance to appreciate all the room's magnificence before he hopped in the shower to freshen up.

The salted body scrub still tingled his skin as he changed into a tight-fitting plaid shirt and chinos. He messed his hair up with a dollop of wax, trimmed the five-o'clock shadow, spritzed some cologne on his chest, air-kissed himself, and then trotted to the elevator.

Out on the street, Blayze drank in London in all its nighttime glory. New city, new mindset. That was what he kept telling himself as he dodged gaggles of people superglued to their phones. The sprawling expanse was exactly as picturesque as he'd imagined, and after he opted against the subway in favor of the short walk, Big Ben chimed 10:00 p.m. the very moment he spotted the electric Adrenaline graphic above the door. It was meant to be.

Offering a smile as he sidestepped a shadow-veiled bouncer, Blayze crossed the threshold and was transported into another universe. Steeped in a graceful vanilla fragrance, every inch of space was aglow with an energetic fluorescence that demanded a fun night out in no uncertain terms. A bass-heavy tropical house playlist filtered throughout the bar, and this time he didn't have to force a smile as he meandered to the sleek counter. This was his happy place. The world might be on the verge of collapse back home, but there wasn't much he craved right then beyond booze and music and hunky men. Sadly it was a little lacking on the guy front at the moment. Maybe they'd only recently opened—which was probably a good thing. He could grab a drink and settle in before the mad rush.

"What'll it be, handsome?" asked a lively girl with a half-shaved hairdo who managed to make eye contact and offer a cheeky wink while fixing a drink mid pour.

Blayze perched on a stool and instantly warmed to her. "Whatever's good. So long as it's got plenty of alcohol, I'm set."

She grinned, passed the drink to a happy customer without pause, and then got to work combining premium label spirits and fresh juices to the point where her hands almost became a blur. "Okay, so, legally I'm not allowed to put this in," she said as she held up a shot glass of amber liquid that was separate from the neon pink cocktail she'd finished fixing. "Trust me when I say it wouldn't be the same."

Blayze shrugged, content to tap his card on the terminal and pour the shot himself in order to bypass the weird excess-measures rule. Then he stirred it with the umbrella straw, sniffed the punchy fruit concoction, took a tentative sip, and melted into his chair.

"Jeez. I see why they call this place Adrenaline. It hits hard."

Satisfied, the girl started to wipe down the bar and left him to it. Blayze swiveled on his seat and eyed the square patch of dance floor. A few people stood around the edge, bopping their heads, cautious about fully committing. There was an older couple getting their groove on in a respectable manner given the tempo of the song, but besides that, there were a few groups sitting and sipping, spaced quite far apart.

In spite of the jolly atmosphere, Blayze tried to stuff down feelings of dejection. More people would come. They had to. He was sure of it.

A few minutes later, Blayze took another sip and came up dry. He stared at his glass, unable to comprehend how quickly it had gone down. Was it because he was anxious or impatient? Both? He didn't like waiting, not for anything or for anyone. He took another look around the disappointingly vacant space and sighed.

"Ahh, fuck it."

He signaled the nice girl for another one of her special drinks and bit the bullet. On his cell phone he searched CharmD on the app store for the millionth time. He'd typed it in so often it was permanently on his autofill, yet in the two years since its inception, something had always stopped him downloading. It had a very respectable 4.8 out of 5 rating, so the hesitancy didn't come from risk of malicious software or even a janky interface. His reluctance came from the fact that the app was made by the partner of his ex-boyfriend.

Jasper's wealthy human beau, Finn, was a dab hand at coding, and apparently his technological prowess now extended to a dating app intended for mages. Blayze had run into them a couple years ago when Jasper managed to get himself magically imprisoned inside his own apartment. They were lucky Blayze had the means and generosity to source him an Oathstone, or Finn would've had his memory wiped and would be none the wiser about the millions of mages wandering the world.

Still, Blayze had never been one for hookup apps. He preferred face-to-face meets and the immediate gratification that went along with them. While he wasn't half as bitter about Jasper breaking up with him anymore—he'd probably always hold a candle for the guy somewhere somehow—but he always imagined it would be weird to actively benefit by his indirect success. Sometimes desperate times called for desperate measures, and before the guilt of leaving the States kicked in and made him regret his decision, he had to combat the growing feeling that this trip was for naught. So he clicked on the wand logo that served as blatant innuendo and put in some basic credentials.

When he dug out the ancient referral code Jasper had given him soon after its inception, things got a little tricky with the five-point security encryption that would prove he was of supernatural descent. It included a live captcha code, a fingerprint scanner, and facial identification to match the picture he was required to upload. As well as the mage security number assigned at birth, he also had to upload the nature of his ability, though it was explicitly specified that this was currently not on display and might soon be on a toggle system if the safety of displaying such information got approval by the MRF. Right now they probably had bigger things to deal with.

When Blayze got through to the main page, he had to swallow his pride and raise his glass to Finn, wherever he was back in New York. For normal humans it would simply exist as your run-of-the-mill hookup app, but the decidedly more VIP members had access to an impressive spread of profiles, and to signify that they were mages, they had little wizard hats in the corner of their profiles. Cute. Even if he was definitely on there for a clear and obvious purpose, Blayze couldn't help but wonder how much longer it would be necessary to have those protocols. What would the world be like if mages could walk around without hiding their intrinsic selves? The thought was even more intoxicating than his rapidly dwindling drink.

Because he was too much of a horny devil to have a specific type, Blayze didn't bother playing with filters. There were plenty of guys who would happily fit the bill—mage or otherwise. But nobody seemed to be in a decent radius. What was up with that? Wasn't this bar supposed to be, like, super popular? Agitated, Blayze sipped hard and ended up draining his drink again. Best not to grab another one right away. When he did eventually get some action, he didn't want to make an ass of himself by going all limp dick.

When he refreshed the feed, Blayze's chest fluttered and his mouth actually fell open when he saw the newest profile. He clicked onto it to get a better view and peered down at the Vikingesque redhead on his screen. Dane Peterson. Bold of him to use his full name. He had soft brown eyes framed by bright, cleanly cut eyebrows. That angular and fluffy ginger beard alone was worth the Looking ping he sent without hesitation. Blayze bet his muscles had muscles, and he probably knew a pocketful of tricks in the bedroom.

"He'll do nicely," Blayze said to himself, imagining the two of them in all sorts of salacious scenarios.

According to the app, Dane was only a few feet away, and yet, when he whipped his head around the room like a watchful meerkat, he couldn't spot anyone half as godlike as that. Either it was a catfish situation or a wonky GPS situation, and Blayze wasn't happy about either. "How freaking typical."

"Woss that, mate?" said someone next to him. Right as Blayze was about to wave him off, the reedy guy spilled a fresh tumbler of rum and coke in his lap.

"Aw, Jesus, man!" Blayze shot up from his stool, dripping black liquid over the tiles. "Look what you've gone and done!"

"Hey, hey, so sorry! No harm... dun... is it?" the guy slurred. Though he was clearly way too canned to have even been served another drink, his subservient body language made him look apologetic. "Probs a bit cold and sticky, I'll bet? Here...." He grabbed a wad of napkins and started dabbing at Blayze's crotch. "Lemme help."

"It's fine!" Blayze rolled his eyes and backed up. "I've—I got it."

He pocketed his phone, slammed his empty plastic glass on the counter, and marched away to find the restroom, trying his best to block out all the people staring at the massive wet patch on his pants.

As he finger-scrubbed the remains of the gooey syrup with some particularly lathery soap, he began to wish he'd never gotten on the plane. It was never this hard to secure some harmless fun back his way, and that bit of napkin foreplay was probably as intimate as he would get with any guy tonight. Why had he bothered to come all this way? He could have saved himself a truckload of time and effort—not to mention heaps of money he didn't even have.

Angling his crotch up to the hand dryer wasn't an easy task, and it took a full five minutes before his pants began to dry. As they did, he got to thinking about home, and when he pictured the rapid decline of his once-affluent lifestyle, he longed for a distraction. It wasn't in his nature to give up on the hunt so easily, but when he headed back upstairs with plans to try some authentic British ale, Blayze took some measured breaths to realign his chakras, and scoffed at the idea of spilling beer on himself just for attention.

CHAPTER TWO

DANE CHECKED his watch for the fiftieth time that day and breathed a small sigh of relief. Only a quarter of an hour until he could punch out and shrug off the damned monkey suit. Dealing with a horde of prissy partygoers had taken its toll, and although he made a effort to keep his guard up, he'd already caught himself accidentally amping a nearby guest. And since his mind had been firmly elsewhere over the last few days, it was happening again.

"What did you call me?" a shrill voice cut above the freeform jazz, causing heads to turn.

A petite Hispanic woman wearing an exquisite crimson scoop neck was standing in a circle of other well-dressed ladies, and while they had been quietly sipping merlot and wearing practiced smiles, the accusatory snarl evolving on her face didn't quite befit the chic tone.

"Seriously, Jennifer," she continued, brandishing her Chanel purse like a boxing glove. "You so much as breathe those words again and you'll be wearing this wine, I don't care how rare the grapes are."

"Fuck my life," Dane whispered.

Since he hadn't done it on purpose, the amped emotion had been up for grabs, and for the second time that night, the hands of fate had chosen anger. Maybe it was a not-so-subtle sign from his internal manifestation. Maybe there was something in the air in the wake of that shocking video that he couldn't stop thinking about. Whatever the cause, he needed to settle this woman before things got too wild. He didn't have the energy to hang around and provide yet another police statement if she acted on her temper and ended up in a full-on catfight.

Dane closed his eyes for a brief moment and reached out with his aura, like with an unseen third hand traveling through the spiritual ether. To a novice mage in a room full of so many bodies, it would be like searching for a needle in a haystack. But it was easy for him to detect the pillars of people's emotions simply by their heat level. There were the usual smatterings of tepid boredom, lukewarm pleasure, stone-cold drunken content, and a handful of new toasty blends of confusion and alarm. But when he reached the source of a blisteringly hot totem of inexplicable rage, he grasped hold of it and immediately worked on dialing it back.

Normally when he wanted to cool off someone's anger, he pictured a well-loved watering can sprinkling a light drizzle. But this woman had gone from zero to a hundred in all of three seconds, and to manipulate her back to normal he had to imagine dousing her aura with an industrial hosepipe.

"Huh," said the woman. He opened his eyes and looked across the room. A frown dipped at her brows, and she wobbled on the spot from such a disarming comedown—something Dane hadn't had time to avoid. "I'm... I don't know what came over me. Please accept my apology. Perhaps I ought to go find somewhere to lie down."

As she slowly made her exit and gave the party something tangible to gossip about beyond politics, investment opportunities, and trending holiday destinations, Dane contemplated his mistake. It had been more than twenty-one years since the interview where he was officially categorized as a mage who can amplify other people's emotions at will, but lately he'd been struggling with the *at will* part. Losing control during sex was one thing. Letting it slip during daily life was inexcusable.

Where telepaths hear voices in their heads, Dane felt auras, and even though he could choose any emotion in the known spectrum to enhance and fine-tune by varying sets of select degrees if he was careful enough, sometimes his own emotions got in the way. And it wasn't like he could simply turn off his brain and go about his day—not for lack of trying, anyway. Extensive elective therapy had cost a tidy fifty thousand pounds, eaten up a whole year of his life, and accomplished precisely fuck all. Only more money in the MRF's back pocket.

There were times when gently manipulating someone's emotions came in handy, sure, but those moments were few and far between because his moral compass was a little too rigid. Using people for personal gain was plain wrong, and yet on days like this he wished he had the balls to be a bank robber. Or a corporate spy. Or an assassin. He could think of a thousand ways his ability would aid him in such careers, and maybe then he'd feel like his ability had some actual purpose.

Regardless, he needed to work on his focus. Especially after the video that had found its way onto everyone's screens. There was ample doubt right now, what with the major advancements in CGI, yet every mage in the city had their butthole clenched. It would only be a matter of time before things were confirmed for good. Dane would be damned if he was the one to slip up and be responsible.

Some kind of clicking noise threatened to break his reverie. When Dane looked down at Norman Harwell, the organizer of this posh pandemonium, he was literally clicking his fingers at his face.

"Doorman, hello? Earth to doorman?"

Dane stared at the semipermanent scowl of a pinched-in face shaped by wealth and an ignorance of the slightest hardships.

"Yes… sir?" The man before him was easily twice his age, and yet he begrudged addressing him like that. People should earn the right to formal titles—not simply attain them through social status. "How can I help?"

"Kenny needs more of that Fiji Water in his SodaStream. Andrea and Zeke are nowhere to be found after that strange outburst from that woman—Lord knows what I pay them for—and I simply haven't the time to run down to the wine cellar."

Forcing a smile, Dane swallowed his initial response. Kenny could use the perfectly serviceable water from the tap instead of the artisanal twelve pounds per bottle, but who was Dane to suggest such things? He was merely the monkey in the monkey suit. And who needed a bouncer at a sixteen-year-old's birthday party anyway? Like, seriously. The event was being held inside an executive townhouse and needed both a physical key and passcode to gain access. Was Norman really that worried someone might hop along to swipe the mountain of untouched foie gras?

"Sir—" Dane glanced at his watch—five minutes and counting. "—the basement is like a labyrinth, and I'm almost off duty."

Norman arched a bushy graying eyebrow. "Listen here, young man, I'm almost at my limit. Entertaining a bunch of spoiled brats isn't all that fun when they're surrounded by cutthroat bankers who keep on eye me like I'm expired meat about to die just so they can take a peek at my will." When he paused for breath, Dane almost admired his candor. Then his scowl returned where it belonged, and he changed his mind right back. "My patience is wearing thin. If you do this for me, I'll pay you time and a half for this last hour. And if you don't… I need only put out a few words to my colleagues and you'll be struck off any upcoming events quicker than you can say *redundancy*. Winter is a busy time for lads like you, am I right?"

Dane couldn't hold back an eye roll. Someone caught him scrolling through CharmD during his last event, and whether the comment was referring to his profession or his sexual orientation hardly mattered. He was used to threats from rich assholes who never learned how not to get their way... and he really ought to straighten his spine, stick two fingers up, and politely tell them where to shove it. The temptation to heighten the man's sexual desires right there and then was very strong, though it wasn't the money that dissuaded him, it was the stability. His current security detail was the first job he'd managed to hold down with a corporation, and he needed backup options if his online presence were to take a sudden dip. Though Dane liked to think of his streaming channel as completely drama free, cancel culture was extremely prevalent, and it only took a handful of dedicated internet trolls to undo years of hard work.

"Okay, fine," Dane agreed. "Next time I'm strictly on door duty. Pay someone else to be the errand boy."

"Fair enough," Norman said, already ambling back to the gathering of unsettlingly tame teenagers and their semiwatchful parents. "Better make it snappy, all right? You're correct, it really is a maze down there. Wouldn't want you getting lost or anything."

Dane heaved a sigh and turned on his heels to head downstairs. He had only worked this location two times prior, but that didn't mean he was blind to the lavish playground of the filthy rich, with all their still-life paintings and springy carpets. Even the wallpapers were embossed with Nordic runes nobody had the capacity to read, and because there were jasmine air fresheners strategically placed at five-meter intervals, the house literally stank of wealth.

The cellar, on the other hand, was perhaps the furthest thing from grandiose. Cast into a pit of darkness, the whole place felt eerie and mustier than the gloomiest alleyways in the city, and it didn't take a genius to work out why Norman usually had plenty of helpers to run back and forth to this massive area to fetch wine.

It had been a long time since Dane had been fearful of the dark, and yet something about traversing that place made the hairs on the back of his neck stand to attention. Owing to his Scandinavian descent, he'd always been a big guy, and a wave of claustrophobia crashed down as he squeezed through the narrow passageway and headed for the faintly illuminated rack.

When he reached the drinks, he spotted the glass water bottles underneath the multitude of champagnes, reds, and vermouths that probably cost more than his car. When he heard a scraping to his left, he didn't hang around to appreciate the intricate metalwork.

It was likely a mouse or some other kind of innocent rodent going about their day. Nonetheless, in this space with no sense of being, it was too easy for Dane to imagine he was on the set of *It* and Pennywise the Clown was moments away from initiating a horrifying chase sequence.

Clutching two bottles, Dane raced back the way he came and squeezed out of the cubbyhole and into the open air, hoping and praying nobody was around to see that he'd very nearly crapped his pants.

There wasn't an emotion on the planet that would've saved him from an embarrassment like that.

AFTER SUCH a grating shift, Dane needed a tall rum and cola. Probably two. Depending on how sloshed his friends were, he might even be really naughty and stretch to three. It was the start of a rare weekend off, and he was so eager to get out of that airheaded function that he didn't swing by his place to shower and freshen up. He was also in such better spirits that he didn't even begrudge paying black-cab prices instead of hopping on the Tube.

The glory of London passed by in a blur, mostly because he was glued to his phone, catching up on emails and giving his thumb a workout from an obligatory double-tap session on socials. He also logged in to CharmD to show his face and see who was kicking about. Though there had been many knockoffs since its launch, the original blew all other hookup apps out of the water, likely because there had never been a safe space for mages to connect so easily. Every time he scrolled, a new face popped up, and it never failed to fill him with a certain sense of joy.

He suspected he wasn't the only one wondering how things like that would change in the coming months. There were plenty of overarching concerns he could endlessly toil over, but it was exciting to imagine a stark transformation to the once-sheltered mage culture. Maybe that heart-pounding video was exactly what they needed. On some level, Dane had always hoped his kin might be able to openly coexist with humans. One day, perhaps. Wishful thinking, probably. For now, he'd settle for a decent shag.

Right as he began scrolling through the recently added Visiting tab, the cabbie barked at him.

"Get a move on, pal, it's Friday night, yeah?"

Dane forked over the amount on the screen and didn't bother to wait for change as he got out of the cramped space.

The streetlamps cast a cheerful glow on Adrenaline, and he dug his hands into his pockets as he ambled up to the bouncer. Even if he liked to think he looked good for his thirty-one years, gone were the days when they'd card him. Some did on a blue moon, either for a power trip or because they wanted to creep and find out his name. But his thick ginger beard left little to the imagination in terms of age, regardless of how tidy and trim he kept it.

"Busy?" he asked by way of greeting.

"Nah, mate," the guy said, voice stern. Dane couldn't tell if he was making it lower to show off or if it came naturally to the brick-shithouse cueball. "It'll pick up soon if you're after some delicate peaches. Always does."

He chuckled at that. No need to tell him that he had a tendency to break twinks or that he actually preferred the bar when it was quiet because it afforded a modicum of privacy that he and his mage friends enjoyed. People tended to eavesdrop more when they were sober, though by the time they were fully tanked, they either forget what they were talking about or they straight-up thought they were fangirling over the latest Netflix sci-fi. Either suited him perfectly fine.

When he headed inside, Dane spotted his friends at once. They were deep in conversation, nestled in the farthest corner booth beyond the fuchsia glow of the bar. There were a few dolled-up stragglers dotted around too, and he tried not to feel too self-conscious as he ordered a drink.

"All right, handsome?" The barman, Rob, was a sprightly young addition to the team, and tonight he was kitted out in tight-fitting black leathers and full of welcoming effervescence as he wiped down the sleek mahogany. "What'll it be this time?"

"Rum and cola, no ice. Thanks, man." By the time Dane got his wallet out, someone had slid into the adjacent stool.

"Hey," he said. "How's it going?"

Turning to see the face behind the thick American accent, his jaw almost dropped. He was your typical olive-skinned Abercrombie poster boy with purposefully messed-up hair, except that his was silky black instead of bottle blond. The way he was shamelessly sizing Dane up like a scrap of meat made him feel some type of way. He was mega hot, and he damn well knew it. He was definitely new to the area, and Dane wanted to know whether he was here on vacation or here for the long haul.

"It's going good, thanks," Dane said instead, tapping his card to gain access to the drink. "Just hoping to chill after work, you know?"

"Mm-hmm, you're one of those work drones, then? Never really been much for the nine-to-five." He winked slyly and took a big gulp of beer. "More of a creative type, myself."

Offering a sheepish smile, Dane wasn't sure what to make of that. This guy might as well have NYC tattooed on his forehead, and he didn't know whether to be impressed or freaked out by his directness. There was a fine line between confidence and arrogance, and he seemed like he teetered that line like it was a tightrope.

"Well, um." Dane wanted to stay and chat, but he was frozen by the thought of small talk. "Have a good one, yeah? Hope you find some... creative people."

Then Dane made his way over to his friends, popped the straw into his mouth, and suppressed the urge to drain the whole thing.

"Oi-oi!" called Kitt. He raised his pint and spilled a bit over Ollie, who punched him on the shoulder. "Took ya bloody time!"

Dane perched on the edge of the booth as Terri threw a wink his way, then went right back to mashing out a text message. "Dealing with the 1 percent takes its time. Can you believe I ended up amping two people tonight? Need to get that bloody video off my mind. Where's Violet?"

Once he finished rolling a cigarette, Kitt tucked it behind the silver scaffolding bar on his ear and grinned. "Fixing her hair, probably. You know how she loves to make a grand entrance."

Seeing as Ollie was wrapped in a rubber singlet, Terri was wearing a full face of her favorite greyscale makeup, and Kitt had more metal in his head than Vivienne Westwood's pin cushion, it wasn't like they didn't make entrances of their own. Since he moved to London five years earlier, Dane had been drawn to these people, not because of their edginess or even their ridiculously awesome abilities, but because of their genuine souls and their shared love of partying.

"Did we settle on going to Astro later?" If he didn't already know he had the power of Electrokinesis, he'd swear Ollie was a telepath.

Astro was the current hotspot for the mage gathering that happened once every other month, and where it used to be a place to network and have a good old-fashioned laugh, the more mages that came out of the woodwork, the more rowdy it tended to get. The last couple of times were a bit heavy for Dane's tastes, and he wasn't sure having a big bunch of mages in one spot was the most sensible thing right now.

"Aw, don't do me like this," Ollie said when Dane grimaced. "That guy only wanted to test his limits."

"If by *that guy* you mean the crackpot Transfigurist who very deliberately turned me into a walking eggplant for a full five minutes? Yeah, no thanks. You ever felt what it's like to become a vegetable, Ollie? Everything's all... squishy."

When they all guffawed at his expense, Dane flipped each of them the bird and sipped his drink.

"I hear they're hosting an archery tournament tonight," said Terri. "I've got a couple of Psychokinesis buds, but only one of them can fuck with nonorganics, so I've no idea sure how they'll factor that in."

"Maybe they'll have a bowl of spaghetti to hand?" Kitt joked. "They've gotta figure something out to keep it fair, you know?"

"Isn't it a bit dangerous? And careless?" Dane wondered. When all he got were vacant stares, he spread his hands emphatically. "You know, given what's recently happened over in the States, I... is it really such a good idea to be parading our abilities around?"

"Hardly parading," Ollie brushed him off. "You know the gatherings are always held in a secure facility—there's literally zero chance of any humans getting in. Like, I get what you're saying, but I, for one, think now more than ever, it's important for us to stick together."

Dane definitely agreed, but he was starting to feel out of sorts with the weight of the dilemma. When he side-eyed the bar to check if Abercrombie guy was still kicking about, he was already looking over with a clear line of sight, and he didn't flinch or bother to hide it by breaking eye contact, which was pretty bold. Unpredictably, Dane was the one to wimp out first, and while his friends launched into long-standing conspiracies about the ethics of magical anti-doping, he hopped onto the app to see who was about.

He didn't get far down the list before he stumbled across the Visiting tab again and spotted the artsy American. He had viewed Dane's profile recently, and he'd even sent the cute purple-wink emoji, which was universal code for *hop on my dick*. Dread froze his chest for a second, and when he reached for more of his drink, he suffered a stab of annoyance when there was none left.

The guy's name was Blayze—how vogue—and his bio read:

Just a chill dude fresh out of Boston looking for fun times. Idina Menzel is my spirit animal, pineapple on pizza is a sin, and bad vibes get left at the door. Also, if you're into it, I'm probably into it.

Dane tutted at his screen and scrunched up his face. *Chill* was something of an exaggeration, and the small collection of professional selfies were wildly out of date. Why was Dane even bothered? The dude had basically called him boring, and he didn't exactly exude an overwhelming sense of friendliness. Although, damn, he was fine, and for someone to have as much confidence as that... he was probably packing. It had been way too long since Dane's last fumble, and he could already feel the ache for intimacy.

Screw it. He could be the bigger person by going back to the bar to approach conversation from a different angle. But as much as he fantasized about the idea, it felt risky, so he sent back a smiley emoji and let the powers be.

"I'm telling you, it's all a game of diplomatic chess." Terri laid her hands firmly on the table to emphasize her point. "For years now the MRF have allowed overachievers to soar higher and higher above the big-name humans, and I'm honestly surprised we've not been outed sooner. It's probably intentional. Hell, they could've even orchestrated it themselves."

"Yeah, right!" Ollie cried. "As if they'd risk a full-scale uprising. Not after Salem. There are too many factors that us worker ants aren't privy to. And think of how much work it'll be for them to organize a mass memory wipe."

"You think it'll come to that?" Dane asked, shocked at the train of thought. "I'm sure it's feasible for them to organize that... but would peace really be too much to ask for? Wouldn't our world be a better place if we could all simply get along?"

"Duh, of course it would," Ollie said, smiling softly, shaking his head. "It's naïve to think it'll be as easy as that. Also, I hate to be the bearer of bad news, Terri, but those greedy-ass mages you're talking about? Those ones who are too deep? They want to *stay* there. Take away their penthouses or private jets and there's gonna be hell to pay. Can't say I pity them much, mind you, when they knowingly used their gifts for gain. If the humans find out how they got them, things are gonna get real ugly, real quick."

"Easy for you to say, Mr. Grade A Elemental," she sneered. "Although you'd sooner act like you aren't, you're tremendously valuable, given the current state of our climate. Imagine if everyone knew you could generate 10,000 kilojoules of energy per minute, with zero drain to your life force? They'd worship you like planet Earth's savior. When was the last time anyone gave a shit about those of us who can see into the past?"

"Or influence dreams," Kitt chimed in.

Dane didn't know how best to navigate that area of conversation. Retrocognition and Oneirokinesis were both handy in certain situations. Every ability had value in some way. Sure, heightening people's emotions sometimes felt about as useful as a chocolate dildo, but if there were no ethical concerns, he'd be England's most successful criminal mastermind. But that wasn't the path he'd chosen, and so he had inadvertently resigned himself to always dealing with other people's shit.

"Going for a smoke," Dane said and patted Ollie's arm.

BECAUSE THE bar was practically empty, Dane returned his glass and made sure to grab another drink before heading out to the garden. As he lit up, he was eager to track the progress of the orange and golden fish in the koi pond, but he stopped in his tracks when he spotted a different kind of beautiful specimen—Blayze.

He had one leg crossed over the other, phone and drink on the table, and was vaping a small pen device. The frown on his face also suggested he was unhappy about something. Either that or he had a serious case of resting bitch face. Even though Dane very much wanted to sit next to him, stick out his hand, and introduce himself like the good old times, the fear of rejection made him linger.

Argh. He had to be tough with himself. If Ollie hadn't taken a chance on Dane when he was sitting in that exact spot, he'd never have met his current friends. He had to put on his big-boy pants and bite the bullet. Seize the day. Suck it and see.

"Your clouds smell funky," he said, taking a perch. "Is that real weed, or just flavored juice?"

"It's the real deal, but it's strictly medicinal," Blayze said, back tensing up a little. His leg started to bounce on the spot, and he offered a small smile and kept eye contact. "Helps keep away the crazy."

Smiling purposefully but not so much that it came across creepy, Dane angled away the smoke of his Marlboro in case it offended. "How'd you get it over the border?"

He shrugged nonchalantly. "Think they've got other things on their mind at the moment. Won't be long before you guys have it over here, I guess?"

"Maybe. I mean, I vote Green, but that's mostly 'cause they stand for environmentalism and anti-racism. Grass has lots of validity for being legalized, though I can't say I've ever actually partaken."

Blayze turned up a corner of his mouth and held out the stick. "Have a try. It's key lime pie flavor."

"I'm good, thanks." Tapping his glass, Dane was immensely proud of himself when he sent along a cheeky wink. "Probably best to stick to one vice for the time being, you know?"

A part of him wished he could match the blasé attitude, and when he pictured himself getting intoxicated and confident enough to do a whole host of things to those extraordinarily full lips, he had to consciously look at Blayze's eyes instead.

"So," he started, wishing he didn't have to pause so often to gather his nerves. "Is it just Blayze, or do you have a surname?"

"Just Blayze," he said firmly. "And you're Dane Peterson, right? Don't worry, I'm not a creep or anything. It's on CharmD."

"Oh, of course." Dane grinned sheepishly. "I should know better than to put my full name on these things, but I like being up-front. Things tend to run smoother. Anyways, how are you enjoying London so far, Blayze?"

Blayze gave a little chuckle, then sighed softly. He uncrossed his leg, put the vape in his pocket, and reached for his beer. "It's a gorgeous place, but I expected it to be a little... I don't know... jazzier?"

Dane nodded and took another puff of his cigarette. "Yeah, I get you. Most gay bars have gotten distinctly less queer over the years. Think maybe the pink pound isn't worth all that much anymore."

"Possibly. Unless it's pride season, of course."

"True, true." His phone pinged—probably Terri wondering what was taking so long. "In terms of colorful people, I seem to find the mage gatherings bring a lot of eclectic tastes to the table."

"Oh?" Blayze turned to face Dane head on, clearly intrigued. There was a spark of shock in his sky-blue eyes, and Dane abruptly got the idea that this guy wasn't quite as confident as he wanted everyone to believe. "Only been to a handful in the States. For whatever reasons, there's always a weird political undercurrent that I've never been keen on."

"Hmm," Dane offered. "Doesn't really happen here. It's more of a psychedelic rave, in truth. I'm still of two minds about going tonight. My mates think it's all well and good, but... well... I'm sure you know more than anyone why it's probably a silly idea."

"Maybe that's why we should go?" Blayze said. "As an act of defiance. We as a community have to stick together, don't you think? While I have no idea what's on the horizon, I get the feeling we might need each other real soon."

He wasn't at all wrong, and Dane found the obvious *we* mention very interesting. Either this Blayze guy was actually super into him and already inviting himself to things, or he was already sick of the bar and wanted to find some party action. In either case, over the course of their chat, his smile had gotten bigger, more genuine, and he had relaxed his body considerably—all good signs.

As desperate as Dane was to know what he could do, asking about someone's power was kind of taboo until you knew them well enough. It was like shaking a bus driver's hand after they've dropped you off. Doable, but weird. Mages preferred to show their abilities rather than speak plainly about them, and since they were out in the open of a nonsafe space, he'd simply have to wait.

He bet it was something powerful—useful, fun, creative.

Dane took another pull of his smoke; he was almost down to the label. When it was gone, he'd have no real reason to stay out here, so he needed to be daring.

"Wanna come, then?" he asked. "To the gathering, I mean. I think you're right about sticking together, and my friends have been badgering me for weeks—they aren't gonna let me dip out. If you come with, it's bound to be a lot more fun."

"Uhh, okay." Blayze winked. "Sure. Why the hell not? What's the worst that could happen?"

In celebration of his extroverted victory, Dane downed the rest of his drink simply so he could offer to buy Blayze's next one. He had a grin plastered on his face as they made their way back in, and despite all of the unspoken controversy and uncertainty, he felt good about his chances, and he was hopeful that this was going to be a fun night. Best yet, if Blayze had never been to a British mage party, he wouldn't know his ass from his elbow.

What had he gotten this poor guy into?

CHAPTER THREE

A PARTY SOUNDED like exactly what Blayze needed to perk him up. Dane's buddies were pretty far out, and despite not knowing what any of them could do, they'd fit right in back home, image-wise. What set them apart was the fact they accepted somebody into their close-knit circle right away—even Violet after she burst through the doors so ceremoniously that she almost caught her bouffant lace-front on the backswing.

Then there was Dane himself. Blayze still wasn't sure what to make of the towering and fumbling Brit, but he knew for certain that his fire-red hair and thick fluffy beard was a major turn-on, and he had a curiously awkward charm. He even walked timidly as they made twists and turns through the back alleys of London, heading to their clandestine destination.

Twice he tried to strike up some form of conversation with Blayze and instead ended up gazing right past him. How could someone be so drop-dead gorgeous and so socially inept? It made zero sense.

"Oh shit," said the Hellraiser wannabe as he puffed on some particularly pungent tobacco. "I forgot to ask about the inquiry, Vi. What's the verdict looking like?"

"Mm-hmm," she groaned. "I can't really speak much about active cases, but there's some interdepartmental politics getting in the way of the transfer of case files, and they can say what they like, but it's clouding everyone's judgment."

"Whoa, really?" said the rubber-and-chest-hair guy whose name started with *O* or something. "You could pay me all the cash in the MRF's back pocket and I wouldn't touch human politics with a barge pole. It's always been a messy and long-winded business. Like, how many times a day do you have to cite constitutional law?"

"Umm, we don't have that in this country," Vi scoffed. In spite of her soft Scandinavian accent, her voice was easily the loudest among the group, and despite having turned up last, everyone seemed particularly more present now that she was around. "What do you think we are? Some dumbass Americans?"

"Umm...?" Blayze interrupted, dumbfounded.

"See?" Vi winked. "Case in point. It's, like, I know my shit, right? Yeah, it might've cost me an arm and a leg… but I didn't ace law school simply so the jury can stare at my breastplate all day."

"Oh, hun," Terri piped up. "You think they're expensive? Try getting surgery."

"Am I detecting notes of regret?" Kitt asked as he tossed his cigarette down a nearby drain.

"Not in the slightest," Terri sang. "My puppies are worth every penny. Could you imagine if I was holed up back in that Yank's country? It'd cost more than a mortgage on their healthcare."

"Pay them no mind," Dane said, leaning in. He patted Blayze's arm. "If they're mean to you, it means they like you."

Blayze made a concerted effort not to bite back and kept walking. It wasn't long before they turned down a tight passageway and made another series of lefts. Then everything went quiet as they reached a sour-faced bouncer standing outside a big steel warehouse door.

"Digits."

After everyone took their turn, Blayze listed out his mage number automatically without a hitch. The MRF-assigned numerals were easier to remember than his birthdate, and when the stout guy tapped it into the database and it checked out with a pleasing *beep*, he let him pass. Blayze smiled by way of thanks, and when he got a deadpan stare in return, he turned to see that Dane had held back while the others ran off.

As soon as he crossed the threshold, his body tingled with a wave of electric heat. It was a familiar and pleasant sensation, one that let him know he was in for a good time. He followed Dane down a dimly lit corridor, where the words Careful What You Wish For were written above the next door.

"Hmm, definitely not ominous at all," Blayze muttered.

"Never mind that." Dane placed his hands on Blayze's shoulders and hurried him along. "It's only tonight's theme. They play around with them from time to time. Expect to see lots of genie costumes."

Blayze rolled with it and pushed open the door. Everything was chaos. Not even organized chaos, just pure bedlam—a heaving uproar of lights and sounds and smells. He had a hard time focusing on anything specific, and yet, as Dane pulled him through the crowd, Blayze's panic morphed into awe. These were his people, his kind, and he couldn't help but feel an instant sense of belonging.

"Cool, right?" said Dane. He leaned one arm on the bar with a devil-may-care attitude, and Blayze was shocked he could be so chill when people a few feet away were suspending orbs of water, swapping outfits to the beat of the music, and making out while levitating. Some were even in the middle of conversation with milky-white clairvoyancing eyes.

"Incredible," Blayze said. "I've never seen so many gifts together in one room."

"You don't have these gatherings back in the Big Apple?"

"Sure we do. Though they get pretty cliquey, and it mostly turns into a standoff with the Electros against Earthers, Aquas against Pyros, etc."

"Ah." Dane rolled his eyes. "Sucks to be an elemental, I guess."

"Right." Blayze nodded slowly as Dane ordered the drinks. "Ah, thanks," he said when he remembered the new brand of beer he'd taken to.

There was a Shapeshifter on the dance floor mimicking people's appearances for fun. Every three or four shifts, she went back to a fixed state of ripped blue jeans, flannel tee, and shaved side part. When she caught sight of Blayze staring, she morphed into him and threw out a wink. God*damn* he looked good. Not a hair out of place. She'd even managed to replicate his handsome jaw and olive skin, and as cool as it would be to ask her to turn around so he could get a better look at his bubble butt—because the mirror never did it justice—she looked like she was having the time of her life without lingering on any one person. He sent her a wink and a wave, and she happily returned both, then mimicked an exotic beefcake who walked right by.

"This is great," Blayze said to Dane. "It's refreshing to see people in their natural state, being their unapologetic selves."

"I know, right?" Dane agreed. "Makes me wonder how the world could be if we were truly open. Things would be a lot more liberal, for sure. And confusing. Enough of that tonight. That's a conversation for another time. What about you?"

"Hmm?" Blayze stuck the straw between his lips and sucked hard.

"What's your story? What ticks your boxes?"

"Oh, you know… normal stuff."

A moment after Dane shot up a single eyebrow of disbelief, Blayze was met with an unexpected surge of honesty, and the words rushed up his throat like bile.

"I've yet to have my first foray, but I'm slowly getting into BDSM."

When the other of Dane's eyebrows reached the first, promptly causing both of them to practically tickle his hairline, Blayze's mouth fell open and formed a perfect circle.

"Holy shit." He coughed on his drink when the honesty phase disappeared as quickly as it had come. "You're an amp?"

"Argh, fuck, I'm so sorry." Dane shook his head as his cheeks flushed a pleasing shade of crimson. "I honestly didn't mean to do that. Must be the booze. Damn it, that's the third time today."

"Chill, you're all good. Man, this explains so much."

"It does?"

"Yeah, Amps are usually all timid and quiet-like, because of everyone else's bullshit feelings bouncing around their head. Now I get why you're a bit withdrawn. It's kinda cute, actually."

Dane rolled his eyes and grinned out at the throng of people. "Yeah, I guess we're like Empath mages, except that we read auras instead of minds, then amp those emotions if necessary. How is it you know it so personally? You some sort of mage scholar over here on business?"

"Not in the slightest. I'm simply taking a vested interest in the world we live in." Because Blayze had never met an amp before, the list of questions grew every passing minute. "To that end, do you ever use your power to do weird stuff during sex? Or maybe to *get* sex?"

"No," Dane cried, brow creasing. "I never use my power on people for personal gain. It's wrong. You Americans must know that too, right?"

Blayze held his hands up in surrender. "The thought never crossed my mind. Don't sweat it. Oh, and I totally would, for the record. Do some weird stuff. No telling what I'd do with a power like that."

Dane rolled his eyes toward the ceiling and tanked his drink. Blayze half expected him to ditch him right there and call it a night, but he turned to the bar for another and even got him a refill. Interesting.

"So what's your deal?" Dane probed, breaking etiquette.

Surprised, Blayze offered him a friendly scowl. "And to think I took you for someone with class."

"Pfft. To hell with that. I need to know if we're on an even playing field. Whether your ability is as useless as mine."

"Useless?" Blayze repeated, unsure if he'd really said it or if it was a lyric in the rhythmic trance music. It didn't help that the DJ kept repeating the same string of words in the background, though Blayze wasn't paying the slightest bit of attention. "You think you're useless?"

"Look around," Dane said, sweeping his hands. "There's a dude over there who's literally crawling on the ceiling. And that girl with the yellow sunglasses? Pretty sure she has Land-Based Sonar. Me? I can make someone feel happy or sad, and as a result, I have zero control over the bullshit that goes on in my own head. Whoop-de-fucking-doo."

"Hey." Blayze seized the opportunity for some body contact and laid a hand on Dane's arm. Wow. His biceps were rock hard, and he wasn't even tensing. "Your power is valid and has countless applications. Just because you haven't found your calling yet doesn't mean it isn't out there. Like, okay, you gotta trust me when I say that I don't usually say this... but I'm actually a little bit in awe of you right now."

"Really?"

"For sure." Blayze didn't know why he was coming on so strong. Maybe it was because he'd been royally disappointed with the trip until he ran into Dane. Maybe it was because it hurt to see a lost soul when he had so much to celebrate. Probably it was because all the sweaty dancing dudes had him horny as hell and he needed to get laid. "Have you considered every possible avenue? Not to project on you or anything. Like, what do you do for work?"

"Bodyguard *slash* doorman."

"Ah, that figures."

"Because it's boring and not the slightest bit creative, right?"

"No, because you're a hot fucking stud."

Dane's blush deepened, and as he ducked his head slightly, it was clear that he was taking a reading of the room. It was tricky for Blayze to understand how Dane couldn't share joy in the emotions he dispensed. He downed half his beer and launched into his spiel.

"Every mage on this planet has value in some way or another. Not to go all elitist on you, because you and I are obviously still human, but for the normal folk, as much as I respect their fortitude and all that, I don't know how they muddle through life without that special innate something keeping them going. I'd be nothing without my power. It's been my light in the dark on too many occasions, and even though you might not think so, I'm willing to bet you've felt the same at some point. Fuck what anyone else thinks. Your gift is special, unique, a blessing. There's a thousand different ways you could utilize it that would grant you fulfillment or wealth or a mix of both—"

Dane cut him off with a kiss. It was so unexpected and out of the blue that Blayze got all flustered, pulled back a fist, and was a song's beat away from going all Karate Kid. Then he got a look at the longing in Dane's warm brown eyes. He slammed his drink on the bar, dragged him to the dance floor, and melded their mouths together.

He tasted hot and full of need, and it was a matter of seconds before they were grasping at each other's bodies—waists, backs, asses, napes— both greedy and desperate for more contact.

"Damn," Dane groaned in his ear. "You're such a ball of energy. I wish I was inside you right now."

"Gosh," Blayze laughed. "Bold of you. I like it. And me too, for the record. I wish you were inside me too."

As he experienced the soft touch of his lips again, a striking warmth enveloped Blayze's body. Given that he'd only had a few drinks, the feeling was foreign and scratchy and out of place. Not to mention the fact that he was fully in control of his power at all times, even when highly inebriated, and there was absolutely zero chance he'd ever let it slip so foolishly. He had no idea what that feeling was or where it came from, and he chose not to care. For now, the only priority was getting Dane out of this bar and banging his brains out.

WITHOUT THE need for words, they made the mutual decision to head back to Dane's, and on account of the nonstop kissing and touching each other, the Uber driver couldn't wait to kick them out.

They swiped into his apartment complex, and then the elevator took a while to climb the floors before they made it into a private place. Blayze didn't mind. They were still wrapped up in each other's orbit, and he hadn't been this horny in decades. Was Dane amping him? He seemed very against the idea of using it for personal gain, and yet it was entirely possible he was doing it accidentally.

Something was definitely up. It was as if Blayze was a virgin again, and he barely noticed how swanky Dane's penthouse pad was because he took him straight to the bedroom and pushed him down onto a plush king-size bed.

"Holy fuck, I need you," Blayze said, ripping off Dane's shirt so that the buttons flew around the room. As he got to work undoing his own pants, Blayze raked in the glorious sight of Dane's hunky physique.

His midsection was a bit chunkier than the guys he usually went for, but when he reached out to touch the curly red fur on his chest, he bit his lip at the surprising firmness of his pectorals. "Buckle up, Viking, I'm gonna ride you like there's no tomorrow."

"Is that a promise, short stuff?" Dane asked, practically drooling as Blayze finally freed himself from his cotton confines and let his junk hang out in full view. "You gonna show me how the New Yorkers take a nice fat cock?"

Even though Blayze had spent his first six years in Mexico City and acquired his American tongue later on in life, addressing it would murder the mood. Instead, he licked his lips in anticipation, overjoyed to hear that Dane's timidness didn't extend to the bedroom. Being verbal always made things more exciting, and when he unsheathed Dane's stiff dick and bulging balls, he was even happier to find that this was one of those very pleasant times where size really did scale.

Impulse wanted him to pull out all the stops to make him feel like a walking god. In that moment, Blayze would do just about anything to please this gruff introvert, and as he jumped on Dane and latched his mouth onto him, he was so overcome with lust that one half of him was worried he wouldn't be able to last that long, and the other half really didn't care if he busted in less than two minutes.

He grabbed a rubber off the side table, and it appeared they were in sync because Dane was already fetching the lube. In the space of ten seconds, Dane was jacketed and greased up, and when they found the most suitable position, the hunkiest mage in London let himself get climbed upon like a flagpole.

"Sheesh," Blayze moaned as he closed his eyes and lowered himself. Smiling in delight, he started to jerk his cock, which was growing harder the wider he got opened up. "Feels even bigger than it looks."

"Yeah?" Dane asked, not needing much more permission to start slowly but surely pumping himself. Though he was more or less an exclusive bottom, Blayze knew he was tighter than a vise and felt like liquid velvet at the best of times, and it wasn't long before the rhythmic action of skin on skin had built up a delicious sheen of sweat. "You like that prime British meat?"

Dane grinned emphatically as he took things up a gear and started rocking himself into Blayze full force. There was an obvious goal on the horizon, and because all of the inhibitions were gone now, what remained was pure animal need. Seeing him take charge and feeling him pound Blayze like a fuck toy was such a turn-on, and with the astonishing amount of pleasure he was bestowing upon his prostate, it was like Christmas had come early. Blayze guessed Dane was about ready as well.

"Man, that feels so good," Blayze growled, voice turning hoarse as he grabbed on to Dane's hips and forced himself down deeper and harder, unable to stand the thought of delaying a second longer. "You gonna shoot for me? Do it, man."

"Fuck yeah," Dane called to the ceiling as he rapidly removed himself and the rubber, then let his body lay flat against the bed again as he furiously jerked his shaft. "I'm gonna... fucking... blow."

As soon as Dane's creamy payload shot up and hit Blayze's chest, he needed only a few tugs himself to reach for the stars and keep on soaring as the knot in his balls swiftly undid itself. He had morphed into a wild tiger, roaring at the moon, confronting the very face of ecstasy like he'd never known.

He was so lost in an ocean of blissful satisfaction that when his load rained down on Dane's still-pulsating cock, his groans of appreciation were faraway. At some point, Blayze's eyes had closed of their own accord, and because that ten seconds in picture-perfect paradise felt more like an hour inside the physical embodiment of multidirectional limbo, he was barely able to appreciate exactly how much of his energy was getting sapped.

The laws of equilibrium suggested there would always be a price to pay for an above-average high, and once the strangest orgasm of his life began to ebb away, he collapsed on the bed and genuinely almost passed out.

When Dane scooched over and reached out for some automatic body contact, it sounded like he was either quietly chuckling or sobbing—maybe both.

"Whoa," Blayze said, dog-tired and totally at a loss for words. Having brought himself to climax at least a few thousand times in the past, what he'd just gone through had been decidedly more out-of-body. It didn't seem appropriate to voice his complaints, but he had to admit, it was extremely disconcerting. "Gonna go... grab some water."

Hearing sounds of acknowledgment from behind him, he grinned as he maneuvered off the mattress, feeling like his bones were made of lead.

Reluctantly Blayze trudged to the bathroom, lamenting something of a comedown. Price to pay for such a heavenly session? Or maybe the beers had taken their sweet-ass time to hit? Either way, it was like he'd been on a stretching rack instead of an incredibly luxurious bed, and the burst of emotional overload that randomly popped into his head made him feel like he was in the middle of a dream.

Fortunately he was lucid enough to locate the nightlamp in the bathroom and headed for the sink. The water was a delightful boon on his skin, and he cupped some of it and splashed it on his face. Since he was apparently in real danger of passing out, he had to grip the sides of the porcelain to keep himself steady.

"The fuck is going on?" he asked himself.

Or at least, he thought it was himself. But that couldn't be right, could it? Had he been drugged somewhere across the night? Was he that much of a walking cliché?

When he peered into the mirror, the person staring back wasn't who he'd learned to see for the last thirty-one years. The person he was looking at should be half-asleep in the other room, basking in a similar version of post-orgasmic bliss.

Reaching a very meaty hand out to touch his very bearded cheek, he pinched himself, cursed loudly at the pain, and quickly came to a sickening realization. Blayze had swapped bodies with Dane, and when his head began to swim again for the second time in the space of five minutes, the oncoming bout of nausea crashed down with enough force to knock him straight on his ass.

CHAPTER FOUR

DANE WAS roused by an instant headache, unsettling queasiness, and some relentless thumping. Everything was dark in the bedroom, and it took him a long time to realize that he must've dozed off after the best screw of his life. He was also covered in a thin sheen of sweat from head to toe, and there was a vexing heat radiating from his chest.

"Dane, wake up," he thought he heard.

The voice sounded a lot like his own, except it was outside of his head, as if it were a recording or something. He was probably still dreaming.

"Right now," the voice insisted.

"Dude," Dane moaned. He felt like his brain had been replaced with a colony of bees and like he'd lost over a hundred pounds. "Talk about a rude awakening."

"I'm serious, man, you need to wake the fuck up and take a look at me."

When light filled the bedroom, Blayze's figure was illuminated. Except it wasn't Blayze Dane was looking at, it was himself—*his* naked body, *his* walnut eyes, and *his* face shaped by a thick ginger beard.

"What the shit?" When Dane sprang out of bed, he noted that it was a lot easier than usual. He put his hands out in front of him, and they were thinner than normal, and so were his arms. It was like he'd been shrunk in the tumble dryer, and when he peeked into the floor-length bedroom mirror, it told him everything he needed to know.

Yet his brain still refused to believe it. The only thing it let him entertain was the vast emptiness. There wasn't a single aura to be read, and for the first time in thirty-three years, the void-like ether was entirely gone and the silence left in its wake was blissfully deafening.

"I'm you," Blayze said as he joined him at the mirror, his expression mixed with disbelief and alarm. "And you're me. Jesus wept…. My voice has never been this deep. And I'm guessing the freezing cold shape of terror inside my head is your aura? That's definitely not how I thought it would feel. How the fuck has this happened!"

"*Is* this really happening?" Dane wondered, still not convinced he wasn't locked inside of a really messed-up dream.

If he was no longer in control of other people's emotions, and Blayze was... that left him at his mercy. He was vulnerable. Exposed. Subject to all sorts of exploitation. Blayze had said himself that he would willingly do weird shit if he had Dane's power. Even the thought of being on the other side of the coin was enough to make him feel sick.

"Why have I got the world's worst heartburn?" Dane asked. "Blayze, seriously, if this is really happening, which—what the actual fuck—then I want you to listen to me very carefully. Whatever you do, don't manipulate people's emotions, okay? You have to keep your guard up at all times and shut yourself off. If you don't control it, people will go haywire."

"No shit." Blayze screwed up his face. "I'm not a moron. And, unlike you, who literally admitted they let their power slip a total of three times today, I'm pretty well versed with control."

"This is bad," Dane said. "There's no way this is happening. We've gotta be sharing a dream or something, yeah?"

Dane nodded to himself like he just got the answer, then gave himself a swift slap around the face. It stung like a bitch, and when he didn't immediately wake up, he yanked at his hair.

"Hey!" Blayze shouted. "I already tried pinching myself, like, five times. Doesn't work. That's my moneymaker. Try not to give me a shit-ton of bruises, okay?"

Dane huffed in exasperation. "This is some sort of prank, I know it. Maybe we're still back in the club, never having made it back to my place. With so many varieties of gifts, it wouldn't be out of the question for someone to be holding us in some kind of trance right now."

"The club...?" Blayze said, brow furrowed. "Hang on a sec...." As he paced the carpet, it looked as if a floodlamp had been shone into his eyes. "Do you remember feeling some kind of, I don't know, warmth back when we were dancing?"

"Um...." Dane sat back on the bed and wracked his brain. "Yeah, I guess. That was only the booze, right? Makes you feel all flush and stuff. Happens all the time."

"Sure, sure. But there was something more obvious than that. I brushed it off because I thought it might've been a spot of presex butterflies, but now that I think of it, I'm pretty sure we were hit by a spell."

"Are you serious?" Dane balked. His voice sounded extremely strange to his ears, given that it was all nasally and considerably higher pitched. "You think…?" He had to pause, gather his nerve, and start again. "You think someone's done this to us on purpose?"

"Maybe?" Blayze threw a big set of hands in the air. "People are weird in the head, aren't they? Mages aren't the exception to that. And you London bunch haven't exactly been shy about letting your freak flags fly."

When Dane flipped him the bird by way of thanks, he began to realize there was something very wrong with his skin. The pleasant bonfire inside his chest had grown exponentially, and as he got to his feet and started to tremble, it was like he'd been dipped in a lake of molten lava and somebody forgot to hand over the nuclear suit.

"I'm really fucking hot."

"Gee, thanks, I know that but—"

"No, like, I'm literally burning up." He held out his arms and wondered why he couldn't see that they were on fire, because they certainly felt like it. "What's happening to me?"

A lightbulb might as well have clicked above Blayze's head, and yet when he opened his mouth to speak, he didn't get to voice whatever it was because Dane's entire body burst into flames.

"Oh my God," he screamed as he stared at the burning body in the mirror and flailed about in full-on panic mode.

He was a walking bonfire, a beacon of destruction, a chaotic ball of death born from the center of the sun. He was also pretty scared for his life, but when he tried to see why his skin wasn't melting off, he didn't feel any pain beyond the comfort of a toasty heat, which was oddly curious. The real danger came more from trying to get clearance from anything made of fabric so that the building didn't go up in flames.

"Simmer down," Blayze yelled over the blaring smoke alarm. He had his hands up in surrender as he drew closer to Dane, and because the look on his face echoed the overriding sense of fear, the walls felt like they had begun to close in. "It's okay, Dane, it's just my power!"

When those words finally registered in some small part of his brain, Dane was stunned into silence and the flames died as quick as they came. Even though his skin was no longer ablaze, the little burning entity was quick to take refuge inside his chest, and he could swear he almost felt it laughing at him.

"You're... you've gotta be kidding me. You're a Pyro?" he shouted, aghast as he patted himself down, though there were no ashes or residual smoke, pleased to see that all of his limbs were still attached, even if they weren't *technically* his limbs. Disregarding the dizzying sense of detachment, he focused on the present moment. "How could you...? Why didn't you say something?"

"Because it's not a big deal?" Blayze crossed and uncrossed his arms uncomfortably. "You seriously didn't work it out from my name?"

When the cogs in his brain finally began to work as a functioning machine again, Dane could have kicked himself. He was tempted to ask his doppelganger to do it. The absence of auras made things impressively difficult to focus on, and he craved a tall glass of water to make sure his throat wasn't singed.

"Jeez, stop being so melodramatic," Blayze spat. "I'm sick to the back teeth of this bizarre and frankly age-old prejudice. I thought mages were supposed to stick together, huh? You could end the world in a tidal wave about as easily as wildfire, dude. Don't come for me like that."

"I'm not trying to come for you," Dane said, a small frown pulling at his eyebrows. He stepped away from the mirror and tried to recenter himself. It took more time than he cared to admit, totally unaided by the fact he could barely look at Blayze as he walked around in his skin. Seeing someone take charge of something that had belonged to him his whole life was downright creepy, and he was struggling to not feel embarrassed that he was still walking around buck naked with his dick between his legs. They both were.

"Sorry," Dane said. "I didn't mean to offend or anything. It's simply a shock, is all. Also, I know we're in the middle of something right now, but there's a few reasons why people don't trust Pyros in general. They can be wanton with such a destructive element. In my experience, Water Weavers have a more contemplative perspective."

"Wha? I don't even—" Blayze paused for some deep breathing. "I know 90 percent of the firebugs in the States, and we would never knowingly put anyone at risk because of our power."

"I'll take your word for it," said Dane. He knew that his anger was heavily misplaced and he needed to take a chill pill, find some clothes, and get some perspective. "I'm gonna grab a drink," he said as he rifled through his wardrobe, rolled his eyes to the ceiling, then scooped Blayze's outfit off the floor. "You're welcome to join me."

"Okay," he said, but he looked uncertain.

In the kitchen, Dane fixed himself three fingers of vodka, downed it, then pulled up a stool. When Blayze hovered uneasily in the doorway, looking on the face of it like a stranger in his own home, Dane waved him over and poured him a glass.

"Got any mixer?" he asked, grinning. "Situation definitely calls for it, so no judgment from me. I'm not really the hard-core type."

Dane raised a brow and then planted his head into his hands. "Lemonade's in the fridge. Door gets a bit stiff sometimes, gotta give it a good yanking. Gods, this is… way beyond fucked."

"Sure is."

Hearing someone bustle around the kitchen gave Dane some welcome sense of normalcy. When he looked up and saw his own furtive eyes plagued with a near-permanent state of confusion, the strangeness came right back.

"That's a very thoughtful look on your face," Blayze said as he swiped the vodka and poured out a generous measure. "What are you thinking?"

"I'm thinking that this all started when we fucked," Dane whispered, almost daydreaming. "Or, rather, after we fucked. It was fine during, wasn't it? What would happen if we did it again? Maybe we'll swap back?"

Blayze screwed up his face, took a long sip of his drink, then set it down on the counter. "Yeah, I'm not doing that. Sorry, I don't mean to offend or anything… because it was good and all, but after what's just happened, I'm gonna go ahead and err on the side of caution."

Tilting his head to one side, Dane wanted to clap back. But what was he supposed to do? Demand that he sleep with him again? Starting a massive argument was probably the least smart thing to do, so he tried his best to stay cool.

"This whole aura-reading thing?" Blayze whispered. "It's fucking weird. Like, what happens if I reach out and…?"

All of a sudden, Dane endured a sharp tug in the back of his head, and a jumble of emotions surged throughout his brain to recreate the battle of Hastings—or maybe the battle of Gettysburg, now that he was, at least physically, American. He was both cheerful and miserable and disgusted and enraged, and even if the reason for the mix was impossible to decipher, the presiding feeling of confusion made him feel violently nauseated.

It was both sickening and harrowing to be on the receiving end of something that had been at his disposal for his whole life, and while the experience only lasted a few seconds, he was eternally grateful to himself for practicing a pseudo-pacifist stance, because his natural instinct told him to get up and go thump Blayze over the head.

"Oi!" Dane slammed his hand on the counter, emotion settling on anger even though the tap had been firmly closed. "I told you not to do that. You've had zero training—you might end up making me do something really stupid. What if I got so full of hate I grabbed the kitchen knife and went on a rampage? Huh? What if I set myself on fire again and chose to give you a hug? You aren't impervious to it anymore, and this isn't a game, Blayze. Yeah, it's weird and all, but we're adults. You've gotta be more responsible than that."

"Pfft." Blayze took out a stool, stared dead ahead at the stove, and sipped more of his drink, undoubtedly embarrassed by his imbecilic behavior. "This sucks. I wasn't thinking straight. My bad. How long do you think this is gonna last?"

"Fucked if I know. Could be a few hours or a few days. Maybe longer. Any tips on, you know, not bursting into flames?"

Blayze lifted up his shoulders in an awkward shrug, as if he expected them to go higher but they couldn't because of the muscles upon muscles.

"It's not really something I've had to think about in the last two decades," he said casually. "You need to remember it lies beneath and try your best to not to let it out."

"Wow," Dane said. "Big help, pal."

Blayze turned to make eye contact, then thought better of it. "The flame is ever-present, and even when your emotions tell you otherwise, a big part of control comes from learning to keep that flame at a simmer, not a boil. To be honest, it's been a part of me for so long that I hadn't realized how much I'd miss her if she went away. I feel... empty... without her."

"Her?" Dane repeated.

"Yeah," Blayze said, eyes downcast, looking like they were deep in the throes of a daydream. The frown on his face was heartbreaking. "It's weird. I never really thought about the flame as a feminine being until she left, but... she's definitely a she. So, anyways, what about you?" He looked back up and made a point of clearing his throat. "How do you have space to figure out your own emotions if you're constantly being probed by everyone else's?"

"Lots and lots of training," Dane said. "I've tried a bunch of different therapy techniques over the years, but it doesn't help to be nervous in public, because nerves are harder to fight than fear. Something tells me you aren't the nervous type."

Blayze grinned, confirming a lifetime of nonchalance. For the longest time, Dane envied people who looked so comfortable in their skin, so it was something of a mindfuck to see it in this capacity. "Has someone really done this on purpose?"

"I don't know."

"What are we gonna do when we find them? Ask them to change us back?"

"I don't know, Blayze. I'm as clueless as you are. Damn it to hell, I'm not the enemy here, okay? Less of the accusatory tone, please. We need to put our heads together and try to be reasonable. Here." He refilled his glass with a generous measure of vodka and topped it off with soda. "Have you known this to happen to anyone else?"

"Sort of... my ex, Jasper, got snared in his own apartment for, like, three months because of some metaphysical breakdown."

"Seriously?" Dane marveled. "That's nuts. I tend to go a little batshit whenever I'm sick and bedridden for more than two days."

Doing a pointed three sixty, Blayze hummed in disapproval. "Could think of worse places to be. Your apartment is a helluva lot nicer than his was."

Dane sighed deeply, disappointed in himself. His place *was* very nice, and it was surprisingly easy to forget how good he had it when he was surrounded by luxury all the time. It had become second nature for him to expect heated flooring, eat fresh steak from a well-stocked fridge, and enjoy the glittering cityscape on a daily basis, courtesy of his giant bay windows.

Blayze chuckled softly and downed more of his drink. "In truth, I thought Jasper's snare was fanciful drama at the time. Being the spiritual sort, I assumed he was messing around with master-level spells way beyond his reach and had done it to himself. Or maybe he'd forgotten to align his chakras, or some shit. Didn't think the universe was punishing him because he had unresolved feelings about his life. So, do you think maybe this is somewhere along those lines? Like, we've built up some bad juju and now we need to atone for something?"

"Atone?" Dane repeated, incredulous. "Got a guilty conscience, have you? What have you done that's so wrong?"

"Nothing, obviously." Blayze waved off the idea, and yet the brief hesitation plus the fact that he guzzled his drink gave Dane an altogether different impression.

"Look, I get that we're not anywhere near the deep-and-meaningful stage yet... but this?" Dane wagged a finger between himself and Blayze. "This is going to take some figuring out. Above all else, we've got to be honest with each other, because if we don't communicate, we don't stand a chance in hell at understanding how to fix this."

"Let's just go back to the damned club," Blayze huffed. "Sooner we get this over with, the less painful it is for everyone involved."

"See, that's the thing. It's closed, and it'll be gone for another two weeks. Lucky there's such a demand for the parties, to be honest. Used to only be twice a year. Now *that* would be a nightmare. Still, they're like a pop-up shop—here one minute, gone without a trace the next. Nobody knows where the next one will be until the night of the event. They might even get canceled soon, what with what's going on your end."

"Well, who runs them?"

Dane shrugged, completely at a loss. The fire was definitely simmering beneath his skin, and the thought of being utterly helpless only seemed to fan the flames.

"Never heard any names about the organization?"

He shrugged again, finished his drink in frustration, then sternly reminded himself that pouring another would only serve to worsen the situation. Alcohol plus combustible hands probably didn't equal a good combo.

"There's gotta be someone we can talk to." Blayze ran his hands through his hair, completely messed it up, and didn't bother to put it back in place. "Who else was there last night that you knew?"

"Besides the friends you already met, I only recognized a handful of pretty distant acquaintances."

"Okay, fine. Let's go see your buddies and see what they have to say. Maybe they saw something out of place."

"Something out of place?" Dane guffawed. "In a mage bar? No shit."

The statement was so ridiculous, and added together with their frankly ludicrous circumstances, he couldn't hold back violent shudders of laughter. By the scowl on his face, Blayze didn't share the sense of joviality, and that simply made it funnier.

"All right, all right." Dane made a forceful effort to keep the hilarity under control. "The guys are pretty wild. They'll definitely still be partying somewhere in town. Talking to them is as a good a place to start as any. Okay, how's this for a compromise—if you try your hardest not to send anyone crazy, I'll try not to recreate the Great Fire of London."

"Yeah," Blayze said as he got up off his stool. "Please don't do that. You'll only go and fuck up my holiday visa, and contrary to all signs that say otherwise, I do actually plan to enjoy myself here."

CHAPTER FIVE

CONSIDERING HOW freaked out he was about it earlier, Dane seemed surprisingly calm as he hailed a black cab and got on the phone to Ollie. When he explained that his voice was higher pitched because he was using a funny voice filter—*rude*—they were invited back to his place, and the casual feel was like they were heading back after popping out to grab some smokes.

Blayze, on the other hand, was trying hard not to ramp up the driver's general feelings of boredom as he tore through London. He'd known about how Amps worked for years, at least in theory, but he never expected it to feel so unsettling in practice. In the interest of control, he had envisioned it being something you could toggle on or off when it suited the user, not having a constant directional compass of a stranger's essence whenever they were within arm's reach.

Maybe he simply needed more training. And yet, if this was what it was like all the time, it would be easy to see why Dane came across as reserved if he had to perpetually keep an invisible guard up at all times. He had also been right when he suspected Blayze didn't get nervous all that often. Or at least he didn't until about an hour ago. At present he was a nervous wreck, because as amusing as it was that his reflection had transformed into a hot stud muffin, he wanted his damn body back, and it was super weird that it was literally in touching distance.

"Fuck me sideways, it's cold," Blayze whispered.

His teeth had started to chatter, and the more he thought about how disturbingly alien the sensation was, the more panicked he became. The sound of the car's heater on full blast was unmistakable, and Dane simply stared at him like he'd grown two heads.

"You don't get it," Blayze said. "I haven't felt like this. Ever. I think I might be getting hypothermia."

"Relax." Dane placed the back of his hand against his forehead. "You feel fine to me. It's all in your head, okay? Let's keep calm until we see my friends and try to figure things out from there. Think you can do that?"

Nodding resolutely, he wrapped his arms around himself and focused on the fabric weave of the back seat. Why oh why had he left his vape pen back at the apartment?

"Yeah," he said solemnly, "I can make it."

"You've got a point, though. Why am I completely numb right now? I should feel something, right?"

"Pyros don't need to regulate their temp," Blayze said. "We don't get hot or cold. Admittedly, it's a bit more useful than I ever gave it credit for."

At the mention of its absence, Blayze desperately began missing the curious little flame he'd nurtured his entire life. It seemed evil to part with her and weirder still to hope that Dane was treating her with care, considering she hadn't really been a thing on his radar until the very moment she went missing.

With nothing more to say, they sat in a tight silence for the rest of the journey before the driver kicked them out onto the gradually brightening cobbled streets. Because it was early morning on a Saturday, small groups of people were milling around sipping from cans, and after Dane shoved some cash through the window, he led Blayze to an apartment complex and buzzed for flat number seventeen.

"Yeah?" A gruff tone filtered through the intercom after a solid minute of waiting.

"It's me," Dane said in Blayze's voice.

When a shiver ran up his spine, Blayze reminded himself how everybody hated the sound of their own voice when they heard it played back on video. While this was like that, it was also ten times more annoying, and he wasn't sure how much longer he could take it.

"Let us up," Dane said, "quick-like, yeah?"

"All right, all right," the voice said. Then the intercom sent down a loud buzz that pinged open the latch for the main door.

Climbing three flights of stairs wasn't much fun when he had to avoid the ceiling. "Jeez," Blayze moaned. He put his hands on his hips. "You're fit and all, but I feel like a walking skyscraper. Exactly how many times a day do you suffer mild concussion?"

Dane scowled when he reached the top. "Yeah, well, you're reedier than a bonefish. I'd be shocked if you can lift a pencil."

"Um, when was the last time you even used a pencil?" Blayze quipped back. "Pretty much everything's automated already."

"Whatever," Dane dismissed as they headed down a paisley carpet to knock on a door that had steady yet respectful house music behind it.

Blayze lingered behind him, and when the door swung open, Ollie's bright and cheery face appeared. He had changed into a more casual khaki shorts and white tank top ensemble, and a sloppy grin was stuck on his face.

"Wassup, bros?" he said as he stepped aside and ushered them in. "You came right on time. Violet's about to break the Guinness world record for longest bong hit."

"Fab," Dane said.

The apartment reeked of floral incense with a tinge of weed, but the open-plan layout was much more spacious than Blayze could have pictured from the outside. The dark leather upholstery looked like something out of an *Architectural Digest* magazine, and the walls lined with impressionist pieces totally clashed with all the state-of-the-art appliances... except maybe that was the point—a fuck-you to the norm. Dane's friends were huddled around a monstrous oak coffee table laden with booze, erotic playing cards, and tobacco pouches, and they all cheered when they took notice of their arrival. Their collective delight spoke volumes as to how good a night they were having and how genuinely pleased they were to see them.

Ollie supplied both of them with a bottle of beer and then sat back down cross-legged. Blayze passed along his thanks, then drained his beer as Dane propped himself on the arm of a cuddle chair.

"So," he said, "turns out we've got something of a situation."

Kitt tilted his head as he passed a sizeable chunk of green to Violet, who loaded up the bowl while Terri had her cell poised at the ready.

"One sec, new guy," she said. Then she put her mouth over the rim and struck a silver Zippo. When the plant was practically incinerated, Violet emptied her lungs, then filled them right up with a haze of purple smoke. Blayze was mighty impressed as he lingered around them like a giant in limbo, and the cloud that followed hung in the air as everyone giggled.

"We've swapped bodies," Dane called above the din.

The silence and quizzical looks that followed were ludicrous as everyone turned in his direction, then to Blayze's.

"Come again?" Terri hastily stashed her phone in her pocket.

Blayze groaned. He wished there was a way to get help without having five virtual strangers gawping at him.

"It's true," he said. "I'm in the body of a brick shithouse British dude who has to keep his guard up all the time. Otherwise he'll turn everyone into babbling psychopaths."

"And I'm in the body of a prissy American Pyro who doesn't get the context of social tact."

As much as he'd prefer to pretend otherwise, Blayze didn't miss the collective flinch when Dane mentioned his ability. But he bit his tongue, simply because he didn't have the strength or patience to get into it right then. Bigger fish to fry.

Terri got up from her seat, went over to Dane, and waved her hand in front of his face, as if that was going to solve anything. "How did this happen?"

"At the club, we think." Dane shrugged. "Everything was fine until we went back to mine and...."

"Shagged?" Terri said.

"Banged?" Kitt suggested.

"Hid the sausage?" Ollie joined in.

With both hands, Dane flipped everyone except Violet the bird and brushed their comments off in frustration.

"Look, point is, we've somehow managed to swap bodies, and whilst it's funny for a while, I'd really like to get back to some kind of normality before I start burning buildings down."

"Bros, what did you say at the club?" Violet asked as she set the bong aside, sat forward on the couch, and stared into both of their souls. When the collective response was two silent confused looks, she asked again. "What did you specifically wish for?"

"Wish for?" Dane repeated. "What do you mean?"

"You remember the whole 'be careful what you wish for' theme, right?"

Ears pricking up, Blayze pictured the words above the door. "You mean that stupid sign?"

Violet shot him a withering look as she started to pack another bowl.

"He's right, though," Dane agreed. "What's the sign got to do with the price of piss?"

"Dane, you're not seriously telling us you didn't know about DJ Jinn?" Ollie smirked broadly. "The literal genie with the power to grant wishes?"

"That's a thing?" Blayze shouted, aghast.

"Um, yeah." When she finished packing the bowl, Violet set the glass pipe on the table for later, then sat all the way back against the couch and got comfy. Blayze was sorely tempted to swipe it up and smoke the lot, but he was oddly determined to prove Dane wrong and show that he did, in fact, have social tact. "He travels up and down the country, rarely making appearances," Violet continued, "and when he does, you really gotta be careful what you wish for. You folks done fucked up."

"You honestly didn't know he was playing?" Kitt rolled his eyes. "It was literally above the door."

"We were a little preoccupied talking about our gifts," Dane huffed. "And when he kept saying 'I'll make your wishes come true,' I thought he was talking about fulfilling my Tina Turner setlist fantasies."

Blayze hummed in agreement. "And here I thought he had some kind of stutter. The way he kept saying Dee Jay Jinn is in the house… exactly how have I gotten to thirty-one years of age never knowing genies existed?"

"Wow." Dane shook his head, lost in an ocean of thought. "I can't believe I didn't remember. So unbelievably dumb of me. Wait a sec," he said, turning to Blayze. "Do you recall *actually* wishing for this? Like, speaking the words?"

"Doesn't matter if you did or not," Terri said. "As long as you thought about it concurrently, the result is the same."

Blayze drained the rest of his beer and remembered quite clearly how he had wished to be inside of Dane, and how Dane had wished the same. Well, the Djinn certainly took that wish literally. Was he was stuck for good? Wishmasters were famously fiendish beings, and if he were sitting on the couch right now with all of Dane's friends, he'd probably get a wonderful kick out of seeing the mess he caused.

"This is bullshit," he concluded. "Precisely the opposite of what we need right now. This honestly couldn't have come at a worse time."

"Speaking of," Ollie said. "Would you care to explain why you sodding Americans gotta throw a parade for everything? Ooh, I'm a sixteenth Irish—let's have a party! And hey, guys, by the way, as it turns out I'm a lightning mage, so let's make a huge fuss and disrupt the *entire* bloody planet. Ever heard of the phrase 'Keep calm and carry on'?"

"Hardly my idea, was it?" Blayze defended, longing for the bowl of weed to settle his anxiety. "I spent too many of my teenage years coming out, and I don't relish the idea of doing it again. Also, before anyone dares call me a coward, my ability is the only reason I left. It was a tactical retreat, and I've been deliberately staying away from the news. They don't need me in the mix over there because, after living through what I have, I know myself pretty well by now—if I ended up seeing something I didn't like, I'd be bound to react."

"Guys," Kitt said placatingly. Then he downed a shot of neon green liquid and wiped his mouth. "Have either of you looked in a mirror yet?"

"No, I hadn't noticed anything wrong," Dane scoffed. "What do you think? Seriously, looking at what we already know isn't gonna swap us ba—"

"Not that kind of mirror," Kitt interjected. "*Our* kind of mirror, man. You know, the ones that relay extremely important information to the magical race when it becomes appropriate? Did you hit your head in the body swap or something? Anyways, the MRF made an announcement an hour ago, and it's on repeat, so I'm sure you'll see it soon enough."

"Oh?"

"Yeah, well, to cut a long story short, they're mad as hell that a grade A Electro could be stupid enough to get filmed using their gift, but they can't deny that an opportunity for integration has finally presented itself. They're gonna ride the wave and see how it pans out, and they're urging us to keep quiet like normal. If the shit starts to hit the fan with human government bodies in the coming weeks, they'll arrange for a more drastic workaround."

"Mass memory wipe?" Blayze asked, hoping that his voice didn't betray his apprehension.

Although he had only worked for the MRF for a short stint while he distributed a few Oathstones, the mere thought of all the paperwork involved in something like that was enough to run a chill up his spine. When Kitt nodded, confirming that human-wide memory wipe was, in fact, potentially on the table, the air in the room became decidedly heavier.

"Brilliant." Dane nodded, seeming to also recognize the possible ramifications behind the new information. "Now the pressure is on, I guess. If we're being told to keep a lid on things, it's not gonna look good if I start walking through the street, body ablaze. The last thing we need is a rookie Pyromancer accidentally burning down the London Eye."

"Um," Terri piped up, "isn't it made of metal?"

"Not the point."

"Can we reverse it?" Blayze asked nobody in particular, desperate to change the subject. "Like, surely if we go find this Djinn dude and ask him real nice, he can simply sort this all out?"

"Doesn't work like that," Terri said. She put a filter tip between her lips as she stuffed tobacco onto a paper.

Of the bunch, her emotions were the easiest to detect. She was curious, empathetic, and felt bad for the pair of them.

"I don't pretend to be an expert on this sort of stuff," she said. "I do, however, know that you can't unwish a wish. Kinda defeats the point. And anyways, he's in pretty big demand lately, probably halfway across the continent by now."

"Shit."

"Yep," she said, sparking up. "That sums it up quite nicely."

Ollie whipped out his phone and skipped a couple of tracks to find something with a more suitable tempo, then wrung out his fingers with an audible crack. "Maybe you should go speak to the Seer?"

"Oh," Dane said, looking off into the distance. "That's a great idea. Well done, mate."

Suddenly hope fluttered in Blayze's chest. "You guys have a Seer?"

"You don't?"

"Closest one to me is in Cali, which ain't all that close to NYC. Aren't there, like, only a handful of Seers in the world?"

"Definitely under ten. The shop for ours is nestled at the back of Tottenham Street," Dane said. "We can go first thing tomorrow."

"Tomorrow?" Blayze gawked. "What are we gonna do until then?"

"Take the load off?" Kitt suggested. "Smoke a bowl? I don't know. You guys are tenser than a coiled spring. And hey, would you look at that, you've learned how to synchronize scorn. Such fun. Look, gentlemen, I get it. It's really fucking weird. I'm sure I'd be freaked out too. But there's nothing that can be done right now, so grab another beer each, park your asses, and chill."

Dane breathed a deep sigh and allowed his shoulders to sag in defeat. "Okay. Fine. Makes sense. Oh, and Blayze, we should probably disable the biometrics on our phones, else we can't use them."

"How long do you think this will last?" Blayze bitched. "You're really gonna have to give me some training if you're settling in the for long haul."

"I can assure you that I'm *definitely not* doing that. I merely don't think swapping phones is a great idea, unless of course you want me seeing thousands of your nudes."

When Blayze's mouth fell open, the scratchy beard tickled his neck. "Thousands? You think I'm that vain?"

"Are you going to sit there and tell me you aren't?"

"I'm not," Blayze bit. "There's gotta be a hundred, tops. Though each one is artistic and valid in its own right. And by the way, how do you stand this wig on your chin? Yeah, it looks hot and all, but wow, what a pain. I'm getting rid of it first thing tomorrow."

"You are *bloody well* not," Dane cried, working up such a fuss that he literally started to give off steam from his ears like a freshly boiled kettle. "I work hard to keep it so tidy. Oils aren't exactly cheap either."

"Huh. Who's the vain one now?"

Dane nodded thoughtfully. "Touché."

When he realized where the steam was coming from, he actually cracked a smile, and Blayze found himself quick to return it. As disconcerting as it was to pilot an entirely foreign entity with an incredibly taxing ability, tomorrow was a new day, and he was confident that, with the help of an authentic in-person Seer, they'd soon be on track to getting things sorted.

His time had been unexpectedly eventful ever since he landed in London, and when Ollie handed them a fresh set of drinks, all he had to do now was enjoy the beer and the company of Dane's friends. Mercifully, when Violet also agreed to let him get in on her premium-grade weed, the toll of keeping his guard up lessened considerably and he was happy to find that meeting new people really wasn't much of a challenge after all.

CHAPTER SIX

IT HAD been years since Dane last visited London's most renowned Seer, and it had left a sour taste in his mouth when she was unable to predict his future. Annoyingly, it had less to do with the skill being out of her wheelhouse and more the fact Dane had spent years building up a mental wall—whatever that meant. Maybe things had changed since then. Maybe that wall had been smacked with a sledgehammer now that he no longer belonged to his own body and people's auras weren't constantly getting in the way.

It was dangerous to think about a life free from his power. What if he got so comfortable being alone inside his head for the first time that he would no longer want all those outside influences? Likewise, Blayze might be enjoying the fact he didn't have to actively nurture a peculiar flame entity, though it didn't seem to need much beyond a spare thought here and there. That's what he kept telling himself, anyway, because while it sure as hell required a lot less maintenance than his old power, it was weird having something else actively residing inside his chest.

When they got back to the apartment and opted for iced espressos instead of power naps, Dane's morning routine had been somewhat skewed when he set himself on fire in the shower. At least he now knew to be careful not to idly think about how much he wanted to be scalding hot. Following that, when he went to bring his stubble back down to half a millimeter as per Blayze's request, he almost punched the projected image of the suit-clad man who appeared in the mirror to relay the MRF announcement.

Though he'd been forewarned by Ollie about the message, it hit differently to actually watch the words *stick to the collective and limit use of abilities* come out of the official's mouth. Was that seriously all they were prepared to say on the matter? Where were the directives? What was the plan? Why wasn't there any urgency to rectify the rapidly devolving situation? Reports surrounding the validity of the video had already been translated from online media to physical print, and as far as Dane was concerned, his magical government was doing little to quell anyone's doubts.

Once he eventually managed to get ready for the day, he had been intent on discussing the practically laughable message with Blayze, but he entirely lost his train of thought when he found him spread-eagled on the couch.

As he fixed a big pot of coffee and blended a kale shake, it was hard not to feel a weird tug of attraction to his own physique. Dane wasn't unattractive—he could admit that much without bordering on narcissism—and yet it was still bizarre to see someone walk around in your skin and behave so differently in it.

Blayze was gregarious, opinionated, and charismatic. Those weren't traits Dane often applied to himself, and even if he wondered what Blayze's opinion was in reverse, it was abundantly clear that he was *not* a morning person, and they sat in a cold silence during breakfast. That silence continued until they left the apartment, and when they hopped onto the Tube, Blayze even wedged a pair of AirPods into his ears, clearly in no mood to talk.

Dane stared idly at his phone and wondered if he should take some goofy selfies to commemorate the ludicrous occasion. That and he'd get a wicked kick out of posting them online.

"Caffeine's started doing its thing now," Blayze said as they were on their third connection. "Where's this Seer again?"

"Tottenham Road," Dane reminded. "Not much further. Try to stick to the objective once we're inside, all right?"

Blayze threw a theatrical scowl across the gangway and took out his other earbud. "What do you mean by that? You think I can't focus on one thing at a time?"

"Not necessarily. I merely suspect you get distracted easily."

"Gosh," Blayze snorted. "Some opinion you've got of me."

"Let's not do this right now," Dane dismissed. "It'll all be over soon. Then you can pick up where you left off with your *tactical retreat*, okay?"

"Seriously, I don't think you should test me on that one," Blayze whispered, eyes wild. "Whatever your stance is on the path I chose, I'm telling you right now that I will categorically not entertain discussion on the matter. Not when there's so much doubt flying around."

Shoving his music back in, Blayze slapped on a pouty face and did everything he could to avoid eye contact. In the back of his head, Dane knew he was only being short because of the near-constant threat of spontaneous combustion, but it was tough to shake the paranoia. For what it was worth, Blayze had probably done the smart thing by leaving his kin to deal with the fallout of the video, because if he didn't trust himself not to get mixed up in everything, it was responsible of him to recognize that fact. Too often peaceful protests get out of hand, and if it came down to it, maybe Blayze was better over here, where he was out of harm's way. Even so, mages tended to pride themselves on their sense of community and their ability to exist in secret without going completely insane. As a result, it was hard not to see his behavior as an act of desertion.

Would Dane have been stubborn enough to stay if the roles were reversed? Or would he have been wise enough to take himself out of the situation like Blayze had done?

When their stop came up, he was half tempted to ditch the grumpy American and see how his smart ass figured out the labyrinthine Tube network by himself. Then again, leaving Blayze to his own devices was probably not the best idea, and Dane had a feeling both bodies needed to be present during whatever ritual the Seer would invoke, and so he gestured Blayze to get off his butt and follow.

The overground was pissing down with rain, and weaving between bustling tourists and hasty commuters was almost a full-on workout. Three times Blayze got collared by street vendors selling tacky London merch, and for a second, it looked like he was about to break.

"You should be used to this," Dane said as he pressed the traffic light button and firmly stood his ground. "Isn't New York twice this busy?"

"What's the matter?" Blayze elbowed him when he finally caught up. "Worried one of those baseball caps wouldn't fit your big head?"

Dane chose not to dignify the comment with a response. Instead he navigated from memory past the endless rows of boutiques, bakeries, and information centers, through a sprawling maze of alleyways, until they eventually reached the Seer's shop. On the face of it, Essence and Vigor looked like just another quirky independent place of business that happened to be nestled in the back alley of the capital city. To those in the know, however, the collection of symbols painted on the storefront weren't chosen at random—they were ancient mage insignia, designed specifically to welcome people with abilities into a safe space.

Although it felt slightly ridiculous, he did a quick visual sweep of the area and then pushed at the door. A bell chimed upon entry, and the first thing he noticed was the potent scent of lit sage. Next were ocean waves playing softly overhead, and when Blayze closed the door behind him, Dane relaxed enough to fully appreciate the eclectic spread of wares.

Amid the racks were a bright and exotic selection of feathers and quills, velvet cloaks, dainty pendants, staffs and staves and wands, wooden idols, tarot cards, pendulums, candles and cauldrons, runes, various homeopathic healing gems, crystal balls with prisms so intense they were accompanied with cloth coverings so that people didn't burn down their houses, and of course, shelves upon shelves of spell books.

It was a true feast for the eyes, and for the first time in what seemed like eons, Dane was put at ease. The fire sitting beneath his skin seemed to identify that they were in a secure zone, and they both knew they weren't in any immediate danger.

As a result of sheer blissful ignorance, Mage shops were too often associated with the occult, but Dane wasn't afraid of the unknown. This was a sanctuary for novice mages, and even though his last run-in with the Seer wasn't exactly ideal, he recognized the importance of her work—so much so that he'd donated a sizeable chunk of his savings a few years ago when a handful of exuberant naysayers had tried to shut her down.

Blayze scoffed at the wares. "Look at all this. Think if I light three candles and dance around doing a naked chant we'll swap back?"

"Man," Dane said when Blayze started huffing an ornate pot of herbs. "I knew you'd be like this."

"What?" He turned back around and framed his face with his hands, pretending to be the picture of innocence. "I've only visited a Seer once in my life, and it was great fun poking holes in all his logic. I'll give this one credit where it's due. This stuff is beautiful."

The moment he started to finger a particularly jagged azurite, the Seer materialized behind the front desk. She was dressed in an elaborate off-white chiffon kaftan ensemble, and despite standing safely under five feet and wearing a placid expression on her oval-shaped face, Dane remembered reading that seers could be dangerous when crossed.

"Hi again, Trina," Dane said. "It's been a while."

"Yes, Dane," she agreed in response. "That it has." She looked at the hulking form that was usually Dane's body and inclined her head. "And it's nice to finally meet you, Mr. Martinez."

Blayze took a sharp intake of breath, and his voice was barely a whisper when he next spoke. "You—huh? I... haven't used that name since I was nine years old...."

Whatever crisis he was undergoing would have to wait, because the fire was starting to itch under Dane's skin again. "Look, I'm sorry to be rash about this, but we need your help undoi—"

"I know why you have come," stated the Seer. "Seems you weren't the only ones who were careless with their wishes last night. I have already regrown a full head of hair for a young lady and shrunk a gentleman's member back to its original size, and it's not even nine o'clock. Swapping bodies? Now that... is a particularly interesting one. How are you faring with each other's gifts?"

Blayze eyed her carefully as he moved to stand right next to Dane. "Terribly. I've got people's emotions buzzing around my head, making it practically impossible to untangle my own, and that one over there is minutes away from turning himself into a live firework. How is it you knew—?"

"Can you reverse it?" Dane cut in front, fingers crossed in his pockets. "This is something you've done before, right?"

"Actually, I have not." Trina offered up a genteel smile, one that said she pitied them sincerely. "In all my times on this plane, this is not something I have come across. Nonetheless, fear not, dear ones, as this does not mean we cannot find a resolution. It simply means I will have to get a little creative. This might take some time." She glided across the room to lock the door and flip the sun-bleached Open sign to Closed, then quickly ushered the pair through a set of beaded curtains into the back room.

THE SEER'S private quarters weren't any less magnificent than her storefront, and when Blayze joined Dane at the circular mahogany table, Trina started to rifle through a mountain of wicker baskets.

A row of six black pewter cauldrons lined the far wall, and Dane became fixated on the steady bubbling and heady concoction of aromas coming from within.

"Not going to lie," Blayze said, "I was half expecting to find a Ouija board and a bunch of white pillar candles back here."

Trina gave an audible tut as she gathered up a collection of items in her arms. "That's because you are prone to being shortsighted. My work focuses on the immediate future. It does not bode well to linger on the past."

"Oh right." Blayze narrowed his eyes. "I haven't gotten a super firm grasp of this power yet, but the overriding emotion I get from you is pride. Though that's cool and everything, why is it we can't fix this ourselves? We're mages. Hand over the spell book and we'll learn ourselves."

"Dear child," Trina said, not the least bit offended by his psychoanalysis. "Do you know what Nephilim are?"

"'Course. They're angels, right?"

"Almost. They are those who are born from both angel and human. Whilst I am not a direct offspring, my ancestors' blood courses through my veins, which means I am honor-bound to do no harm. It also means that up here," she said, tapping her temple with two fingers, "lies the intrinsic knowledge which cannot be found in any spell book, to concoct precise remedies for circumstances such as this. So, what will it be?"

Nodding slowly, Blayze smiled. "How many Nephilim are there in the world today? You're telling me nobody considered the idea of putting together a handy little journal for this kinda stuff?"

It was painfully clear that Blayze was a skeptic—natural for a mage who'd grown up in secret, but still quite surprising considering how much of an interest he'd shown in gifts. Maybe he was pissy due to their predicament. He'd probably been expecting her to wave a wand and have done with it already.

"All magics are at the very intersection between science and divinity. I am no child of faith, yet I cannot deny the stock that those before us put in the will of their gods and those who did the same with the supposedly natural marvels of the universe. We are living in a golden age of discovery, and while some believe there is a discourse between science and magic, there is much to be learned from the void between."

"So basically," Blayze said, "people happen across something different, study the fuck out of it, then replicate the results?"

Dane tutted and elbowed him in the side. "You're really not helping. He's being an ass. Sorry. We would very much appreciate your help. This happened when we had an... uhh... exchange... of sorts."

"When you made love?"

Blayze guffawed loudly and shook his head vigorously from side to side. "No, no, no. We screwed, plain and simple. He wants to know if we'll change back if we do it again, but I held off in the interest of caution."

Trina pulled up a thin eyebrow, eyes glittering with humor. "That was wise of you. However, in my humble opinion, I suspect that the joining of your bodies acted as a catalyst for the wish, rather than it being the reason in and of itself."

"Hmm," Dane said, scratching his chin. "So what you're saying is, we're free to do it again if we want?"

When Blayze opened his mouth again, probably to let him know that was exactly the last thing on his mind, Trina pointedly placed a ceramic pot down on the center of the table. Next to it she put a baggie of soil, a small metal watering can, and a little rectangular container, rattling inside of which was a stark white seed about the size of a chestnut.

"Sorry, I've never had much of a green thumb." Dane snorted.

"Too bad," Trina said when she finally took a seat. Eyeing the pair carefully, she clasped her hands and smiled. "The seed set before you is that of a moon lily. Imported from a grove skillfully veiled deep within southern Mexico, it is very rare and very powerful. Once sown, the plant will pledge itself to you, body and soul, and its growth will depend upon the grade of your connection. Embark upon a deep and meaningful journey to create a genuine bond and the flower will bloom and create the most beautiful petals you ever saw. Make light of the task or fail to gain traction within an appropriate time frame, and the plant will wither to dust before your eyes. Bring me but one of the petals, and I will brew a tonic that shall return what was once yours."

There was a good fifteen seconds of silence in the room while the pair digested that, and that silence was soon pierced by Blayze's incredulous hooting.

"For real?" He guffawed. "You're not kidding? Okay, so, let me get this straight… I've gotta force myself to like this guy simply so I can get this magical problem-fixing plant to grow, and with that you'll brew a potion that can get me my body back? No offense…." He held up his hands and turned to Dane. "You were only meant to be a screw. This wasn't supposed to be a long-term thing."

"Same here, bud," Dane admitted. "I'm not exactly thrilled about this myself, but it's not really looking like we've got much of a choice, do we?"

Trina smiled graciously. "Fortunately, there is a way to make the task easier. Owing to the Law of Correspondence within the mystic arts, the plant will grow exponentially quicker if you locate a set of powerful items which correlate to the main elements. Fire—produce a sun stone by absorbing solar essence atop the highest vantage point you can find, to provide the correct climate needed for healthy development. Water—a vial of purified water collected from the well that feeds Aldwych, to offer up the nectar of life needed for all things to flourish. Earth—a dish of fresh sap from a Dryad's grove to act as a catalytic nutrient for the soil."

"A Dryad?" Blayze repeated, astonished. "I… I thought they only existed in myth…."

"They are as real as you or I."

Looking deadpan at Trina, Dane was overwhelmed. He had no idea where to find any of those things, and he was starting to regret ever going to that stupid club when he could've been at home streaming, talking to chat, and building his loyal and drama-free community, where the only wishes came from an Amazon list.

"And what about air?" Blayze asked. "Pretty sure there's an entire division of Air Spinners who might disagree that it isn't a main element."

Trina sighed but did well to keep her composure. "I do not make the rules. I simply lay them out for others to follow. And before you ask, the kind of solar energy the crystal requires cannot be found in a mage's gift."

Disregarding Blayze's insistence of equity among Elementals, Dane silently implored the Seer for an alternative method. He'd probably take anything that didn't involve being forced into spending time with the increasingly abrasive and starchy American.

"Frankly, there is no other choice," she said, effectively reading his mind, energy signatures, or body language. "The wish that has been granted has only a seven-day window of reversal opportunity, and you are already down to six. Despite your misgivings, the pair of you seem shrewd enough, and I'm sure I don't need to spell out what happens when that timer runs out?"

Blayze huffed impatiently. "We'll be stuck, won't we. Forever?"

"Correct," Trina said. "Now, do you seek my help or not? These resources are incredibly scarce, and if you intend on wasting them, I'd sooner channel my efforts into helping those who want it."

"We want it," Dane said hastily, deciding for Blayze. "No way I'm getting shipped off to the States. Yeah, us Brits might be a little quirky, but you Yanks are a whole different kettle of crazy. Please, Trina. We need your help. And thank you, even for trying."

The Seer turned expectantly toward Dane's former flesh and waited patiently for Blayze's input.

"As if I wanna be stuck on this island full of Limeys. Why did I even come here in the first place?" Dane watched as Blayze finished muttering to himself and finally turned the sour look toward Trina. "Yeah, fine, we want it. Thanks, I guess."

The Seer drew in a lengthy, measured breath. With their confirmation now locked in, she reached behind her and fetched a conical glass vial with a cork stopper, a deep plastic petri dish, and a roughly hewn chunk of agate. Even if the crystal was of medium size and was incredibly beautiful in its own right, it was also quite a bit duller than Dane remembered the gemstone to be. Maybe that would change.

"From this point forward," she said, carefully arranging the items equidistant from each other for no apparent reason, "the pair of you must act together, as you must be the ones to sow the seed, not myself. Fear not, for it is not unlike a conventional planting process. It is what's on the inside that counts."

Blayze eyed Dane warily. "I got gifted a cactus once, and even though it only needed watering once a month, it still gave up on me. Are you any good at this sort of thing?"

"Not so much." Dane opened the soil packet. "But this is our only choice, okay? We have to give it a shot. I'll fill the soil, you plant the seed, then we water it together."

"Fine by me," Blayze said. Then he grabbed the box with meaty hands.

Once Dane had poured in the whole packet and leveled off the soil with his fingers, he created a small well for Blayze to pop the seed in. When it was good and buried, they each grabbed ahold of the watering can's handle and poured in a generous measure. Then they sat and gazed at the pot for what felt like minutes. When nothing immediately out of the ordinary happened, Dane let go of a breath he didn't realize he'd been holding.

"Like I said," Trina started, that smile ever-present on her lips, "these things take time. It is ironic, truly, that this is the one thing in which you are lacking. If you put your faith in the lily, it will do the same."

Dane was getting a little tired of riddles, and Blayze was itching to jump out of his seat. "How do we know when it's ready?"

"Once the plant is ready to be harvested, you will certainly know. Now," she said as she passed the crystal in Blayze's direction, "there is a matter I must return to within the astral plane. I hope to see you again very soon, and I bid you both the best of luck."

Dane lifted his finger in the air, about to ask for any more hints or tips that would aid them on this ridiculous and annoyingly time-sensitive journey, but the Seer's eyes glazed over when she went into a meditative-like state, and with that, there was nothing more to be said.

THEY KEPT conversation to a minimum on the way back to Dane's. Mostly because he had been made to carry the plant the whole way when Blayze had refused, thrown a sour face, and promptly jammed in his AirPods to doubtlessly drown out a barrage of outsider emotions.

As he watched him absently rolling the crystal between his fingers, Dane was grateful he hadn't felt the relentless urge to burn everyone and everything in his path. That was a very welcome improvement, and he wondered if it was because the Seer had helped him gain some perspective.

"You've gotta give me something here," Dane said as he closed his apartment door. "What are you thinking right now?"

"I think this is bullshit." Blayze put the crystal on the counter once Dane had put the plant down, then perched on the back of the sofa and crossed his arms as the kettle boiled. "Being forced to spend time with each other and pretending we're all lovey-dovey to grow a stupid little plant? Such garbage. And that collection of things we have to find? How the hell are we gonna get sap from a Dryad? They're supposedly famous for hating Pyros on account of them, you know, being literal tree spirits who think we're gonna burn their forests down?"

"Didn't your Pyro ancestors do exactly that?"

"Allegedly," Blayze said. "I still don't buy it."

"Well, yes, in actual fact, the thought had crossed my mind," Dane said. "Especially since I'm actually going to be the one to have to deal with her. We'll simply have to cross that bridge when we come to it."

"I'm not that patient," Blayze admitted. "We should go find another Seer and look for alternatives."

Dane arched his eyebrow at the mugs, and when he got the tea brewing, he turned back around and crossed his arms. "There isn't another one for at least three hundred miles, and they'd likely tell us a similar version of the exact same thing. Trina didn't have to help us, you know. Notice how she didn't charge us a single penny? That's because she works for the people and always does her best, given the set of circumstances. Yeah, what she told us sounds like old-wives-tale crap, but I trust her, and you should too. We should try to get those items in their exact order as quick as we can. The tallest place I know within reach is the Shard. It's the second-tallest building in the country, actually, right behind Emley Moor, and that's just a giant concrete tower in Huddersfield." The blank look on his reflection told Dane that Blayze had about as much grasp of British geography as Dane had of Native American history. He sighed and pointed in a roughly northern direction "About two hundred miles that way. So, the Shard it is. I reckon if we bring the crystal up there, we can perform the ritual in secret and at least tick that off the list."

"And when was the last time *you* performed a sun ritual?" Blayze wondered. "I'm the one who's supposed to have an affinity with fire, remember? I've never even seen one in person."

"You realize the sun isn't actually on fire, right?" Dane didn't want to come off as superior, but the dude was starting to rub him the wrong way. "It's a ball of gas reacting to nuclear fusion."

"Whatever," Blayze dismissed. "I'm not here for a science lesson, and I sure as shit don't need to tell you how big of a tourist destination the Shard is. Even *I* know that. We won't be able to get five seconds of privacy, let alone however long it takes to do a ritual that you're apparently the master of."

"I never said I'd mastered shit," Dane defended. "Simply that I have this feeling things will turn out the way we want them to."

"Oh, sure thing. Seeing as you're so zen about everything, you might as well bring that Seer up the Shard with you. The way you keep blindly backing her sounds like you've got a thing for her."

"Now you're being ridiculous." Dane rolled his eyes as he poured the milk in, threw out the teabag, and handed over the cup. "We're mages, we have intuitions for this sort of thing, so I'm trusting my gut. You ought to do the same. Drink some tea and chill the hell out, okay? I need you to stream for me in a little under an hour."

Blayze scowled. "Um, what's that now?"

"Streaming, as in content creation? It's something I've been doing on the side of my security job, hoping it will one day garner enough interest so I can resign from babysitter duty and actually turn my passion into a full-time thing."

"Right. And what do you typically stream? Sweaty workout videos for a bunch of thirsty gays?"

"No, actually. I have a VR setup that allows me to play all sorts of interesting titles. Latest one I've been adventuring through is an RPG called *CyberBane*, which is perhaps the best future-forward sword-and-sorcery game I've ever come across. Come to think of it, we should probably set you up with something I haven't played before. That way it won't look weird when you don't know what you're doing."

"Sure, sure." By the look on Blayze's face, he was trying hard not to feel inadequate. "Exactly how necessary is this? I thought we had bigger things to focus on. Like, don't get all mad and stuff, I'm only wondering how imperative this stream lark really is."

"Um... very," Dane said, stone-faced. "I've been keeping to a steady schedule for the last three years, and I don't want anything to jeopardize the momentum I've been gaining. Least of all because of this. You get that, right? You've got a job and all that?"

Blayze scrunched his eyebrows and fixated on his teacup. "I mean, yes and no. Because I've always been the artistic type, I tend not to punch a clock. Admin jobs get boring, retail work lets me experience the disillusionment of human nature, and yeah, I might be good with my hands, but carpentry is too fiddly."

"So what do you do?"

"Well, I *used* to be an Incident Administrational Analyst. Remember my ex who got trapped in his own apartment? I was the one who provided the Oathstone that allowed his lover to remain safe in our world. The job started out fine, but there was so much admin, and as cool as it was to help facilitate someone's destiny, I got bored with the tedious work. I worked under Jasper's mom, who can use Tranquility at will. She made it all the way up the ladder to work for the MRF's public relations division, and not so long ago, it was my life's goal to become a powerhouse like her. I thought being high up the chain of a powerful environment would fit me like a glove, but the bureaucracy was too distasteful, even for me. I don't know what I was expecting when I signed up. Maybe I had this image in my head that I'd get to use my power every day. Or maybe be something cool like an enforcer. Those things were far from the case—it was more a subtle game of diplomatic chess under the guise of incident reports and infractions paperwork, and so I dipped out pretty quick and promised myself I'd never work in an office ever again. I can't stand being a data monkey."

"Hang on a sec," Dane whispered, scarcely able to comprehend what he'd just heard. "You used to work for the MRF?"

How had he not known about this sooner? If he was still affiliated with their magical government, he might be privy to information about their current state of affairs. Being in the dark about global-level decisions had been biting at Dane like a vicious rash, and now that he knew some of Blayze's background, he didn't know if it made more or less sense for him to have been in such a hurry to flee the States. Maybe he'd burned bridges with old colleagues and the thought of seeing them again was too painful. Maybe the day wasn't too far off when they would need to conscript more Memory Wipers, and given that he'd have been in close proximity, he could have been high up on the list.

"Like I said," Blayze continued. "I left a long time ago, and I'd prefer not to talk about it right now if that's okay. I'm a different person nowadays from what I was back then. Which is why, for the last few years, I've been focusing on my Etsy shop that sells blown-glass trinkets. I mean, they're not technically blown because, thanks to my power, I can heat my hands to around two thousand degrees, which I find shortens the process very nicely."

"Wow." Dane smiled broadly. "That's a brave swerve in career choice. I've never known someone who worked for the MRF before, and as many questions as I have, I respect your choice in not wanting to rehash it. The trinkets biz sounds mega interesting. Can I see your page?"

As he pulled his phone from his pocket and handed it over, Blayze's cheeks started to flush crimson. It was the first time Dane had seen him get outwardly shy, and as he took a perch next to him, he was surprised how endearing it was.

"Don't get used to it," Blayze said. "I can feel you pitying me because I'm embarrassed. Trust me when I say it doesn't happen often. Yeah, it hasn't been the most fruitful of careers, but I'm nothing if not persistent."

"Holy crap." Dane scrolled through page after page of expertly crafted glass ornaments. While the flowers and birds and architecture shared an abstract theme, each item was a purposely different color or attitude, and it was almost impossible to believe that some of the designs held their own weight because they were so dainty. "These are incredible, man. You really make these by hand?" When Blayze nodded softly, Dane noticed that the nervousness lingered long after he'd supposed it would. Though reading people in the blink of an eye was second nature to him, it was strangely refreshing to get a feel for Blayze without the use of a gift.

"Remarkable," he said. "I'd love to see the process sometime."

"Glad you think so," he said. "I won't lie. I wish others thought the same. I haven't had an order in about three weeks, which makes me wonder if I'm pricing them too high. Not taking enough high-res photos? Or am I lacking in searchable buzzwords? Maybe I should've gone to business school. Could still do that, I guess, but you know how it is once you get your mind set on something and you can't let go."

"Honestly? In this golden age of social media, I don't think you need to. The prices seem fair given how beautiful they are. Hell, I'm gonna add at least three of these to my basket later on. You've got the talent part nailed. All you need now is a bit of recognition and the ball will start rolling so fast you'll have to get some new sneakers to keep up with it." Dane gave Blayze back his phone and resisted the urge to place a hand on his thigh. "Maybe I could put a word in at work. Better yet, actually show them off to all the swanky rich folk? They jump at any chance to brag about fancy ornamental pieces, especially the one-of-a-kind variety. Never underestimate the value of word of mouth."

"Um, it might be a little difficult producing new wares given our present situation." Blayze gave a sarcastic grin, which was a big step up from how he'd been acting about everything so far. "And I didn't bring any with me on my vacation. Thanks for the offer. Sweet of you. Okay, so where's this console of yours?"

As he paced over to the kitchen to put his mug on the side, Blayze seemed to relax for the first time that morning, and though he could no longer feel his body temperature, it was ten times easier to be around him when the breathing air didn't feel sticky and hot. "I've had my nice British cuppa, you've made me feel decidedly less like a useless piece of garbage, and I think I'm ready to get to work."

"Try not to think of it as work," Dane advised as he washed both cups. "It's a video game—it's fun. Trust me. And don't worry about chatting to the viewers too much. We can say I'm feeling under the weather if it comes to it."

"Hey," Blayze said, gazing down at the pot on the table. "Is that…? Am I imagining that?"

Concerned, Dane dried his hands and turned around to peer at the potted plant, and he could've sworn his heart skipped a beat when he saw a tiny shoot peeking up from the soil.

"Whoa." Dane picked the base up to examine it and make sure it wasn't just wishful thinking. "I guess we're making progress already. Looks like we're doing something right for once, huh? I don't know about you, but that's put me in a really good mood. All right, follow me and I'll show you my gaming room."

Blayze cracked his knuckles and followed Dane into the office attached to his bedroom, where he was met with an arrangement of interconnected desks and curved monitors. The room was cast in relative darkness until he switched the power on, and when the screens came alive, they illuminated a gaming chair with the most up-to-date VR console sitting patiently on the headrest. All the cables were meticulously kept out of sight, and because he even kept a miniature vacuum cleaner hanging from a hook on the wall, Dane liked to believe it was a sleek little at-home setup, and he was often at his happiest in this very room.

"Wow, talk about man cave, and here I was thinking this would be your sex dungeon," Blayze laughed. "How much did all this cost? You know what, never mind. I don't think I want to know."

"Lemme set up a go-live timer." Dane paced over to his main computer with the standing-desk adaptation and found that he almost had to get on his tiptoes because of his new height. "Okay, this will automatically get you streaming in exactly twenty minutes. Should give you enough time to acclimate yourself to the simulated world. If you haven't used one of these before, I'm telling you right now that this is gonna be weird. Try not to give the game away by being a complete noob, okay?"

Blayze sneered as he put on the headset and took a seat in the gaming chair. Once he was fully strapped in and booted up the subterranean platformer Dane had set aside for a special charity stream, the look of sheer wonder on his face was absolutely priceless.

CHAPTER SEVEN

THE HEADSET had been surprisingly comfortable to wear, given that it had been plastered to Blayze's face for the past three hours. The game itself, on the other hand, had been a complete whirlwind of insensibility, and the strangers chatting in the box at the bottom of the screen were quick to discern his ineptitude at piloting an avatar across an endless maze of cave systems.

Still, Dane had been right about the calming nature of streaming. Blayze had been able to interact with people in a way that meant he didn't have to actively control their auras, and after how challenging it had been to manage thus far, it was a blessing to simply let go and be himself without outside influence. The simulated world was also dangerously compelling, and it was easy to see why Dane had become so passionate about building a career on something that was fun and put him at ease.

As he walked into the kitchen, Blayze began to feel a bit remorseful about giving Dane so much shit. He was also completely wiped, and considering he'd just done him a pretty big favor and gotten a boat load of donations and subscriptions in the process, he didn't bother hunting him down to ask whether he could grab an iced latte from the fridge. He'd damn well earned it.

As the liquid caffeine worked its magic, Blayze eyed the plant. He was pleased to see it had grown maybe an inch in his absence, but it wasn't exactly instantaneous progress. He'd never seen a moon lily before, so it was kind of hard to guestimate their fully blossomed size. Even so, he suspected it had a long way to go.

Blayze gulped down the drink and chucked the container in the recycling bin, then moved over to the lounge to get some chill time and maybe catch up on a show. An intensely warm emotion of feverish joy hit him like a wall before he saw the reason why, and he stopped dead in his tracks when he found Dane spread-eagled on the sofa, eyes closed, hands down his pants.

"Bro," Blayze said, jaw swinging. "The fuck're you doing?"

Dane's eyes snapped open, and as the expression changed on his face, he looked like he'd been caught shoplifting at Ann Summers. "I— sorry, I was only trying…," he stammered as he slowly removed his hand and sat up, anxiously looking around the room at nothing in particular. "I was watching the stream for a while, keeping an eye out and whatnot, and then a really powerful urge grabbed hold of me. It's weird. It's like I got possessed or something. Are you always this horny?"

Standing there gawping, about to catch flies, Blayze became the embodiment of confusion. He was instantly turned on, and he could very perceptibly feel that Dane was even more aroused than he had been before. Suddenly Blayze started to feel weird about it. That was his own body in front of him, and while he could admit he might be egotistical at times, this was a whole other level of narcissism he had yet to untangle.

Then he started to get a little mad. It was *his* cock this dude was fumbling with, right? Why should he get to play with it without asking first? How many times had he touched his junk in secret? And, in the interest of not being a total hothead, was it acceptable for him to feel this way? Granted, the situation was far from normal… and yet Blayze couldn't help feeling a certain sense of possessiveness over his body.

When Dane noticed his hesitation, he made a move to get up off the couch, but after a swift change of mind, Blayze got down to his knees and held him there. "Fuck it," he said. "Turns out I'm horny as well. And I always wanted to suck my own dick but was never flexible enough. How about it?"

After a small shrug of his shoulders, Dane grinned. "Works for me. It's kinda hot, when you think about it."

Blayze nodded noncommittally, trying to shove the creepiness out of his mind as Dane unsheathed a cock he had looked at for thirty-one years. It was odd seeing the underside of his dick from this point of view, and even after having taken hundreds of pictures from all different angles in the past, he'd never quite realized how droopy his balls were in comparison to his long shaft. They looked like two low-hanging apricots, and when the excitement got the better of him, he gave them a few strong licks, then fixed his mouth on the tip. It tasted of lemony soap with a faint hint of musk.

Scarcely able to believe what he was doing, Blayze opened his throat and took his own cock to the base. It was pretty weird to suck a dick with a different-sized mouth than what he was used to, but he plowed on, gently deep-throating Dane and grabbing a firm hold of his giant nut sack and giving it a sharp tug, hoping to cause the all-over sensation he was very fond of. Though Dane wasn't all the way hard yet, he'd soon change that. Blayze was an expert cocksucker, and just because he had a new set of teeth and slightly meatier hands didn't mean that was going to change. He was also sorely tempted to heighten the experience by amping a few emotions here or there, but after last time in the kitchen, he gave the thought a wide berth.

"Mm-hmm," Dane moaned in appreciation and placed both hands behind his head, totally at ease.

A stirring in Blayze's pants let him know he needed to free himself or run the risk of snapping his new dick in half. As he was doing so, Dane leaned forward and watched eagerly.

"You like that?" Blayze asked. He got up to perform a mini striptease and then gently stroked himself. Somewhere along the mystifying timeline he'd actually forgotten how thick Dane was, and the weightiness of all the cock meat felt incredible in the palm of his hand. "Tell me—how bad do you wanna suck yourself right now?"

"Real bad," Dane said, practically panting.

With one purpose in mind, Blayze made short work of stripping himself, and by the time he was buck naked and about to drip precum on the couch, he grabbed the back of Dane's head and pushed him to the base of his cock.

Wow, he felt amazing. Like a warm cloud, if only that cloud had the ability to grip like a spacecraft airlock and suck like a 2,000 rpm vacuum cleaner. Dane's body was hotter than if he'd been sunbathing for the entire day without a single shade break, but if he was aware or not didn't matter much, because the only emotions radiating from him were pleasure and intent.

"Jeez," Blayze said, absently combing his silky head of hair, admiring the view of someone playing with a foreskin he'd never had. It was like he had taken control of someone else in VR or something, and it just so happened that the hunk on the other end was himself. "Keep going like that and you'll give me a run for my money."

Dane chuckled softly, and since his mouth was full of dick, the vibrations on the base of his shaft felt beyond incredible. Whether the gag reflex was in the mind or not was of no concern, because in that moment, it was only the two of them, and body swapping be damned, they were simply two men enjoying each other's bodies, ferociously pawing at each other, making themselves feel good in the best way they knew how.

He wondered what it would be like to eat his own ass. He bet it tasted great. How weird would it be to fuck himself? Although he often labeled himself as versatile on most hookup apps, he was really a pretty exclusive bottom. Maybe now that his body had Dane's brain, things would be different. They'd probably have to discuss some ground rules if they wanted to keep things civil over the course of their absurd scavenger hunt… but all of that could wait, because this man was working some real voodoo magic with his too-hot mouth, and Blayze quickly recognized that he needed to shoot his load really fucking bad.

"Keep going," he demanded, not that his throat would let him go any deeper. Dane didn't need much more encouragement to suck even harder, and he started groaning long and deep as he jerked himself with one simple objective in mind.

As those groans morphed into something distinctly more carnal, Blayze lavished the balmy heat of his tremendously tangible joy as it swiftly evolved into a white-hot beacon of ecstasy. When Dane started to shoot so fast and hard that it volleyed up to Blayze's stomach and balls, he clamped his eyes shut and reached for Jupiter as a million nerve endings began to explode from the head of his dick.

As he emptied his load down Dane's throat and felt him swallow every drop, Blayze's heart started to pound out of his chest. The overload of emotions was enough to make him dizzy, and because he was in fairly serious danger of passing out, he gracelessly fell back onto the couch, chuckling hysterically, drunk on pleasure.

"Fuck," was all he could manage when the breath finally came back to him. "That was hot as hell. Why are my orgasms ten times more potent when with you?"

"Fucked if I know," Dane breathed next to him. The sky-high temperature he'd built up on the couch was gradually subsiding, and Blayze was mega proud of him for not setting anything alight. "Shame we didn't get to do anything else. Got carried away, I guess. Always a next time, eh?"

It was curious that they'd had such a close parallel of thought, but in the cold light of day, amid the postorgasm awakening, Blayze was craving something sugary. Before he could entertain such ideas, he started to itch for a shower.

"Mind if I go clean up?" he asked, already getting up. When Dane gave a nod of approval, he bent down to pick up his clothes. "Could do with a snack afterward. Oh, and I'm gonna have to bring my suitcase over from the hotel. Easy there, I'm not asking to move in. Just think you could do with more than the one pair of my clothes."

"Good thinking." Dane tried to act all nonchalant even though he'd quite clearly had a mini meltdown. "Probably best if you check out and come crash on the couch? That way you don't have to pay stupid amounts of money for something you aren't using."

Blayze nodded, apparently rooted to the spot from secondhand awkwardness. When he finally broke free of the invisible chains, he spun around to hunt for the bathroom, then stopped in his tracks when he side-eyed the potted plant on the kitchen counter.

"Dude, you're not gonna believe this," he said, voice low. "This damned plant has gone and grown leaves."

CHAPTER EIGHT

DANE WAS ready to call bullshit until he sprang up off the couch and paced across the apartment to examine the plant. As well as shooting up a couple of inches, the lily had, in fact, produced two bright green leaves. Their significance didn't go unnoticed, and yet as happy as he was to see them, they also left him and the flickering flame in a conflicted state of mind.

"So, what?" Dane asked, incredulous, forgetting that the curtains for his bay windows were wide open and he was still stark bollock naked. "What do you make of this? Are we supposed to simply fuck it out until the plant grows big enough, then we're safe and sound?"

"Possibly?" Blayze shrugged. "Who knows at this point? Maybe that's really what the Seer meant when she talked about forming a bond. Maybe it was a kinky kind of thing. If you give me a few, I'll be ready to go again if you wanna try."

Dane eyed him cautiously and considered it for a few seconds. "Nah." He shook his head. "I'm not buying it. There's gotta be more to it than that. Trina knows what she's talking about. She seemed confident in that list of items, and she laid out the order pretty explicitly. She also implied that we need to get to know each other's minds as well as each other's bodies. Or our own bodies, as it apparently were."

Blayze didn't look convinced. "I'm not so sure. Yeah, she was helpful, but that woman seemed to enjoy the whole cloak-and-dagger approach a little too much. She prides herself on being vague and mysterious."

"Sure, she's a little theatrical. Wouldn't you be?" Dane stared at the plant again and wondered if it would grow in front of his eyes if they made a hard effort to bond. "I think maybe the fact we actually got to have sex like that was the turning point. I don't know. Whatever the case, I'm glad we're onto something. It was starting to drive me mad, not getting anywhere. Go take your shower. I'll make us some pancakes. Then we need to put our heads together and work out how we're gonna get this essence of sunlight."

Blayze offered a lazy smile as he trudged off to the bathroom, and Dane practically skipped as he bustled around the kitchen and threw ingredients into a bowl. Because he had the luxury of an open-flame stove, once the batter was made and a few ladles' worth were in the pan, he had the urge to try cooking them with his power.

What was it Blayze had said before? Try to keep the flame at a simmer, not a boil? Dane could do that. He reached out with one hand and switched the extractor fan on with the other while he stared pointedly at the twin burners. He called upon the flame in his mind, pictured it with his third eye exactly how he did every day with his aura-reading power. Instead of reaching out with a hand that didn't exist, however, he tried to actively will the flame to materialize.

When a small and steady fire appeared on the burners, Dane's heart leaped into his throat. But he was overjoyed for all of half a second, because the fire was quick to expand beyond the limits of the pan. As soon as it touched the batter, it scorched the food, and the flame promptly died.

"Shit," Dane said.

Awash with deflation, he scraped off the shriveled black disks and cleaned the pan. Determined, he took a breather and tried again, but batch number two turned out even less successful than the first because of his mounting impatience. And no matter how hard he tried to summon the flame with a soft, carefree mind, the fire always grew far too big and only served to incinerate the food.

"Oh, for fuck's sake. Why are you being like this?"

Dane rolled his eyes, hardly able to believe he'd actually just addressed the flame directly. When the fire alarm on the ceiling began to shriek a high-pitched wail, a shirtless, towel-wrapped Blayze came to casually waft a tea towel under the detector. He looked alert yet unrattled as he scanned the stack of burnt pancakes on the counter, and owing to his power, Dane wondered how many thousands of fire alarms he had heard in his lifetime. Surely it was dangerous to be desensitized to such a thing? Then again, if a housefire ever crept up on him at some point, it's not like Blayze himself would actually be in any real danger.

When silence finally came, Blayze threw the towel aside, then stuck his hands on his hips. "When you offered to cook pancakes, I didn't realize you were intent on burning the place down in my absence."

"Ha bloody ha," Dane mocked. "I was *trying* to get to grips with this stupid, finicky power. How the hell do you put up with it on a daily basis? It's damned near impossible to control."

"Hard? Yes." Blayze said. "Impossible? No. Now you're starting to see what I felt like with yours. Why don't you cook some the old-fashioned way while I raid your wardrobe. Then afterwards I can help guide you through a few things, okay?"

After Dane begrudgingly cooked up a fresh batch of perfectly golden-brown cakes the entirely boring way, he placed them on the island and was layering maple syrup when Blayze rejoined him. The outfit he had rummaged for was an odd pairing of burgundy pants and cream cable-knit sweatshirt with sleeves rolled back. His sense of style was interesting to say the least, and in his hands, he had also brought a pair of boxers and a tee Dane got from the Glastonbury Festival about seven years back. It was much too small for him now, and yet he couldn't stand to part with it because of the amazing memories he'd made.

"My body's great and all," Blayze said as he handed them over, "but you might wanna cover up while we eat."

Dane threw the clothes on and took a seat on the barstool. "Thanks. I'm not a nudist, I swear. Slipped my mind for a sec there."

"No worries," he said as he tucked in. "Wow, these are yummy. Do you cook often?"

"Not as often as I should," Dane said as he stabbed a forkful. He hadn't realized how famished he was until he started. "The trouble with being in the literal center of London is that there's, like, a thousand takeout places I can order from, and because the best ones are all in a one-mile radius, all the naughty food can get here in, like, fifteen minutes tops."

Blayze nodded absently and kept his thoughts to himself as he finished his meal. That was a first.

When they were done, Dane loaded everything into the dishwasher, then trotted back to the main room, eager to learn.

"Okay, I know we've got this sun-stone lark to deal with soon, but if I want to safely spend a whole minute outside of this apartment without worrying about imminent combustion, some training is in order. Where do we start?"

Blayze pursed his lips, and a pensive expression crossed his face. "At the risk of sounding counterproductive, we should start with something complicated, then work our way backward. Hopefully it'll give you a quicker understanding of what's involved."

"If you say so," Dane said. "You mean like something from your trinket catalogue? Works in theory, I suppose, except I don't exactly have a stack of raw glass lying around for an occasion like this."

"Fair," Blayze said. "Got any cereal bowls you can reconstitute? There's gotta be one you aren't super precious about."

Dane rooted through his cupboard, impressed with the resourcefulness. "This big enough?" he asked as he pulled out a deep casserole dish he'd gotten from IKEA a few months ago and never used. When Blayze nodded, he also grabbed a tea towel from a drawer in case things got messy.

"Best to do it on the couch, because you can sit comfortably and get in the zone." Blayze found a spot first, then patted the space next to him. Anxious, Dane carried the bowl over, and when he sat down, he closed his eyes and tried to empty his brain. "That's a good start... but you're gonna need to pick which ornament you want to replicate."

"Ahh, yeah," Dane said. "Duh."

When Blayze started a slow scroll of his wares, it didn't take long for Dane to find a favorite. The rainbow-colored bird of paradise perching on a freshly hewn tree was probably somewhat optimistic... and yet he felt a joyous sort of tug toward it, and he figured it was important to pay attention to that.

"Brave man," Blayze said. "I dig it. All right, close your eyes again and really try to feel the warmth in your hands. It's always there, but you've gotta will it out bit by bit. When you feel them get up to temp, open your eyes again and start to craft. But try not to overthink it. The beauty of fluid art is that the work will speak for itself and take shape as you guide it. Got it?"

Dane nodded, then did his best to block out the world around him and the sound of the cars below. When he pictured in his mind the ever-present warmth coursing throughout his body, he tried to channel it specifically to his palms, his fingers, and his fingertips. This time around he opted for a distinctly gentler approach and treated the flickering foreign entity with the calm sort of tenderness it so obviously craved. Though he'd been mortified to address it directly like it was a genuinely separate individual, when he spoke to it in his mind, she seemed far more willing to cooperate.

All of a sudden, heat surged in his hands. It wasn't an uncomfortable feeling; he simply knew it was there and chose to let it exist. As straightforward as that was, he did start to panic when the casserole dish began to melt. But he reined himself in, and instead of letting it all slip through his hands, he was actually able to pluck shapes from the giant liquid ball. It wasn't anywhere near close to resembling a bird—it was more like a sea urchin, and even then, he had to use artistic license to call it that. But he was doing it. He was creating fluid art, which was something he'd assumed could only exist on canvas... and yet, here it was in physical form.

It was beyond satisfying to be in control of such a wild power, but the very second he allowed himself to relax and play around a little, the creation imploded.

"Aw, Jesus," Dane moaned as the glass melted through his hands, then ended up as solid shards on the floor. "I thought I was doing it. I'll never understand how this works."

"Hey, you did good considering it was your first try," Blayze encouraged. "You gotta be proud of the small victories and not be so hard on yourself. This method of mine isn't common among Pyros. Pretty sure I'm the only one in NYC who can do it so well. Everyone starts out somewhere, and it's not realistic to expect perfection the first time around. Now, I'm not saying I was wrong, but maybe the big approach wasn't the best idea. I fancy another cuppa. Wanna make me one?"

"Um. Didn't we literally just have one?"

The look on Blayze's face was not to be tested, so Dane scraped up all the shards with the towel, tossed it into the trash, and readied the ingredients for two brews.

"Put cold water in the cups," Blayze demanded. "Then bring them over here."

Confused, Dane did as he was told, and the penny didn't drop until he was seated back on the couch with Blayze looking at him expectantly.

"Oh! I get it. You want me to heat up the liquid?"

Blayze nodded and then watched as Dane summoned a toasty heat in his hands, trying extremely hard this time not to reach a temperature anywhere near what he had before. Eventually, after straining so hard he almost burst a vein in his forehead, it was very pleasing to see a boiling cup of tea water and even more pleasing when he managed to put a firm stop to it.

"Oh wow." Dane celebrated his success with a grin. "That's super handy. Screw making trinkets, you should start your own barista business. The overheads would be so cheap. Hah," he said when he saw Blayze's face. "Kidding."

Blayze frowned. "I know it's a long shot, being an artist for a living. If I could only get a bit of traction with my store, it would all be fine, you know? It's not dissimilar to what you want to do with your streaming, but it's so hard these days for small businesses to emerge when the bigger brands undercut everyone because they can buy in bulk. There's no room for the little guys anymore unless you wanna make fifty cents per item. Not being greedy or anything, but how is that sustainable when it takes a decent portion of time to make these things? Let alone make any kind of profit for a living."

"Yeah, I hear you. This company that I partner with, SciCo? They might look small now, but give it a couple years and they're gonna be tech giants. They have the drive for it, and it's so exciting to see what the future holds for the gaming world. And hey, I know I said about showing off your wares to the rich folk... maybe I could add a link to your site on my stream as well? My following isn't huge, but the people in my chat are loyal. I don't see why they wouldn't love your stuff. They look like they're great for having around the house and giving as gifts. Everyone needs gift ideas. People tend to get booze and chocolate from me at Christmas time nowadays."

"That's... wow." Blayze was stumped at his kindness. "That's really nice of you."

"No probs. Give it time. I know it's a grind. You'll get there."

"Thanks for believing in me. I guess I need to start doing the same for myself."

"I think so too," Dane said. Then he got up off the couch, went over to the plant, and picked up the agate. He examined it in the sunlight beaming through the window. "All right. Let's get the ball rolling and go charge this thing. It won't be too long before sunset, so we should get moving."

"Whatever you say, boss." When Blayze stood up and lingered by the front door, he eyed Dane carefully. "I know we're in on this together and whatnot, but if you end up getting sent to jail for occult practices in public, you're on your own."

Dane rolled his eyes, pocketed the crystal, and headed out of the apartment.

CHAPTER NINE

BEING THE tallest building in the city, the Shard was fundamentally impossible to miss as they wove their way through the streets. Blayze counted their lucky stars that Dane had snagged a couple of last-minute tickets, and once they took time to admire the Golden Corgis and life-size Beefeaters, they crammed into the elevator again and sailed up to the sixty-eighth floor.

They filed their way into the main area and became a part of the herd who automatically drifted toward the sprawling windows. Dane's penthouse apartment was dizzyingly tall in its own right, but it was nothing compared to the view of London in all its glory, basking in the slowly dwindling light of the sun. Blayze took pleasure in the collective delight from the auras of those next to him, and he felt a strong echo of that emotion inside himself when he pinpointed countless famous monuments and lesser-known achievements within modern architecture. From this vantage point, with all the cars and construction work and people milling about the streets, he swore he could see the city breathing.

"Wow," Blayze stated. "Really puts things into perspective, huh? We're like ants running around an elaborate maze down there. Too caught up in our own business to realize how small we actually are."

Dane chuckled at his side. "That's very profound. And to be honest, disturbingly true."

"I mean, ants are pretty awesome. It never ceases to amaze me that they can lift three thousand times their body weight. Plus, they work as one unit in service of the queen. Do you think humans will ever achieve harmony like that?"

"Metaphorically speaking, it's possible. In practice I'm not so sure. Guess we'll find out soon enough, won't we? I know you don't want to talk about it, but people are getting restless, and the speculation is getting hard to ignore. Interviews from supposed witnesses have made the front page of the biggest newspapers in the country. Usually it's nothing but thinly veiled political drivel, so if the lefties are giving this a spotlight, shit's really getting real."

Blayze turned around to hide the sudden tear that had sprung to his eye. He needed a distraction, and while a large chunk of people had broken off to find good selfie opportunities, he tugged at Dane's arm, asking him to follow. Once they made their way up to the sky deck, Blayze was blown away by the spectacular arrangement of flora. In front of yet another breathtaking vista were rows of poppies, fox gloves, lavender, marigolds, and even birch trees. Clearly a lot of thought and care had gone into the design of this space, and he could already feel inspiration stirring for new trinket ideas.

"Whoa." Blayze took out his phone to snap a quick panorama. "Elijah would love this."

"Who's that?" Dane wondered. As he took in the beauty of the plants, the look on his face said he was more intrigued than jealous.

"A friend of my ex—a quiet and reserved guy. Nice enough, though. And a damn good Biomancer. Man, I haven't seen him in, what? Four or five years? I wonder what he's up to."

"Biomancer?" Dane repeated. "As in, the ability to make plants?"

"I think it's more to do with healing living matter than making it, but it just so happens most Bios work in either botany or medical fields. Come to think of it, would we really have to be doing all this if we had that gift? Because we could simply grow ourselves a perfectly healthy moon lily...."

"Best not to think about it too much," Dane said, then he placed a hand on Blayze's shoulder. "How are you doing? In the here and now, I mean, not metaphysically."

"If I'm being honest, I could do with a snack from a vending machine, but I'm guessing this place is probably too fancy for that. Isn't there supposed to be some sort of Sky Garden restaurant up here?"

"No, no." Turning back to the window, Dane pointed a finger toward another building that was half the height of their current vantage point. "That's over there at the Walkie Talkie. Ate there once on a date a long time ago—would highly recommend the rib eye. Another time, perhaps? So, I'm usually fine with heights, but I'm starting to feel a little nervous all of a sudden. Let's go grab a drink."

Blayze's throat pinched at the thought of a passion fruit martini, but he was ever-conscious of their mission. "Do we have time for that?"

"A quick one, yeah. Would help us to blend in. Second-tallest point in the country, remember? We've got a bit of time before the sun goes down."

When they got back down to the main area, they joined a rapidly moving queue, and Blayze almost had heart failure when he saw the prices on the menu. His credit score would hit rock bottom by the time he made it back to the States, but because he was being put up by Dane, at least he no longer had to pay the Savoy's eye-watering rates. That was something. When it was their turn to be served, Dane didn't seem too bothered to fork over the handful of cash, and maybe that was due to circumstance, or maybe his bank account was simply that full of savings. Either way, when they brought two brightly colored cocktails over to a standing table, Blayze took a sip, reluctant to admit it was easily the best-tasting drink he'd had since the cocktail at Adrenaline.

"Wow," he said, practically going bug-eyed. "This is dangerously good. I could probably drink this like orange juice. What's yours?"

"Something adjacent to a Blue Lagoon," Dane said, smiling. "Reminds me of kicking back on a sun lounger in Spain, which is often my happy place. D'you wanna trade sips?"

Blayze nodded eagerly and passed his glass over the table. When he received Dane's and took a small sip, the explosion of flavor in his mouth was enough to make him momentarily forget why they were there. "Okay, so I'm gonna need at least six more of these."

Dane swapped back and cast a furtive glance out the window. A minute passed in which they didn't speak, simply listened to everyone else's animated blabbering. When a quartet of dolled-up ladies started speaking at length about the video on everyone's lips, citing that even Marvel Studios couldn't reproduce such realism, Dane turned back to face Blayze, and there was apology written in his eyes.

Even if it certainly wasn't the time or place, Blayze knew he had to speak on the matter eventually. "I don't feel qualified to talk about the video of that Stormcaller. For them it's fine—they're doing the perfectly normal thing by speculating what they think might be in front of their eyes. For us, we know the truth. We know what it means if that video gets the blue checkmark, and I wouldn't even know where to begin in terms of passing judgment on what should or shouldn't happen. That in itself kinda worries me."

"Okay, I get that. Truly. And yet, why not at least entertain ideas? Where's the harm in that?" Dane pressed. "He's been identified as Jeremy Lane, by the way. And not to sound like a total simp or anything, but this news is only, like, the *most* exciting thing to literally ever happen to our community. Why aren't you bothered by it?"

Blayze heaved a sigh, gulped half of his drink, and then instantly regretted it. There was a very real chance he'd only be getting one of those cocktails in his lifetime, and he'd planned to make it last. "Yes, it's exciting. However, going from what we already touched on before, much as I'm trying not to act, I am very bothered by it. The full scope of what we're talking about here is mildly terrifying, and I can't stand to 'entertain ideas' for the very same reason I left the MRF. And for that matter, it's the same reason I left my home country. It wasn't an easy decision to up and leave my place of birth during a monumental time like this. You get that, right?"

"I do."

"Are you sure? Because I don't think you do get it. You're acting like I'm this callous piece of shit who went along and thought, *Oh hey, this is getting a bit much, think I'm gonna dip.* Spoiler alert—that wasn't the case at all. I've got fire in my blood, and I'm not just talking about my gift. I don't do things halfhearted. It's not in my nature. Maybe I should blame my ancestry for that, but I don't want to see the news or listen to any MRF mirror messages until there's a clear-cut way forward. There's too much ambiguity right now going on in my own head—I don't need to see and hear it from everyone else."

"That's fair enough," Dane said. "And for the record, I don't think you're a callous piece of shit. Most people wouldn't have recognized the severity of the situation. You did, and you didn't give in to irrationality, which must have been tempting. That can't have been easy."

To his credit, he was really trying to understand where Blayze was coming from, but he'd only been living in a Pyro's skin for a couple of days. He would never be able to fully understand the toll it took being a living time bomb for thirty-one years, and even if he could, Blayze didn't want that for him. He didn't want it for anyone.

"How are you holding up?" Blayze asked. "Flame-wise, I mean."

"I'm good." Dane stroked his own arm gently and became pensive as he examined the invisible fire-threaded current that ran through his veins. "I can tell she's there—she's always there. Though the pyromaniac urges are getting somewhat easier to manage. Maybe it's because I'm kinda getting over the denial part? I don't know."

"Maybe. That's a good sign, and I'm glad you're a little more comfortable."

Looking back up, Dane offered a sly smile. "How are you faring, Mr. Martinez?"

Blayze tightened his lips paper thin, huffed through his nose, and tried very hard not to slam his fist on the table. "Ability-wise, I'm fine. Oh, but please don't make a habit of calling me that. I get that it might not be a well-used name over here, but it was as widespread as mosquitoes in Mexico City, and that was a whole lifetime ago."

"So where did Blayze come from? How did your parents know you'd be a Pyro?"

"They didn't. They named me Mateo—which, again, is pretty common. After I discovered my inherent power at age eight, I rebranded myself to fit my intended identity, and I legally called myself Blayze as soon as I was able. Even though I can't forget my heritage, I prefer to go by that name because all of my life I've worked to be able to hold myself to a certain standard, and by now I like to think that I'm anything but common."

"You had your prepubescent discovery at age eight?" Dane asked, screwing up his face. "Holy crap, everyone in my school was around ten or eleven. Oh, and you definitely hit the nail on the head there. You are anything besides common. I've sure as shit not met anyone like you before."

"Huh." Blayze blushed at the unexpected compliment. "Thanks."

Even though they were here for a substantial and time-sensitive task, hearing about a mage's magical awakening was always intriguing, and now that Blayze had started to open up, he found that he didn't want to stop.

"Let's imagine for a second that the MRF don't deny the existence of the video," Blayze suggested. "Let's say they come out with their hands up and admit that we've been walking alongside them for eons. What then?"

Dane shrugged and sipped his drink. "I don't know, Blayze. I wish I could sit here and tell you that everything will be fine, that we'll make this grand entrance and everyone will be jumping at the chance to dish us out warm hugs. But I can't do that in good conscience. People are more complicated than that."

"I'm only doing what you asked me to do," Blayze said. "Entertain ideas, remember? See, as much as I want to believe otherwise, I think our relative freedom is just an illusion. There's enough lunatics in this world already without giving them real ammunition to throw at us. Yeah, there will be loads of people who will look up to us and show us the respect we deserve, but how long before the mages themselves abuse that power?"

"Pfft." Dane made a move to shrug his shoulder again but thought better of it. "Maybe you're right. We've gone this long without needing any kind of permission to practice or other forms of external validation. Why shouldn't we carry on living in secret? Yeah, we might make more genuine connections if we were allowed to be our authentic selves, but as you pointed out, it's too easy for people to get a power trip on either side of the coin. Not to mention how much of a spanner that would throw in the works of mage culture. You know what we're like, always conducting our business in clandestine locations and using mirrors to communicate events that have a global impact. Sometimes I think it adds to the drama, but what happens when everyone gets a say in how we govern our own people? What's that age-old saying? Don't rock the boat? Yeah, that's it. Our community has always managed to flourish under our day-to-day masquerades, so where's the need to upset the natural order?"

"I don't want to be right," Blayze decided all of a sudden. "What we've had to go through over the course of our lives shouldn't *be* the natural order, and that doesn't sound like a world I want to live in anymore. I'm done looking over my shoulder all the time. Sorry to get out my tiny violin again, but it's bad enough being a Pyro. I've never been wholly accepted for the things I can't change, so the pros definitely outweigh the cons in this potentially not-so-hypothetical scenario."

"You think so?" Dane asked.

"I do," Blayze said resolutely. "I can't exactly go back to the States and help right now, not given our present condition, at any rate. But if there does come a time when I can make a difference, you can bet your ass I will do my best."

Dane nodded and appeared to agree wholeheartedly, but something in his cheeky little smile suggested he might have been pushing Blayze to that very conclusion in the first place.

"OKAY, LET'S do this." Sucking up the last of his cocktail, Blayze took a mental picture of the taste in case they got arrested in the next half hour. "There's an area over there that's closed for maintenance. That's probably our best shot of getting somewhere quiet, so let's head to the toilet, slip out, and get this done."

"Sure," Dane agreed. "Let's not actually go into the toilets, okay? Oh, not because of any funny business. I just don't want to break the seal because I've no idea how long this is gonna take."

The thought hadn't even crossed Blayze's mind, but it was an interesting image to hold on to as he made his way to the door with a very obvious no-go sign plastered on it. Trying hard not to look over his shoulder and arouse suspicion where there wasn't any, he pushed on the door, ignored the strong gust of wind, and sidestepped to the left-hand side, making sure to keep out of sight from the window as he held the door ajar.

Though the area was in a state of disrepair, it was seemingly intended to become one of those deranged setups where people lean off the side of the building for the viewing pleasure of social media. Fortunately for Blayze, there were no staff to be seen anywhere, and the space was mostly open-air and therefore likely suited for a sun ritual. Unfortunately for Blayze, while the view of the city was largely the same as from the inside, there was an altogether different feel at the gargantuan height now that there wasn't a physical barrier between him and the ground.

As Dane promptly joined him and cursed under his breath, he closed the door, then grinned. "Dude, this is batshit," he said as he leaned across to take a quick peek through the window. "I don't think anyone noticed, but that draft might have ruffled some feathers. Let's shuffle over before we get blown like trees in a tornado."

Blayze made sure to keep his back against the building as he shimmied like a crab across a narrow passageway that was absolutely not built for foot traffic. Of all the times to be in a different body, this was perhaps the least favorable one. While he found it extremely arousing in the bedroom, being stout and burly wasn't all that useful when it came to doing parkour eight hundred feet up. Also, to add insult to injury, the sheer increase in scale made the chill in the air painfully hard to ignore.

When he finally came across a wider section that also happened to have a large clearing of sunlight, he doubled over and blew out a sigh of relief. No doubt the flooring was just as solid as on the inside, but he couldn't shake the mental image of a sudden collapse.

"Thought I was gonna be sick," he said when Dane joined him, having had a considerably easier time wearing Blayze's more nimble skin.

"Yeah, me too." When Dane retrieved the stone from his pocket, he held it up to the late afternoon rays and watched in awe as it glinted like an iridescent diamond. "Let's sit down opposite each other and try to get this done as quick as possible."

Still having no idea how they were supposed to fulfill this ritual or how long it was supposed to take, Blayze put his trust in Dane's faith as they sat crossed-legged in the sunlit patch. When he laid the crystal on its side against the metal paneling, something did seem to change in the air, but if there was an incantation to be spoken, then they were pretty much fucked. His mind had gone entirely blank.

"What now?" Blayze asked, worried they'd wasted their time.

Dane tore his eyes away from the crystal and peered at him. "Could we make something up? I'm not all that in tune with the mystic arts, but I'm pretty sure the words don't matter so much as the intent. As long as we're channeling the same energy, willing this gemstone to take on the form that we need it to, then we'll be golden. Okay? Take my hands."

Blayze grasped Dane's hands and waited for the words to repeat.

"Gaia," Dane said, closing his eyes as he turned his head up to the sky to address mother nature herself. "We call to you for aid. Grant our request and we will be in your debt. Transform this lowly crystal into a sun stone."

While he didn't relish the idea of being indebted to a heavenly body who may or may not exist, it was surprisingly easy to share in Dane's unexpected sense of invigoration, and Blayze kept the bigger picture in his head as he repeated the latter half of his speech.

"Transform this lowly crystal into a sun stone."

The Law of Correspondence didn't fail them, and the moment the last word left their lips, the agate made a *whoosh* as it began to spin so fast on the spot that it became a blur.

Waiting for the next phase was like watching a pot boil, and he should probably mimic Dane's closed-eye approach and let it do its thing, but Blayze couldn't keep his eyes off the gem as it literally drank in the sunlight before his very eyes. Even though he wasn't touching it, some of his energy was pouring in, and the abrupt change in Dane's aura told him it was happening to him too. It wasn't painful in the slightest, and it didn't exactly feel like anything crucial was getting sapped from him; it was more of a friendly handshake as the new artifact was gradually being birthed.

As it spun, the gem started to change shape. The hard, jagged edges were hammered out where it *cricked* and *cracked* every so often, and it steadily grew in size as it absorbed the essence of life itself. It took just over a minute for the process to finish, and when it came to a decisive halt, Blayze watched Dane crank open his eyes and grin ear to ear.

"Oh my," he said, instantly reaching for it. Even if it was a thousand degrees, Dane wouldn't feel a thing as he grabbed ahold of it, and Blayze was unexpectedly envious of the fact that he was cradling their creation in his hands. "It's... magnificent."

It really was. Having gone from a small and random chunk of a dull beige color, it was now a big, bold, and beautifully smooth orb, mottled in a gradually shifting semitranslucent shade of pale honey. Blayze had never seen something so extraordinarily elegant, and he was instantly inspired to theme a whole new line of handmade trinkets around it.

"Let's get this back to the plant," Dane suggested. "It should be cool to the touch by now. Would you like to hold it?"

"Yes," Blayze said without hesitation.

He held out his hand, and Dane carefully placed it in his palm. It was a lot heavier than he'd expected, and as soon as it made contact, a bizarre notion of pride enveloped him from head to toe. It was the same sort of feeling he got when he learned to embrace his gift as a kid, but it was also distinct in its own right.

As the power emanated from his hands once again, it was almost like every interaction up to this very moment had led him to the creation of this ethereal relic. Though he considered mage rites to be very important, now more than ever, Blayze didn't often pay attention to otherworldly signs. This time things were different. Pouring their combined energies into something like that had changed them. Or, at the very least, it had changed *him*, and as they sneaked back into the building and headed to the apartment, Blayze had never taken greater care of anything in his entire life.

CHAPTER TEN

DANE WAS more amazed than anyone at how smoothly things had gone at the Shard. He had totally winged it when it came to the incantation, and he was mighty proud of himself for holding his wits together, considering he'd been a plastic bag inside a cyclone. Maybe one day he could give Trina a run for her money.

Once they made their way down, it hurt to leave the intoxicating smells of the various restaurants behind when his stomach was doing a great job of eating itself alive, but when Blayze swung by his hotel to get a bag of his clothes, Dane made sure they swung by his favorite Chinese takeout on the way back to the apartment.

"You sure you got enough?" he asked Blayze when they were back inside. "There's not much there—my appetite normally calls for more than just chicken and noodles. You didn't even order any wontons."

"All good," Blayze said. "I'm not all that hungry."

"You sure? It'd take all of two minutes to order some more."

"Yes, Dane, I'm sure."

Blayze was being short because he was distracted. Had been ever since he first took hold of the sun stone. It wasn't like he was possessed or anything. At least, Dane sincerely hoped not. More that he had displayed an uncharacteristic amount of care in transporting the spectral gem. He had insisted on keeping it with him when he dipped into his hotel room and made Dane wait outside, and now that he lingered by the plant, which had grown about an inch since that morning, he seemed hesitant to relinquish his stewardship.

"You ready?" Dane asked. "We could always eat first and do this afterward if you'd prefer?"

Shaking his head, Blayze breathed through his nose and squared his shoulders. "No. Let's get this over with."

He held out his palm with the stone in it and carefully hovered it over the top of the plant. Once his hand began to vibrate, Dane wondered if it was down to cosmic intervention, but it was simply Blayze trembling in anticipation. When nothing seemed likely to happen, he tried a different position and slowly rested it on the counter. Over the course of about a minute where both of them simply ogled the plant, nerves building, its stem jerked slightly, the young leaves shook like they were a puppy coming in from a snowstorm, and that was it. No otherworldly spectacle of light, no rapid burst of growth, and no tangible progress to reward them for their efforts.

"Well that's—" Blayze started.

"Anticlimactic?" Dane suggested.

Blayze became dejected, and when he reached out a hand to grasp the sun stone back off the counter, he evidently thought better of it and chose to leave it where it was.

"I'm sure it'll take effect soon," Dane promised as he fetched the dinnerware, took to the couch, and promptly dove into his steaming kung pao chicken.

For some reason, Blayze's tongue wasn't very familiar with spicy food, and the irony of that was nothing short of hilarious. The hotter-than-usual stabbing on his tongue put a different spin on something Dane had eaten a minimum of fifty times, and when Blayze tucked into his noodles and made soft sounds of appreciation, it was nice for them to sit together in relative silence and enjoy the multifaceted wonders of oriental cuisine.

"Okay." Dane put his cutlery to the side when he was adequately full to bursting. "Don't go blowing your lid or anything. Now that that's all over with, I am gonna need a big favor from you."

Blayze narrowed his eyes to slits, already unimpressed.

"I need you to go do a shift for me."

"Do you stream games that regularly?"

"I don't mean that kind of shift," Dane said tentatively. "I'm talking about my actual, physical job."

When he finally understood, Blayze's jaw hit the floor, and when the plate nearly fell off his lap, an artery almost burst in his forehead.

"As a bodyguard? Please tell me you're joking?" Putting his food on the coffee table, Blayze looked like he was half expecting Dane to elbow him in the ribs and laugh it off. When half a minute passed and he did no such thing, he rounded on him. "You're not seriously expecting me to go do a security job when I have zero training *and* I've got this damned curse of a power?"

"I'm more of a doorman. And I don't know what to say," Dane admitted. "Not to guilt trip you or anything, but I'll get the sack if you don't. That's kinda how normal jobs work."

Blayze got up from the couch and put some distance between them. "Phone in sick. Say you've got the shits. Or that your granny's got the shits and you need to look after her."

"Can't do that. If you're sick too many times, they don't offer more contracts, and I'm already on thin ice from the time I had glandular fever a couple months back when I kissed too many guys at the Manchester Bearbash."

"Ergh," Blayze moaned, over it. "Don't you have enough savings to cover this one loss? Look around you, Dane. Your pad is next-level swanky. I think you'll be fine to take the hit."

Dane shrugged, drained his tea, then slung both cups into the dishwasher. When he turned back around, he tried to soften his expression, which must have come as quite a shock, seeing as Blayze usually had something of a resting bitch face.

"It's not all about the short-term money. I'm self-employed, which means, much like my streaming platform, the reputation I've built up is done so off of my own back. And if you become a liability in this city, people talk. Quick. Look, I know this is far from perfect, but it's honestly not that big of a deal. Nothing ever happens—you simply stand there and look pretty most of the time. I really need you to do this for me. I promise I'll make it up to you afterward."

"Too right you will," Blayze said, locking his bulky arms together. "You'd better be on all fours waiting for me to pound the living daylights out of you by the time I get back. And I'm keeping whatever you earn tonight. You cool with that?"

Dane offered an ear-to-ear grin, crotch already beginning to stir at the hasty collection of mental images. "All right, Mr. Dom Daddy Top. A favor and a fuck. I am very much cool with that."

CHAPTER ELEVEN

BLAYZE HAD worn a handful of suits in the past, but he had never donned one so expertly tailored, and he tried to hold on to the wondrous sense of comfort in his perfectly cupped ass as he climbed out of the cab and trotted up to a Victorian-style chateau.

Tonight's function was for a Linda Belfry and her frankly superfluous entourage of bridesmaids, and it was a small miracle that Dane had never worked with them before, because that meant Blayze didn't have to try and act any different. Having said that, he'd made a pact with himself on the ride over to actively try and be less *Blayze* so that Dane didn't end up getting fired because of a random outburst.

Managing people's auras, on the other hand, was going to be an altogether different task, and as soon as he walked through the doors and detected a slew of hyped-up emotions, he spied the open bar positively laden with booze and was sorely tempted to swipe some vodka.

He let the thought go and assumed his post by a patio door that led to a lush fifty acres of garden sprawl, and it wasn't long before a gaggle of well-dressed ladies rained down on him. They were in a tipsy state of merriment and still fairly coherent, not quite… what was it the British said? Plastered? Trollied? Gazeboed? Whatever the case, the outpour of compliments would have been flattering were his current body not the complete polar opposite to the one back in Dane's apartment. As it were, it was starting to get on his nerves.

"So," said one of the ladies who was wearing the most tight-fitting version of the Spice Girls dress code. "You ready to get that kit off?"

Their collective aura was like a crushing wave on the East Coast surf, yet through the mix he could still detect unrestrained ecstasy and loyal pride, with only a slight twinge of jealous-based resentment. Above those, the most palpable emotion was ravenous desire, and exactly as Dane had taught him, he tried to separate each of these emotions and secure them based on their heat signatures. Being a Pyro his whole life should have given him an advantage when it came to dealing with temperatures. But this was new territory, and everything was hitting him like a military barrage. He could already feel an oncoming migraine and he'd been there less than five minutes.

"Oh shoot, sorry, gals, I'm not the stripper...." Blayze chuckled and held his hands up in surrender, itching all over with immense restraint. "Just the bouncer."

"Aww," another of the women booed. She stuck out her tongue, then raced back to the makeshift dance floor with wineglass in hand.

She was swiftly joined by the remainder of the horde, and Blayze sagged in relief. The aura reading was evidently dependent on physical range, so he placed both his arms behind his back in a firm *I'm working* stance, crossed his fingers, and prayed nobody got anywhere near him again.

With any luck, Dane's words would ring true, and all he'd have to do was stand there and look pretty for the rest of the evening. That, he could do.

EVERY SINGLE person who did door duty as a full-time profession deserved a medal of honor. Blayze hadn't really known what to expect of the job, never having guarded more than a rum and coke in the club... and yet, as it turned out, watching other people get hammered and sloppy-dance to '80s cheese was pretty dull.

When they played the Macarena and it transitioned into kinky charades, he almost wished for an actual security incident simply so he could get away from the door. At least the real stripper gave him a reprieve when he turned up in a policeman's outfit. His moves were a little stiff, and the dirty talk left a lot to be desired, but he was a real crowd-pleaser, especially when he took off his shirt, drenched it in a bottle of vintage white wine, and then wrung it out into people's mouths.

It was almost ten thirty when the function wrapped. The gang couldn't decide whether to tear up G-A-Y or Heaven—not that they stood a chance in hell of getting into either nightclub. But that wasn't any of Blayze's concern, and once they filed out of the house and crammed into a hot-pink minibus, the only thing left to do was collect the check, make a beeline for the Tube, and go get laid.

A balding gentleman in a mauve trench coat stood at the end of the bar sipping whiskey from a ridged tumbler. Stanley Belfry, if Blayze recalled Dane's less-than-stellar briefing. He was the one facilitating every detail of his daughter's wedding, and when he wagged his finger, Blayze obeyed. He even put on a little subservient smile and wondered how proud Dane would be of him for that.

"Sir Stanley." Against every single instinct in his body, he resisted the urge to offer a sarcastic bow. "I trust the evening went well?"

"Well enough, I suppose. I will, however, be deducting some of your pay, as I'm sure you're no doubt aware."

"Um," Blayze said, feeling his eyebrows shoot halfway down his face. "I'm definitely not aware of that. What gives?"

Stanley's eyebrows, in turn, shot up, and the look of astonishment on his face as he paused the check writing was genuine. "Oh. Right. Well, for one, you failed to get involved in the party games when Chantelle asked you on numerous occasions."

Blayze opened his mouth to speak, then was instantly cut off.

"For two, you failed to report that there was a mangey-looking fox on the front lawn, and it unnerved my darling daughter so much that she had to go adjust her makeup, and that ate up precious dancing time. Please tell me that you did, in fact, notice her absence."

Blayze could not believe his ears. Was this guy serious? He simply gazed at him, totally at a loss. Though he wanted to keep his distance for his own reasons, he hadn't joined in the activities because he was supposed to be doing his job. And who gets scared of a damned fox? Mangey or not, they were probably one of the cutest animals to grace the planet, and Blayze remembered longing for one as a pet when he was little and had visited the Japanese fox village.

Ever since he landed in London, he'd had his back up, and it was very hard not to feel put out when he was out here busting his gut while Dane was at home simply trying to avoid a house fire. Blayze was supposed to be on vacation, for Christ's sake. So why did it feel like work, work, work all the damn time?

Fuck the body swap, fuck Dane, and fuck keeping his shitty power on the inside when all it so obviously craved was to be let loose.

Stanley's face had remained impassive during Blayze's inner monologue, still expecting an answer to his dumbass question, but then it changed abruptly. Without even realizing why, Blayze watched as the graying man before him went from mildly bothered to enormously bewildered. His eyes were practically bouncing around his head as he ripped the check into four pieces, bent down to scribble out a new one, then shoved it into Blayze's hand as he pushed him out of the door with a creepy half smile.

"The fuck...?" Blayze said to himself as he stared after him. As much as he'd definitely considered it, he hadn't meant to let go of his power, and it had all happened so quickly that he hadn't even realized he was the reason for the bizarre change in interaction.

As he walked down to the streetlamp, he unfurled the piece of paper and very nearly walked into the post when he saw the amount penned in remarkably precise handwriting. There were two extra zeroes on top of the figure Dane had approximated. What a score!

In a vastly better mood, Blayze whipped out his phone and texted Dane. The sex could wait; he had other another idea that would satisfy him just as well.

I'm starved. Know anywhere good to eat?

Thankfully it was less than a minute before the dots appeared and Dane texted back.

Yeah, ping me your location and I'll taxi to you. I know exactly the place.

THE PSYCHEDELIC retro diner wasn't the extravagant slap-up image he'd had in his head, but after struggling to keep his power in check for such a prolonged period of the evening, they could serve up roasted horse and he'd have no issue chowing down.

"How'd it go?" Dane asked. He took another sip of Italian beer and propped his head up with his hand, elbow resting on the table. "Make any new lady friends?"

Blayze sneered and narrowed his eyes to slits. He was so antsy he'd taken to shredding the stack of napkins, and before he could even appreciate the absurdity of something he hadn't done in many years, an amateur Jackson Pollock recreation sat between them.

"Won't catch me doing that again." He firmly clasped his beer and made a mindful effort to keep his hands there. "No way, no how. A bunch of horny women I can deal with. This power of yours? Nah, not so much. Dude, how do you put up with it? It's a fucking nightmare."

Dane frowned, probably more upset by his language choice than anything else. "You're telling me. I'm the one who's had to deal with it the last two decades. On a scale of one to ten, how messed up do you think I became when I first felt them in my head? Actually, don't answer that. Yours isn't much fun either, by the way. I set the alarm off three more times, so there's gonna be a wonderfully needless bill slapped onto my rent this month. Even managed to burn five bits of cookware to the point of no return. So yeah, it's been a hoot."

"Wait until someone rubs you the wrong way in a bar," Blayze said, grinning. "Then the real fun begins."

"I'll bet. Have you made a scene before?"

"Once or twice," Blayze said. "It's common knowledge that Elementals have to do an extra year at wizard college, right? But did you know that on top of that they also now enforce a six-month 'real-world preparation' course for all postgraduates? It's remote working you do online, but still, sometimes all the namaste-practiced-patience bullshit fails to work, and it's lucky one of my pals back home has the power to erase short-term memories, really. Else the MRF would have a few things to say about me for sure."

The look on Dane's face said he wasn't impressed at the flagrant misuse of power. "I only know about that extra training because of Ollie. Sounds like it must've sucked ass, no doubt. Except, well, not that this is a pissing contest or anything... you haven't had other people's emotions invading your head for the better part of twenty years, have you? Some people are messed up in the head, Blayze, and I have to block their dark auras on a daily basis. Honestly, I should just go live out the rest of my days on a private island somewhere. And speaking of being honest, it's a pretty good job this body of yours is hot."

"Thanks," Blayze chirped. Then he caught on. "Hang on a sec, what's that supposed to mean?"

"You know what I mean."

"Let's say for argument's sake that I don't," Blayze said, tone dropping. "Would you then care to clarify?"

"Sure. For someone who can innately manipulate fire, you're a bit lacking in self-control."

"Is that so?"

"Yep," said Dane. Blayze leaned back in his chair as far as it would go, creating as much distance as possible without getting up and heaving the thing across the room. "And, by the way, you can't cash that check."

"Why the hell not?" Blayze yelled, instantly seeing red. "I earned it fair and square."

"You absolutely didn't," Dane said calmly. "Rich people stay rich because they're stingy and tend not to give their money away, and unless you're now the proud fiancé of Linda Belfry, there's no way you managed to earn that amount of dough unless you let your power slip. *My* power, Blayze. It'll be *my* neck on the line if you decide you can't handle this, because *I'll* be the one stuck in a padded cell by the time we get our bodies back."

Unsure how to respond to that, Blayze hissed, furious.

How could this guy sit there so judgmental after what he'd done for him? He was positively livid, and when the waiter loaded their table up with food, Blayze demanded another beer, then asked for three different kinds of sauces simply to give the guy the runaround. Once he'd run out of things to pick holes in, he began to prod at his dinner while Dane showed no shame in wolfing it all down. The beefburger was really quite delicious, but Blayze's appetite had vanished in the heat of his anger, and it was hard to enjoy the layered tastes on his tongue when all he could taste was tart bitterness.

He drank the rest of his beer and ruminated on his complete runaround of a day. How dare Dane tell him what to do? What right did he have to talk to him like a piece of shit? Just because they'd swapped bodies didn't mean he owned him, or vice versa, for that matter. They both had their own free will, and he knew very well that if they wanted to see an end to this madness, they had to work together instead of actively trying to thwart each other.

Above all, he was mad because Dane was right. If he cashed the check, it'd be as good as fraud, and even if the MRF were always very quick to weed them out, he would be no better than the lowlife criminals who, even after extensive rehabilitation, continued to use their powers for gain. Still, he was mighty pissed that he had shit all to show for his frankly monumental efforts, and when they left the diner in relative silence, he trudged back with a sour face, doing his best to keep at least five yards from Dane.

A part of him really wanted to turn in the other direction and catch the Tube back to his own hotel so he could get a break from all the nonstop fuckery. Even if it might do them good in the long run, deep down he knew the ever-ticking timer wouldn't allow for a luxury like that. Being apart from Dane for even a few hours meant they stood even less of a chance of getting back to normal.

It was like they were two different ingredients from two corners of the world inside a pressure cooker, but they refused to emulsify, the flavors didn't blend well with each other, and no matter how many herbs and spices they added, it would always leave an unsavory taste on the palate.

When they got back into the apartment and the lights clicked on, Blayze found himself walking on autopilot as he was drawn to the potted plant on the counter. He already had a sneaking suspicion as to the outcome, and while it had grown some since he'd last seen it, the stem had also started to wilt and sag, and one of the leaves that had only recently started growing was already lying dead in the soil.

"Wonderful," he said, defeated. "That's absolutely wonderful."

The hampered progress was no doubt because of their argument over dinner. In light of that, what was he supposed to do differently? *Not* share his thoughts? Didn't brutal honesty play a pretty big part in getting to know someone?

He wished Trina the Seer had written them some kind of handbook or quick-fix guide or something. Maybe he ought to Google how best to get to know someone when you first start dating them—not that they were actually doing that, of course. Whatever this was shaping up to be was far from dating.

"Fucking magic." He shrugged off his suit and threw it onto the couch. "I remember the days when being different used to be fun. Now it's all monotonous, has this weird political edge, and it's become a never-ending chore to keep everything under wraps. Honestly? Sometimes I swear it feels less like a gift and more a curse."

Dane hummed in agreement in the background, and after he stripped down to his boxer shorts, Blayze didn't bother to ask for permission as he fetched a glass, strode with purpose across the room, and raided the liquor cabinet.

CHAPTER TWELVE

"POUR ME one?" Dane asked as he took off his coat and put it on the same chair where Blayze had left his suit jacket.

As fun as it was to watch him parade in his underwear, Dane didn't immediately feel the need to join him, and he took that as a good sign because it didn't feel awkward or uncomfortable.

"No offense," Blayze said. Then he took a long swig and plopped himself down on the couch. "I'm a little bit over taking orders from you."

"Orders…? I don't mean to come across like that."

Dane sighed and nodded thoughtfully, making sure to keep eye contact as he deliberated how to deal with this new development. Though he was a little stung that Blayze had taken him for being bossy when he thought he'd been asking nicely, he made a conscious effort not to snap back as he fixed himself three fingers of bourbon.

Despite having behaved like a jackass at dinner and making Dane pay for it in full, he took a minute to try to better understand Blayze's position. To him, it felt like the mage world had been against him for as long as he could remember, and trying to validate your own place in New York, of all places, must be tough. That and he had to flee his country, hide his power, get a whole *new* power, then try to deal with suppressing that too. In addition to that, the tangible relief on his face when he dragged his suitcase in from his hotel let Dane know that he was very clearly broke and his diehard pride refused to let him admit it.

"All right." Dane placed himself in the armchair across from the couch, which afforded Blayze the space he so obviously wanted. "Let's cut the crap and sort some things out. We need to start being nicer to each other, and I'll be the first to hold my hands up and say yeah, I've asked a lot of you, and I'm probably not doing enough in return. Also, I'm apparently not asking you in the right way. To that end, what would you like to do while you're here? Would it help to brainstorm some new trinket ideas for your store? Maybe we could go on a tour of London? Or take a train over to Stonehenge to see if we can cross over to the spirit world? I feel bad if I upset you, and I want you to know that the choice is yours. If I can facilitate it, I'll make it happen."

"Gosh, how swell it must be to have so much money you can simply click your fingers and make shit happen," Blayze said. After a few seconds of silence while he let that sink in, his face started to soften, and his shoulders sank a few inches. "Okay, that was uncalled for. Sorry. I'm probably just being jealous or something. And believe it or not, I'm also sorry for being such an asshat in general. What with everything that's going on, I'm so tightly strung at the moment, and I feel like I'm a few breaths away from doing something stupid."

"You don't have anything to apologize for," said Dane. "Seriously. It's taken me a while, but I feel like I'm finally starting to see you, and what I'm seeing is that you're not a bad person. Even if we're a little different in our approach to life, that doesn't mean we have to be at each other's throats all the time."

Blayze grinned, mercifully stumped for words as he sat on the couch and sipped his drink.

"Also," Dane said, "not to bear a grudge or anything, because I know you already apologized... I'd just like to set the record straight by saying I have money because I work bloody hard for it. It didn't fall into my lap from inheritance or a lottery win. In fact, my luck is pretty shit to be honest—never won more than a tenner."

"You lucked out meeting me." Blayze winked flamboyantly. It was great to see his bold charm right back where it belonged, and he even flashed a toothy grin at Dane when he finished his drink.

When Dane moved over to the couch, he had hoped to show some physical affection, but Blayze jumped out of his skin when his cell suddenly blasted out a bouncy dance remix of Gloria Gaynor's "I Will Survive." He looked at the screen, frowned, rolled his eyes, and silenced it. "Ugh, gimme a break."

"Spam caller?" Dane wondered. "I get them so often that I have to change my number every few months."

"Just someone from back home," Blayze said with a distant tone. "Totally not important right now."

Once Blayze shoved the phone into his pocket, Dane placed a hand on his thigh, resolved to stick to his guns and not let the moment pass him by. "I'm serious, though. About being honest with my feelings. I've been selfish without even realizing it, and I promise to focus on you and your needs more."

"Yeah?" Blayze asked, gaze absently drifting back and forth from Dane's eyes to his lips. "What if I said I really needed to make out with you right now? Could we focus on that for a bit?"

In his more than agreeable state, Dane nodded slowly and took in a small breath as he closed the distance between them, licked his lips, and then pressed them against Blayze's. Almost instantly, the flame inside him awoke and ignited his very core, and after he let out a soft moan, Blayze adjusted his position and turned to face him head-on as he wrapped his arms around Dane's neck, locking himself in.

As they made out under the first swell of a semidrunken haze, it was a lot different than the two previous times where things were rushed with the urgency of desire, and as much as the curious little light inside him was steadily growing stronger with need, making his skin get warmer and warmer, he wanted to make the moment last.

Dane let his hand travel from Blayze's thigh up to his crotch, and he relished the stiffness of Blayze's cock beneath his boxers. In return, his own pants instantly started to stretch with the rapid growth inside them, but true to his word, he put everything else out of mind for the time being as he removed that hand and placed it firmly on the side of Blayze's head and pulled him even deeper into the kiss.

Last time, when Dane had been jerking off on the couch, he hadn't actually expected Blayze to walk in on him and be bold enough to initiate the sucking session that followed. He'd been pretty quiet about how arousing it had been to have sex with himself, and yet he'd been yearning to do it again.

It helped that Blayze was a really good kisser. Sure, those might have been Dane's lips he was using, but the way he was delicately slipping his tongue around in combination with a forceful yet subtle blend of touch was all new, and it served up an altogether different level of intimacy.

"You're good at this," Dane said when they finally came up for air.

Blayze chuckled as he peppered kisses up the side of Dane's neck and onto his ear, sending a curious wave of gooseflesh across his skin. "Things feel better when you want them bad enough, and you're strong enough to draw it out."

As he pulled away so he could lift his shirt up over his head and toss it on the floor, Dane was pleased to find he had very nearly gotten used to seeing himself exposed like this. He wanted to pause to celebrate the half win, but he was also eager to take things up a notch, and he point-blank refused to get in his head about logistics anymore.

Once he gave Blayze the honors of undoing his shirt, he sprung up from the couch and climbed out of his pants. The giant bulge didn't leave much to the imagination, and he experienced a rush of delight when Blayze took his hand and followed him into the bedroom.

A few minutes after they collapsed on the bed and went right back to making out and feeling each other up, Dane became motionless as another realization smacked him across the face.

"What is it?" Blayze asked, alarmed. "You okay?"

Dane hummed in agreement with his eyes closed. His initial inclination was to go ahead and top like nothing had changed, but for some reason, that didn't seem right. He'd only gone and forgotten that, since they'd swapped bodies, they'd also have to swap roles. The more he thought about it, the quicker he realized he hadn't bent over for anyone in at least a decade, and anxiety began to squeeze his chest.

"I'm fine," he said, "it's just… it makes sense for me to be the bottom, doesn't it?"

"Damn, of course. Man, I don't know how to top." The dread on Blayze's face made it look like he was about to give a parliamentary speech on budget cuts. "What do we do? Ignore it and go back to our preferred positions?"

"We could do…," Dane said, more than a little stumped. "Though my ass won't be used to it. It'd probably take a good while to stretch me out. I mean, I haven't got anywhere to be except here with you… but I don't know about you, I'm so damn horny right now."

"Same here," said Blayze, and he proved himself by getting out his cock and grabbing ahold of it to show off the thick veins beneath the foreskin. "Maybe… maybe I could try to use your power to put you at ease while I'm sinking myself in? Couldn't hurt to try, could it?"

"Hmm," Dane said, dubious. Despite Blayze not seeming to having the best track record with his power, it would be wrong to not let him practice when he'd taken the time to help out when the shoe was on the other foot. "It definitely *could* hurt if you lost control and sent me the wrong emotion… but I trust you enough by now. Just try to keep things linear, okay? Focus on happy emotions and don't blur the lines."

"Of course. And bottoming is definitely a mind-over-matter thing anyways, right? Like, I know how I enjoy my hole being treated, so if there's anyone good enough to top me, it's me."

Dane grinned as he freed his dick again. How strange that sentence would be if heard out of context.

"Go easy on me, okay?" he asked as they melded mouths again. "My safeword is pineapple."

As they frantically grasped each other's bodies, a thin sheen of sweat began to slick their skin, and Dane wondered if it was down to him or Blayze or both. There was definitely a steady increase in heat on the flame's part, but now that Blayze knew he was set to be the star of the show, he treated Dane with an interesting level of care.

"Where's the rubber?" he asked, tone dipping, eyes almost fully glazed over with lust.

When Dane gestured to the top drawer, he willfully squashed down any hint of anxiety as he turned himself over and assumed the position. As the drawer clicked open and shut and a packet rustled, he buried his face into the pillow and told himself how much he wanted this. Though he was still a little pissed at Blayze, that simply fueled his passion for sex, and even if it did hurt, he'd probably be fine to let the man take out his resentment against the world because, above all else, he really did want to please him.

"You good?" Blayze asked behind him in a distant voice.

"Yep," he said, glad to find that it wasn't a lie. "Could you maybe start with a finger?"

"Sure thing," Blayze said, squelching the familiar sound of lube. When it made contact between his cheeks, Dane bucked with surprise at the ice-cold sensation.

"I can tell you don't do this often," Dane said, sniggering. "You're supposed to massage it between your fingers first."

When Blayze hummed awkwardly, Dane arched his back again and felt a meaty digit gently circling his hole. He took his time to trail his fingers along the muscle, and given how objectively sexy Dane knew Blayze's hole was, it was a testament to Blayze's patience that he didn't cram everything in right away. Having been inside Blayze's ass on that first night they hooked up, it really was a wondrous thing to behold, and Dane wasn't sure he could've been so restrained.

One of these days he'd have to install a ceiling mirror so he could see things from all angles, but for now he was content to focus on the darkness of the pillow, the curious mounting of his body heat as well as the eager rising of inner flame, and the fact that, because of Blayze's careful and tender nature, his hole had very easily accepted what was given without any outside emotion manipulation.

"Oh," Dane said, wondering why it had sounded kind of like a question. "Oh fuck, that's good. Give me another."

Not needing to be asked twice, Blayze slid another finger in and began to widen him up as he motioned in and out ever so gently.

"That's good," Blayze said, praising his efforts. "You're doing real well. How long before you can take this fat cock?"

So much for patience. Whatever. Dane didn't want to wait much longer anyway, and he needed to take the plunge and move on to the next stage sooner rather than later.

"Now. I'd like you to ease me," he said, giving his explicit permission for Blayze to use his power.

Dane waited patiently as the first vestiges of contentment entered his brain waves. It started out like he was on vacation, catching the first waves of a soft surf, but then he was steadily enveloped by the entirety of the afternoon ocean in a blissful calm. Suddenly, all of his troubles and concerns evaporated from the scorching yet cozy heat of the silken water, and what remained in its stead was the dire need for bodily connection.

"Now," Dane moaned, voice hoarse and drunk with lust as he backed up like a tow truck, practically begging for it. "Give it to me now, Blayze, and don't you dare think of holding back."

He was taking his time to line it up, and once the bulbous head made contact with his hole, Dane's eyes pinged to the back of his brain as his ass stretched out to accommodate the very wide and very stiff prick. The fiery sensation had nothing to do with the flame inside of him, and he half expected to feel some jealousy from it because it seemed selfish enough to hog the limelight. But after they sized each other up and reached out for the first embrace, the two sensations were quick to coincide and offer up twofold droves of sheer pleasure.

"Holy fuuuck," Dane groaned.

Above all, Dane found that he wanted, *no*, needed to be filled up. The mystical slackening of nervousness was better than if he'd sniffed an entire bottle of poppers, and right then and there, he was transformed into a greedy power bottom. Every miniscule movement caused another stab of glory, and as much as he wanted to savor every single second of it, there was something more tantalizing on the horizon, and without the need for words, he rammed himself back onto his own cock and buried himself to the base.

"Argh," he roared. Would it make a difference to him or the flame if the world called it quits and imploded? Probably not. As long as Blayze's cock stayed where it was, it was unlikely they'd even notice.

Although Blayze was only softly massaging his prostate and had yet to trust himself by really going for it, Dane didn't care how much of an amateur top he was, because having someone go this deep and touch places that rarely got touched was truly fucking incredible. Why had he put off doing this for so long? Was it because of personal image or because of stubborn pride? Or was it because he preferred to be the one in control? The delicate balancing act between vulnerability and intimacy was euphoric, and when his mind unlocked itself like a Mesopotamian casket, he mentally kicked himself for cutting experiences like this out of his life for so long. In that moment, he happily pigeonholed himself as vers, and as soon as he cashed his next paycheck, he was going to order an expensive fuck machine with all the bells and whistles and start giving himself the pleasure he deserved.

"Hang on a sec," Dane said, very reluctantly taking himself off the pole. "Yeah, I'm all good, just gotta see you," he said, voice oozing with lust as he did a one-eighty on the bed and turned over to face Blayze.

His hair was comically disheveled, and the look of raw need in his eyes was wild and almost bordered on scary, but the fact that he was so into it simply added to the overall sexiness as Dane heaved his legs in the air and bared himself to a man like he hadn't done in years. Blayze bit his lip and locked eyes as he grabbed a fistful of dick and found his target again, filling him right back up.

"That's it," Dane groaned, reveling in the sheer rightness as the delicious heat returned to him. He was back where he belonged, and even if they were actively trying to get their bodies back, a part of him hoped he'd never leave. Not while he kept that delightfully devilish look in his eyes. If all went to plan, it wasn't like they'd ever get the chance to do this again, so he wanted to make this moment count. "That's it, oh yeah, right there. Fuck me, Blayze. Fuck me with my own dick."

Spurred on by his words, Blayze finally got the hint and found himself a steady rhythm. Bouncing around so much that he was almost hitting the headboard, Dane was nearly at full temp, completely covered in sweat by now, and because his cock was rock hard and simply begging to be stroked, he could put it off no longer.

As soon as he grabbed hold of himself, the duo of dancing flames collided. Where the one in his ass had been begging for more fullness, the one in his chest had been actively looking for the culmination of their unification, and as Dane began to firmly massage his dick, it came to him in perfect clarity that there was no sense in procrastinating about something he had such a deep longing for.

"Are you getting close?" Blayze called over the sound of balls slapping skin. He eyed him cautiously as he waited for a response, not daring to stop the pounding even for a millisecond.

"Yeah," Dane moaned. It was hard to pay attention to anything other than the mounting pressure in the base of his groin, but in the interest of spurring on pleasure, he made sure to clench his hole on the stiff cock deep inside him. "I'm gonna blow right... fucking... now."

"Please," Blayze begged, strands of hair flying everywhere as he roared at the ceiling, quivered all over, and pulsated inside of Dane.

Unable to hold back, Dane gave himself one final stroke and was met with what might as well have been every atom of energy from the entirety of the universe. It just so happened that that energy wanted to burst out of his dick, and Blayze was kind enough to stay inside him as he jumped atop a monstrous surfboard and rode the five-hundred-foot wave.

There was no way to describe his and Blayze's union other than precisely correct. Getting back his offering of trust twofold was the most magnificent feeling, and the wads of his essence kept on coming as his two flames continued their friendly warfare.

The meaning of reality stretched sideways without purpose or sense, and the transcendent orgasm resonated so deeply and so wholly that Dane wondered if he was in real danger of being sent to another plane. It was impossible to tell how long it was before reality faded back into existence, and yet somewhere during that time, Blayze had collapsed on the bed. He was chuckling softly, chest rising and falling as he panted like he'd sprinted the whole London Marathon in one go.

"Well, one thing's for sure." Going entirely limp, Dane closed his eyes and tried very hard to stay conscious while brushing Blayze's cheek with the back of his hand. "You can do that again."

CHAPTER THIRTEEN

THE MORNING after what was arguably the best screw of his life, Blayze was taken aback when Dane planned to make good on his promise. Blayze hadn't been sure if Dane made the plans with lust in his eyes or if he was faking sincerity because he desperately wanted the plant to grow. Once they took turns showering and changing into pants and sweatshirts appropriate for the weather, they hopped into another black cab, and Blayze decided not to put much stock in either notion.

The plant had realigned itself and was in the process of developing another three healthy leaves, but he was starting to find that he cared less about its progress. Sharing mind-blowing sex was probably a contributing factor, but Blayze suspected there might be more at play than that. Sure, he'd hooked up with a fair share of guys in his time, but they'd mostly been a means to an end. Never before had he felt so connected, so seen, or so wholly satisfied. It was an interesting combination of feelings, and it only served to put him in a better mood when Blayze took Dane up on his offer to get out of the apartment and actually start enjoying his vacation.

"So," Blayze said, "where's the first spot on your list for our grand tour of London?"

"The National Gallery, of course."

Once he'd seen enough awe-inspiring portraits to joke that it ought to be renamed the National Portrait Gallery—which Dane told him was around the corner—they strolled along the Mall until they got to Buckingham Palace. From there they went to Westminster Abbey, then located the Houses of Parliament and Big Ben. They crossed Westminster Bridge and spied the Tate Modern, came across Shakespeare's Globe Theatre, then headed across the Millennium Bridge until they reached St. Paul's Cathedral. Even after seeing it online so many times, Blayze couldn't quite fathom the scope of the Tower of London up close, and the glorious architecture of Tower Bridge was equally impressive.

When their feet started to complain, they hopped onto the Underground and planned a route to Soho for a big mug of coffee.

"Hot damn," Blayze said as he practically collapsed in the chair and took a long sip of his mocha frappe. "It's good to take the load off. I forgot how exhausting it is being a tourist."

"No kidding," Dane said as he began to people watch. "I've lived in this city my whole life, and sometimes it still feels like I've barely scratched the surface."

Blayze held New York in the same regard. It was similar in the nonstop bustling, though that was about where the similarities ended. People were much more reserved and private over the pond, and there was distinctly less street food. And, as cute as the British accent was, Blayze was starting to miss the friendly ease of his home city's tongue. Countless times he'd struck up conversations with randomers in the street and ended up being enriched by their crazy stories. Doing that over here probably meant you were the wrong kind of crazy.

"Speaking of crazy," Blayze said, deciding to voice his feelings out loud for the sake of context. "How do you deal with so many voices at one time? Like, yeah, their energies were all contemplative and peaceful and shit, but I almost had a meltdown in the gallery simply because there were so many people in my head. Wouldn't it be hella easier to move somewhere really remote so you can hear yourself think every once in a while?"

"Probably," Dane agreed. "That's not the point—I'm not going to cut myself off from a life I enjoy because of my power. I've learned to adapt over time, and for what it's worth, I'm glad I stuck it out. I'd have missed out on so many opportunities if I paid attention to my inner saboteur."

Blayze grinned at the throwback, then grew pensive. "I appreciate how tough it must have been in those beginning stages, and I totally get your stance. Same goes for me, I guess. It's one of those things that's so easily said rather than done. My life would probably be exponentially easier if I lived out on a ranch somewhere, but I like city life. Though our home cities are realistically only a few thousand miles apart, it does feel like we're from a different world sometimes."

"How so?"

"London and New York are the big boys, right? Even so, the life you've got down here couldn't be more different from mine." Blayze chose to trust his gut enough to roll with the vulnerability he was about to put on the plate. "You've got money and friends and a high-tech apartment that you obviously adore living in. I don't have any of that back home. In fact, I'm barely making ends meet, and I can't say I blame any of my friends for ditching me. Sometimes I'm a nightmare to be around."

"Sometimes?" Dane jabbed, but he grinned above the rim of his teacup. "Only kidding. You're not all bad once people get to know you. Though you've gotta do something about that resting bitch face." When he put his cup back on the saucer, he checked his watch, and his back straightened in surprise. "Aw, shit. Look, I'm glad you're starting to open up and everything, and I'm sorry to cut this short, but we've gotta get going."

"Going where?" Blayze asked, eyes narrowing to slits. "My feet will probably get a mind of their own and start a revolt if I do any more sightseeing today."

"It's not on the official itinerary," Dane whispered as he got out of his seat and offered his hand to get Blayze to do the same. "I did some googling last night, and the Holy Well Aldwych is right outside of Australia House, which is pretty close by. It'll be getting dark soon, and if we get there after people are clocking off, we should be able to sneak in and get that vial of water."

"Ah," Blayze said. His body wasn't in the mood to undertake a full-scale heist for a measly bottle of water, especially after he'd just admitted he was poor and had no friends. He kind of wanted to sit there, talk about it, and see what nuggets of wisdom Dane had for him. "Isn't there a giant river running through this city? Why not go scoop some out of the Thames?"

"Ew." The look of disgust on Dane's face was like he'd accidentally chomped on a moldy slice of toast. "Have you *seen* that river? We're trying to water this plant, Blayze, not kill it."

"Right, but surely that's the water that feeds all the witches?"

"Huh?" Dane asked, head slanting to one side. "What are you going on about?"

Confused, Blayze frowned. "What the Seer said, remember? We need to get a vial of water which feeds all the witches."

"Man, don't you ever pay attention? She said Aldwych. It's a place. A holy well, actually."

"Oh. My bad. Must've misheard. I thought it was like green witch?"

"Greenwich," Dane corrected. "As in, Gren-itch."

"Pfft. English is dumb sometimes." Because he was utterly mortified and could feel himself going red in the face, Blayze spun on the spot, stormed off down the street, then promptly realized he didn't have the first clue where he was going. When he turned back, Dane offered him a smug grin. "Whatever, smartass. Well go on, then. Lead the way."

CHAPTER FOURTEEN

BECAUSE ALDWYCH station had been discontinued over two decades ago, their journey on foot was longer than Dane would have liked, and pacing through rapidly darkening Westminster past a handful of theaters made him ache to see a camped-up production. As much as he'd rather be doing basically anything other than listening to Blayze moan about how sore his feet were, he was confident that by the end of the night, with another relic found, they would be well on their way to reversing their errant wish.

It was very nearly full dark by the time they reached Australia House, and if luck was finally on their side, there would only be a couple of hard-core desk jockeys left. And hopefully they would be at the back of the building rather than sitting in the row of windows at the front.

The web had told him the well was accessed by a manhole, but given that the city had a good few thousand of those, it wasn't much to go on. Pulling up the blog post in his head, he remembered seeing a small picture of it, and because it was so ancient, it was almost completely rusted over.

"Aha," Dane said when he finally spotted it. "Gotcha. Right. Now we gotta climb down this dark hole here. No biggie. Let's hope the ambassadors of Australia don't come prosecute us and ship us over there for the sentence." Getting into a squat, he prepared to pop it open and hop inside. "I don't do well with spiders. Or alligators. Or extreme heat… now that I'm really thinking about it."

"Can you get on with it?" Blayze tutted. He was probably still pissy after getting so vulnerable at the coffee shop and getting nothing in return, but now wasn't the time to respond in kind.

The recessed lid was practically rusted shut and far stiffer than Dane had imagined, and after the first attempt, he flexed his fingers and properly ramped his triceps up. The subsequent try was just as fruitless as the first, and two more separate attempts achieved sweet fuck all besides grinding away tooth enamel when there was absolutely no give.

"Oi." Dane looked up at Blayze, who was busy gawping at the building. "Care to help? At this moment in time, it seems your muscles are bigger than mine."

"Ugh," Blayze groaned, obviously not keen on the idea of getting dirty on his hands and knees. "This sucks. I would honestly rather be back at the apartment getting inside *your* manhole."

Amazed by his candor, Dane almost lost his grip for a second as Blayze grabbed on. He tried to ignore the unexpected stirring in his pants as they pulled on the ancient disk, and with combined force, they popped the lid open on the first try.

"Yeah, well, I loosened it for you." Dane cringed from the stench of dank mildew.

"Whose manhole are we talking about now?" Blayze smirked.

Save for what little remained of the daylight, the hole was pitch black and might as well have stretched to the center of the earth. There was a rusted metal ladder that, after he gave it a shake, seemed stable enough. Dane rotated his body, put one foot on the rung, and tested its weight. When it didn't immediately collapse, he put his faith in a higher power and began a slow descent.

"Okay," he said. "Here goes nothing."

"What would you say…," Blayze said, voice quivering as he peered down, "if I told you I wasn't great with tight spaces?"

Dane huffed as he looked back up the small amount of distance he'd made. "I'd say that's tough titties. Get your—I mean, get *my* ass in here. And don't forget to slide the lid back over when you do, though not all the way. We don't wanna be trapped down here."

Blayze deliberated for ten precious seconds more and then begrudgingly did as he was told. Dane had a spectacular view of his backside, but it didn't last for long. Once the metal ground against the concrete, darkness eclipsed everything.

"Fuck," Blayze said barely three heartbeats later. "I don't like this. It's too tight."

"Everything's fine," Dane assured. "And I don't recall you ever complaining about a tight space until now."

"Ha-ha, jackass," Blayze said, laughing it off.

In truth, it *was* weird—getting cast in near-total darkness, heading into a murky pit where the only sounds were the clinking of their shoes against the ladder and faint rushing water. Though he was evidently concerned with other things, Dane hoped Blayze wasn't reading Dane's aura right now, because he wasn't coping as well as he cared to admit.

"I think I finally see some light," Dane said after about twenty more steps. "You getting that?"

"Nope," Blayze said. "Nothing at all."

"Are you looking down?"

"No, duh. I'm focusing on my technique."

In spite of his clipped tone, Dane tried not to snap back. Claustrophobia was no joke, and he was doing well given the circumstances.

"So, as it turns out," Blayze started, voice quivering, "it's not just cramped spaces I'm afraid of."

"Hmm?" Dane prompted.

When Blayze let out a small moan, it echoed throughout the space, but he was quick to cover it up by clearing his throat. "You promise not to laugh?"

"Yes," said Dane. "I'm not a five-year-old."

"I—I'm scared of the dark."

"Oh, for real?" It had been so long since Dane had grown out of the notion, and he genuinely didn't know how to respond. "How does that even happen? What with your power, I mean?"

"Now's not really the time. Please, can we get this over with?" Blayze asked, probably taking Dane's silence as mockery.

"Well, nothing's actually changed, right?" Dane said, trying to encourage with logic and reasoning without making it sound patronizing. "The only thing that has changed is our visibility levels. Everything that was there before is still here now. All you gotta do is keep your hold on the ladder and work your way down one rung at a time. It's a simple and doable task, okay? Keep listening to my voice. It won't be long before we reach the bottom."

Blayze hummed in acknowledgment, but given how frail it sounded, it was likely he was trying to convince himself more than Dane. "When you get down, cast a flame so I can see where the fuck I'm putting my feet."

"Cast a flame?" Dane paused his descent. "You want me to burn down a historical and religious monument?"

"No, I want you to summon the most basic flame in your hands. You can do that. It's just like we talked about before. Simmer, not a boil. Do it for me, Dane. Hate to admit it, but I'm shitting bricks here, and if I slip, you'll be the one who takes the weight of my fall."

Considering himself adequately warned, Dane got moving again, and when he eventually reached the bottom of the ladder, his mini workout was rewarded with stepping in something squelchy and slimy. It was probably only mossy undergrowth, but in the dark depths of the unknown, it could just as easily have been a pile of slugs.

"Bollocks," he said, suddenly a nervous wreck at the thought of setting himself on fire again. The few times it had happened already went without too much consequence, but even so, if she was summoned again, there was every chance the flame might simply decide to stay where she was if the whim suited her.

Off to the side was a far-reaching tunnel, the tail end of which was illuminated by a pale and distant light. The origin of the light was impossible to discern, but while the passageway was considerably wider and didn't appear too hazardous, Blayze was practically whimpering at this point. Even without much visibility, it was obvious he had stopped moving altogether.

Out of nowhere, Dane felt his own fear levels start to skyrocket. It was as if he was staring at a rapidly approaching meteor on an unavoidable collision, but because he had spent well over twenty years at the helm of an emotion-adjusting ability, he knew the exact reason for the abrupt spike. Blayze was losing his grip on his borrowed power, and even if it was laughably easy for Dane to put up a mental barrier and get himself back down to a healthy state, the same probably couldn't be said for Blayze.

"Listen to me," Dane said with measured authority. "You need to calm down right now, otherwise you'll get yourself worked up into a headspace that's almost impossible to come down from. I know you're going through it, and you're starting to spiral, but you're a lot stronger than you think. I'm right here with you, and nothing's going to happen to you so long as I am."

Instead of chastising him, Dane was determined to get his own shit together and embrace his new, wild power. Even without Amping, it was easy to sense how scared Blayze had to be, clinging to the ladder while slowly losing his wits. More than anything, Dane wanted him to feel safe. Not just in their current situation, but also in his presence. He wanted him to feel comfortable enough to share things like phobias without worry of rejection. Every being—mage or otherwise—was different and unique in their own way, and just because he had yet to work through some more seemingly adolescent fears, that didn't mean Blayze couldn't excel in other areas.

As he closed his physical eyes and paid acute attention to what lay beneath his skin, Dane instantly underwent a full-body tingling. In the space between one breath and the next, he was cast into the heart of an all-out battle of wills, and in order to contain the itching heat to his left hand and only his left hand, he pictured the gentle flame igniting like a bonfire, except on a much smaller scale. Desperately, more than anything else, he needed to contain her wild energy, but that was a demanding task when she was clamoring to be set free.

She was a formidable and determined adversary, and given that Blayze was putting himself through a traumatic experience at his behest, Dane owed it to him to treat his power with care. Though he didn't have the first clue about how she had transferred in the first place, much less how the eventual reunion would go down, the last thing he wanted to do was cause irreparable damage. Shuffling through life as a Pyro was challenging enough, and he would not be responsible for making things harder.

The next thing he knew, Dane felt the flame appear before he opened his eyes again. In the center of his palm, a small cone of fire was simply sitting there, gently roiling, not threatening to expand an inch unless he asked it to. Wow. What had he done differently this time around? Had he succeeded through sheer dumb luck? Or had he finally managed to tame the flame because he had taken the time to tread with more care and respect?

Cheering for joy, Dane basked in satisfaction. "Hey, look, I did it."

"Nice work," Blayze called. "Shine the light on me for a sec, okay? Think I'm nearly there."

He had actually barely made it halfway down, but when the flickering orange light revealed the full extent of the tight passage, he breathed a very audible sigh of relief and sped his pace up considerably. The place was even grimier and more dismal than it first seemed, like something out of a Blumhouse creature feature, and when Blayze got to the bottom and took Dane's free hand, there was no way to avoid the puddle of boggy mud.

Blayze winced as he brushed himself off and made a massive deal of shaking himself out. "Thank you. I'm sorry for getting antsy. That wasn't pretty."

"No problem. You don't need to apologize for anything at all. Shall we?"

Holding out his hand to indicate him to go first, Dane made the conscious decision to keep the flame going as they advanced. It was fascinating how much more willing she was to behave now that he afforded her more reverence, and as they crept through the tunnel and tried not to bash their heads on the patchwork of bricks, he couldn't help wondering if the flame recognized that its original master had need of her. Maybe Dane's intent had been purer than previous times, or maybe practice really did make perfect. Whatever the case, though he was insanely curious, these were things better not dwelled on for long, given they were already embarking on a sizeable task.

The sound of running water grew louder with every step, and while he hadn't spared a second to think about what they might face when they reached the end of the tunnel, Dane hadn't imagined the space around the well to be so breathtakingly beautiful.

"Gods," Blayze said, summing up the sentiment quite nicely.

It was a cave, though not in the normal grotty sense. Though the domed ceiling reached quite a height, somebody had gone to great lengths to line the walls and floor with golden tiles, and as they lingered by the entrance, Dane's flame ricocheted off the polished surface. It was like they'd been transported into another realm. There was no other explanation for why the space before them was so clean and untouched— modern in its design and yet ancient in feel.

Then there was the well itself. It stood on a raised platform about six feet off the ground and was carved out of roughly hewn granite, each stone of which interlocked with the next in perfect unison to form a solid purpose-built structure. Whatever body of water was beneath glowed an intensely bright shade of neon cerulean, enough to light up the whole area.

Dane switched off his flame and studied the winch on top that was paired with a battered old bucket. Who was the last person who journeyed down here? How many decades had it been? And what happened to them?

In perfect synch, Blayze and Dane stepped off the ledge and onto the path and slowly gravitated toward the well. Upon reaching it, they got on their tiptoes, grabbed on to the concrete, and got a good look at the water. In the center of the pool, it looked like a bunch of fireflies had gotten trapped somehow, except their struggle wasn't endless torment.

It seemed as though they had been waiting unwearyingly for them to arrive, and now that they had, they were content. Happy, even.

"Quickly now," said Blayze as he reached for the winch. "I'll focus on cranking the handle. Your job will be to scoop it up."

The mechanism creaked something fierce, and as the bucket made its way down, Dane came to understand that the liquid wasn't a random grouping of fireflies, but a trick of the light where it bent at such sharp angles. It churned slowly back and forth of its own accord, entirely defying the laws of physics, and as soon as the pail breached the surface, the water began to swell and glisten with more fluorescence as a generous amount began to pool into the wood.

In all of his life, Dane couldn't remember stumbling across anything so outwardly divine, and he wasn't the least bit surprised to recall that this was holy water. Even if it weren't the key to solving their current condition, he'd have been eager to capture its essence for a keepsake.

None too gently, Blayze elbowed his ribs. "Hey, man. Get with it. Do you have the vial?"

"Hmm?" Dane turned to him, yet didn't quite see him. He was wafting dreamily in and out of existence as if he were a mirage, which was ironic, since this was the realest thing to happen to Dane in weeks. "Yeah." H pulled it from his pocket and stared at the water through the conical glass. "It's funny... I'd almost forgotten I had it."

"Well?" Blayze prompted. "Get ready. I'm gonna pull the bucket back up now."

"Don't rush me," Dane said quietly and calmly. "It's too precious."

Once he'd taken a mental photograph, Dane popped the cap on the vial and nodded like he'd just solved the toughest riddle in the universe. As Blayze began to crank the winch to haul up the bucket, the sound of rusted metal grinding against itself reverberated around the walls. The journey upward was slower going than down—likely because of the added weight—but the closer the water got, the more the urge took hold of Dane to throw himself in and be at one with it.

"Get ready," Blayze warned when the bucket was about halfway up. "And... now."

Driven by pure lizard-brain instinct, Dane tilted the glass at a ninety-degree angle and reached down. Right as he skimmed the surface and scooped up what was hopefully a sufficient measure, he was met with pure, searing cold—a sensation completely arresting and unlike anything he had ever experienced. It was fresh and biting and dangerously curious as it rapidly sent his brain into an unsolicited frenzy. It was hard to fathom the grip this spectral entity had seized on his body and mind, and it refused to waver.

Even though his new ability permitted him to regulate his temperature at all times, the shock of feeling something so arresting only served to make the pain that much more terrifying. He hadn't felt so much as a breeze over the last few days. Now, he might as well be wedged inside an Antarctic iceberg.

"Blayze," Dane muttered, drunk on pain, head lolling from side to side. "Help me."

"I'm right here," Blayze said resolutely. "Just like you said to me before, remember? I'm not going anywhere either. You helped me when you calmed me down, right? Now I guess it's about time I repaid the favor. What do you need me to do?"

"Yank me out," Dane begged. "But don't let the water touch you. If you do, it'll pull you under as well, and I really don't want to think about what happens after that."

Every limb of Dane's body had been frozen to the point of total numbness, and yet he could still feel it happening as his arm was slowly getting pulled into the well. The little dancing firefly illusion had grown its own set of grossly disproportional hands, and it was using them to fumble and grasp and tug at him, determined to submerge him into the ceaseless pool of black that had become the antithesis of everything the light represented.

"How am I supposed to get you out?" Blayze asked, still holding on to the winch, visibly rooted with fear and indecision. Without the use of any extra spool of rope, there wasn't a clear way for him to be the hero without getting any liquid on himself. But he needed to make some moves as soon as possible. There was nothing else for it. Dane's forearm was already lost to the bowels of the liquified demon, and it was probably only a matter of seconds before his shoulder and head would begin to follow suit.

"Just do… something," he called, despising the raw desperation in his voice. Somehow, amid some inextricable turn of events, Dane had found himself stripped bare, hovering on the precipice of oblivion as he was forced to tear out his soul and display it in the palm of his hands.

His fate was categorically out of his control, and he couldn't remember a time when he'd felt more vulnerable. "Blayze, please. *Anything.*"

The sudden rise in volume seemed to act like an uppercut to the face, because something inside Blayze snapped. He pulled down the cuffs of his sweatshirt so they acted like mittens, seized ahold of Dane, and pulled with all his might. The first attempt was worthless, and the following only served to make the water angrier.

On the third and final tug, Dane's arm finally separated itself from the well, and although he made a conscious effort to keep a thumb on the lid of the vial, the strength of his newfound freedom was so forceful that they both stumbled off the platform, skittered back across the golden tiles, and fell into a tangled heap.

When they were cast into total darkness and instinctively started unraveling themselves, Dane felt something crunch underneath him, and a new breed of terror grasped hold of his chest like an anaconda squeezing him into lunch. If the vial had broken, the hellish endeavor would have been for naught, and there wasn't a chance in hell he would step a foot near that malignant body of water ever again.

"Everything's fine, everything's fine," Blayze said with a particularly strained tone, probably reassuring himself as much as Dane as they finally separated limbs. "What was there before is still here now."

"I wouldn't be so sure," Dane said solemnly. He held out his free hand, flicked the flame onto his palm, then held the vial up to light. When he got a good look at it, the lump in his throat ceased to exist, and he was eternally grateful to find the glass undamaged and glittering with a modest quantity of strangely sentient water. "Oh, thank fuck." Heaving a deep sigh of relief, Dane clicked the lid shut, thudded his head to the floor, and gazed idly at their reflections as they flickered in the ceiling. "Well, that's two out of three," he said, dog-tired, practically gasping for breath. "You're doing the next one."

CHAPTER FIFTEEN

WHEN BLAYZE found Dane the next day, he was out on the balcony sipping tea in the soft glow of postdawn rays. He was wearing a pair of dark blue Levi's along with Blayze's favorite Nirvana tee, and his eyes were bleary, yet unmistakably cheerful as he beckoned him over.

"Morning," he said by way of greeting.

"Yes it is." Blayze promptly took the vacant seat before he could get vertigo from all the many, many floors beneath them. "Man, you gotta start hitting the gym more often."

"Huh?" Dane pretended to be shocked, but there was a ghost of a grin on his face. "I'll have you know I signed up to the best gym in the city as soon as I moved."

Blayze poured himself a steaming cup of tea from the pot. "Yeah, well, holding a membership card and actually attending are two different things."

Heaving Dane out of that cursed well had taken its toll on the body Blayze had on loan, and when they brought the vial of water next to the plant only to experience an all-too similar version of what happened with the sun stone, it had fully wiped him out. Had he been a little more with it, he'd have followed Dane into bed to see if he liked being the big spoon or the little spoon. As it was, he had simply retreated to the couch and slept like a rock without a single hitch.

Once he had a sip of his drink, Blayze pulled his vape pen out of his pocket, took a deep draw, and shut his eyes as the swift onset of anxiety began to melt away.

"Let's see," he said as he breathed out an indigo plume. "We're two down with one to go. For all the good it's doing."

"Speaking of." With a slightly upturned mouth, Dane pointed at the sky. "There's supposed to be a full moon tonight, and when it hits its apex, that's pretty much the only window we have to get into the Dryad's grove. Call it coincidence, call it fate, it's tonight or never."

Blayze's mouth popped open and closed shut a few times. "I—are we…? Okay. Fine. Let's go pay her a visit and find out what version of despair she'll be in when she sees us. Hold up, do you even know where she is?"

"Oxfordshire," Dane said smugly. "I used a VPN last night to do some online sleuthing, and I came across a pretty startling wealth of mage history. Made me think I should do it more often."

"Why bother?" Blayze wondered. "Using encryption, I mean. Your search history is gonna be the least of people's worries when they realize who they're walking the planet with."

Over the rim of his cup, Dane arched an eyebrow. "I thought you didn't want to talk about it."

"I do and I don't. Just because I don't like to think about what's going on right now, doesn't mean I can't, maybe, ya know, look forward to the future."

It was a heavy topic for early morning chat, and yet, after their conversation at the Shard, Blayze was coming to realize that open discussions couldn't be avoided forever. It was the most prevalent news to have ever happened to their kind, and as scary as it was, that didn't mean he couldn't maintain a positive outlook on it.

Dane took his eyes off the city and offered him his full attention. "What do *you* think is going to happen?"

"Is peace too much to ask for?" Blayze shrugged. "Probably. It'd be nice to live our best lives without hiding our fundamental selves. Like, yeah, even though being a Pyro is cool and everything, it's not my entire identity, you know? Much the same as being gay isn't. There's so much more to me than these things, but people are so quick to judge what's on the surface without realizing everyone has multiple levels to them. And to be honest, I'm not sure what's gonna happen. I don't have a crystal ball. Maybe we should go ask Trina."

When he finished his drink, Blayze felt a little less like a crudely reanimated corpse, and the thought of visiting a potentially treacherous tree spirit was gradually beginning to turn from a joke in bad taste into a semifeasible task.

"Oh, for the love of God," Blayze said when his ringtone chimed. "Man, why does she keep on—hello?"

"Mr. Martinez," said the wintry tone of Mrs. Evangeline Wight, someone he had fully expected to never hear from again. "How are you?"

"How am I?" Blayze repeated, offering Dane his best *what the fuck* face. Not one single time during his employment had she asked such a personal question, and he wasn't the first bit prepared for it. Given that phone lines were so easily breached, he also had no idea how much information he should share with regard to his individual situation or the more general one at large. "I'm fine… relatively speaking. Um, how are you?"

"As well as can be," she said, tone softening, sounding almost bored. "We're understaffed, underfunded, and well and truly up shit creek. Pardon my French. At any rate, this whole business with the Stormcaller has shaken things up in ways I can't even describe, and I wanted to know if you'd be interested in helping out."

"Huh?" Blayze said, dumbfounded. Dane was wide-eyed as he tried to get his attention and indicated with his fingers that he should put her on speaker. As he did, he tried not to bark his response, even though he very much wanted to. "You want me to help out? After that bullshit job you stiffed me with under the promise of climbing the ladder?"

"Excuse me?" Evangeline implored, aghast. "Apologies if I'm misunderstanding, but didn't you have the privilege of distributing Oathstones to those in dire need of them? My son being one of them? Look, all that's in the past now. I'm sorry the job wasn't what you thought it was, but we need all hands on deck over here in preparation for the backlash, and there's plenty of roles to pick from. Enforcers, Adjudicators, Erasers. You name it, we want it."

"Well, I'm in London anyways," Blayze dismissed, "so I'm afraid I can't help you even if I wanted to."

"Ah," she said, clearly dismayed. "I knew it was a long shot, but it was only on the off chance. I must have called a hundred people by now, and I've even had to coopt Jasper into helping. You'd be surprised how many hungry mouths need feeding during a crisis."

"Is that what this is?" Dane asked, unable to help himself. "Are the MRF officially labeling this incident as a crisis?"

After a beat, Evangeline's tone was right back to ice. "Who is that? This is an extremely sensitive topic, Mr. Martinez, and I had expected you to treat is a such."

"Don't worry," Blayze assured. "It's just my… friend. He's a mage too, and well, we kinda swap—"

Dane grabbed Blayze's forearm and gripped it tight. Then he sent his eyebrows upward and shook his head gravely.

"Uhh, never mind," Blayze corrected. "We're handling it. But what's the plan? I mean, what are we supposed to do? What's happening is kinda huge, and we can't be expected to be kept in the dark about it. You said about backlash, which I'm taking to mean that you guys are preparing for the worst."

"Sit tight for now," Evangeline said, impatience rising, very likely about to sign off. "I'm told there will be a new announcement appearing on mirrors very soon, so you should have more information at that point. Good talking."

With that, the line went dead. It was a good minute or so before Blayze made eye contact with Dane again, and when he did, there was apology written in his eyes.

"Sorry," he said. "You're an adult, and I didn't want to cut you off or anything, but the fewer people who know about what we're going through the better. She has indisputable ties with our government, and I haven't a clue what they're about to announce, but something tells me they won't take kindly to the risk our predicament poses."

"Agreed." Blayze rose from his seat and leaned on the balcony bars, heart still hammering. "Well, shit. I had a feeling the MRF wouldn't be able to keep a lid on this situation for much longer, but I kinda hoped we had more time. As soon as they realize the scope of what we can do, the world will change forever."

In light of Evangeline's conversation, there was a renewed sense of urgency to get their bodies back, so they dressed in complete silence, slung some extra clothes in an overnight bag, and got out on the streets. With an unswerving sense of purpose, Dane made sure to dodge the flow of people traffic, then actively maneuvered Blayze to do the same as they headed down a roughly cobbled street. It didn't take them long to find a Tube station, and once they'd tapped the prepaid Oyster cards Dane had gifted Blayze for the day, they jumped onto the Northern Line and eventually found their way to the overground.

The minute they found some seats on a train out of London, the reality of the immediate future settled in, and Blayze gave a voice to his ruminations. "What's going to happen now? Do we offer ourselves up on a platter? Are we days away from facing an all-out war?"

"Nothing's been confirmed yet." Dane raised both his hands, then pushed the air down in a calming motion. "Let's just take this one step at a time, okay? Try not to jump to conclusions, especially ones as extreme as that. We need to work through things as they come, and first up is a meeting with this Dryad."

"But that's the thing, Dane. My head is so full of vivid scenarios that I can barely concentrate on our current task. How's this visit going to pan out?" Blayze asked, wondering if it wouldn't be long before the frown on his forehead would stay for good. "Like, what are we actually gonna say or do if and when we find her? And where are we gonna stay in the interim? Something tells me this isn't gonna be a quick-dip-in-and-out type of deal. Though it pains me to admit it, I don't have bags of money like you. Needless to say, I'm getting a bit worried over here."

"Chill out for a sec." Dane held up his phone. "See this modern marvel of technology? There's this really special app that lets me browse hotels and B and Bs, so how's about we find a place to stay for the night, then start from there? Does that make you feel better?"

Blayze nodded and relaxed some. It was a good ten minutes before Dane put away his phone with a cheeky little smile, and because there weren't all that many people on the off-peak journey, they were afforded some privacy in their booth. Blayze recognized an opportunity, placed a hand on Dane's thigh, and tried very hard to keep it strictly casual. It was pretty good going, given Dane's slightly bristled but overall accepting reaction, and he was content to watch the remarkable span of greenery flit by as they headed toward an unknown destination for an entirely unknown outcome.

"Hey," Dane whispered. "As much as all of this runaround might be a royal pain in the ass, if there's one takeaway from the whole ordeal, it's that you can fuck like a champ."

"Huh," Blayze said, effectively stunned. "Thanks. I mean, I can't take all the credit. It's your tools I'm working with, after all."

"True. And I'm serious, by the way. You should top more often."

Pulse quickening, Blayze winked, happy to have a mental image worth thinking about. "You know what? Maybe I will."

SOMEWHERE IN the two hours it took them to get out of London and reach Oxfordshire, Blayze had dozed off on Dane's shoulder. He awoke with a start when the announcer's voice boomed over the speaker and called for their final stop, and Dane did a wonderful job of acting like he wasn't at all bothered by the invasion of space.

"How far is it?" Blayze asked as they clambered off the train and onto the main thoroughfare. "Are you gonna use maps on your phone? I don't have any data over here."

"Don't be silly," Dane laughed. "We'll get a taxi."

"Ah," Blayze said, once again totally forgetting how much disposable income the guy had.

Because he wasn't in much of a rush to sit down again after so long, Blayze wanted to stretch his legs as they waited on yet more transport. There was also a kickboxing match going on in his stomach, and when he spied a grocery store among the cute little boutique shops in the quirky town, he instantly longed for a 7-Eleven cheese dog.

"Back in two ticks." He pointed across the street and made a quick dash for it.

He shoved a hand in his pocket and fingered what little change he had left. There was maybe enough to buy lunch for them both, but it wouldn't be anything extravagant.

The store was bigger on the inside than the façade suggested and full to the brim of eclectic world foods Blayze had never seen. What the hell was a Jaffa Cake? They looked good and were relatively cheap, so he grabbed a basket and tossed in a carton. The sandwich selection wasn't anything to write home about, but there were a few boxes of chicken Caesar salad that looked passable, and at this point he didn't really care what he ate so long as it nourished the void. He chucked them in along with some beef-flavored chips and scanned the shelves, hoping for something to spark joy. His search paused when he came across a little box of rose-scented tealights.

Blayze thought it was interesting how he was attracted to fire-related things now that he'd spent the better part of a week unable to summon it himself. But... was it only that? Or was there a deeper reason for him staring at these tealights with his brain about to start World War III? Maybe it was because of the image that popped into his head—using them later on with Dane in whatever charming location they were set to stay at. Was that too forward-thinking? Would Dane even care for such a gesture? And did it actually matter if he did or not? The growth of that dumbass plant was throwing him off. He wasn't sure if their success with it so far was based on true merit or if they'd put the effort in because they *wanted* to make it grow. Surely acting on instinct had more value than some wholly gratuitous act?

Screw it. Going with his gut had gotten Blayze to where he was today, and if it turned out that the moment never made itself apparent, at least he'd have a cute souvenir to bring home.

Once he'd gone through the highly embarrassing motions of counting out his change into the palm of a sweet yet painfully pitiful clerk, he ducked his head and returned outside to where Dane was leaning against the taxi.

"After you." He opened the door and motioned him in.

Blayze climbed inside and balanced the haul on his lap as Dane came to sit next to him. Then they sped off into the rapidly darkening countryside.

"I never knew England had so much greenery," Blayze said as he marveled at how the fields and meadows spread on endlessly. He could clearly see lands that were actively used for agriculture and livestock, and yet the grasslands didn't seem to have any immediate use. They were simply there, lush and bountiful in their own right. It was magnificent.

They tucked into their salads with some handy wooden cutlery, and the journey was even more pleasant now that Blayze's stomach wasn't threatening to cave in.

As they diverged from the main road and eventually came up on a swanky estate, the driver whistled a short tune. "Fancy-lookin' spot, lads."

Two rows of expertly pruned bushes lined a long and effortlessly straight road, at the foot of which stood a slender guardian angel water fountain sculpture that greeted them with outspread arms. Then there was the building itself. It was impressive and well preserved—each of the fifty Victorian-style windows were free from wild growth and were so sparkly clean that they were thrilled to bounce back the afternoon rays. While it was doubtlessly an old building with plenty of history, the bricks of the foundation looked like they were freshly laid, and the blend of old-fashioned yet modern gave the place a welcoming feel.

"Jesus, Dane," Blayze groaned. "This is fit for the royal family. Isn't it a little overkill for just one night?"

Dane shrugged as the car came to a halt. He had a butter-wouldn't-melt grin on his face as he took the bag, jumped out, and went to get the other door like a gentleman in an old Hollywood movie.

"Someone's in good spirits," said Blayze as he got out and performed a full-body stretch. "Planning to get laid or something?"

"No," Dane said, instantly blushing. "I'm simply excited for this trip. You know, getting things sorted and all."

As Dane opened his wallet and pushed a tip through the driver's window, a pause of silence befell them.

"I see," Blayze muttered, surprised at the tide of disappointment that washed over him. They both knew that "getting things sorted" meant they'd get their bodies back, and when that happened, there was precisely no reason for them to stay in each other's company. Why did that feel like a punch to the gut?

"So." Dane bounced awkwardly on his heels as the car drove off. "Shall we, um, go check in?"

With a slightly sour taste in his mouth, Blayze squared his shoulders, mentally kicked himself in the ass, and headed for reception.

CHAPTER SIXTEEN

THE BED-AND-BREAKFAST was everything Dane had hoped for and more, and yet, while it thoroughly exceeded his expectations from what he'd seen on the booking app, he wasn't fully able to bask in the joys of a mini vacation. If only he could stop replaying the moment by the car when he'd put his foot in his mouth.

Letting his enthusiasm show like that was a careless mistake, and instead of rectifying the situation by telling Blayze he was actually excited for some quality one-on-one time in a private and ostentatious location, Dane had simply rolled with it when Blayze assumed he'd been talking about their predicament.

How different the mood would be if he just owned up to it and set the record straight… but as they padded through the marble foyer, eyes widening at all the extravagant finery in gold trim, the moment was long past and the correction would end up seeming disingenuous. He'd have to use his actions instead of his words.

"Gosh," Blayze whispered under his breath. "I've seen, like, seven crystal chandeliers already. How much did you fork over for this? Actually, never mind. I'm probably better off not knowing."

"You're worth it," Dane said. When that was rewarded with a heartfelt smile, he tried pushing his luck. "So, do you want to explore some more, or do you want to head straight up to the room?"

"Or we could go out into the woods," Blayze said as they stood behind the desk and rang a bell.

Dane was amazed at how deadpan serious he was for such a kinky request, and he tilted his head and offered a quizzical look.

"You know," Blayze continued. "To go find the Dryad's grove?"

Casting his eyes to the floor, Dane tried and failed to not let his humiliation show.

"Oh my God," Blayze said, "you *are* hoping to get laid! Jeez, talk about a one-track mind. It was your idea to come here, remember? Let's go get it done so we can get things back to normal, like you said."

Dane greeted the tuxedo-clad receptionist when he finally graced them with his presence, and as he filled out the paperwork and tapped in his debit-card details, he tried very hard not to elbow Blayze and make him uncross his arms.

"Thanks a lot," Dane said when everything was in order. Then he turned to Blayze and nodded back the way they'd come. "Okay, let's do this. It's getting dark, so I hope you've got some juice in your phone, because mine's almost out. We're gonna need a flashlight if we're set to aimlessly wander around these woods."

"Have to say I'm not crazy big on that idea." Blayze gave Dane the lead as they began to prowl through the sumptuous garden estate and headed for the thick blanket of trees in the distance. "You sure this is the right thing to do? How do we know that Seer of yours hasn't set us up to be the stars in a hyperrealistic found-footage slasher? Maybe the plant will be fine after what we've done today."

"Maybe you're right," Dane agreed as he opened a cute little wooden kissing gate and fought back the urge to purse his lips. "But we've come all this way. Look how much clearer the water is up here." They veered off to the right, and he took them down a small embankment to a wide lake. When he bent down to see a stark image of his reflection, he couldn't resist running his hands through the water. "I feel connected to this place, for some reason. I know this seems like a bit of a crapshoot, so please just trust me. We'll follow the river until the moon reaches its apex, and then something tells me things will start to make more sense. If they don't, we can head back, get a good night's sleep, then do things your way. How does that sound?"

Blayze's body language had been deflated ever since they arrived, and if he wanted to go straight back to the hotel to enjoy each other's company in whatever capacity, then that's what they'd do. But Blayze smiled and stretched his hand out to the woods.

"I ran track in college," Blayze said as he put his hands on his hips. "Body swap be damned, if we end up getting chased by a psychotic axe murderer, don't expect me to hang around."

"UM, COULD we take a quick breather?" Blayze asked, brows pinched inward. "Gym shoes were a terrible idea."

They had been following the stream for the better part of an hour, and it had been a good while since the hotel behind them disappeared. What was left was the semisodden dirt beneath their feet, relentless thick groves at their side, and an infinite span of aspen trees. Because it was the height of autumn, there wasn't much of a canopy, and it turned out they didn't need a flashlight, because the glow of the moon was bright and far-reaching. It was almost creepy how well lit the woods were, but if things did suddenly change, Dane's ability to summon flame would come in handy—assuming he could keep it under control again and not start a wildfire.

"What're you doing?" Blayze asked when Dane started gathering a bunch of loose twigs and stuck them in the ground at forty-five-degree angles.

"This stream is straight as an arrow," Dane said. "Which is lucky for us, really, because it also means we're far less likely to get lost. I'm only being cautious, is all, by marking our way. Can never be too careful, right?"

Blayze grinned, then shook his head. "Smartass. Man, I know I said it before, but this would be so much easier if I had Elijah's power. Could've grown myself a moon lily in two seconds flat."

Dane shrugged as he dug another twig in. "The Biomancer? I don't know. Trina seemed pretty convinced that we have to follow a certain set of rules. Using a mage's gift probably wouldn't do much."

"True," Blayze said. "I wonder what other obstacles mages have come across in the past. Why don't you come sit with me for a sec and take a load off?"

When he finished poking in the last stick, Dane found a clear spot next to Blayze where he could cross his legs and lean against a tree trunk. He looked positively radiant in the eerie moonlight, and he didn't break eye contact. It looked like there was something on his mind, and it wasn't long before he acted on it.

"Don't you think it'll be weird when we get our bodies back?"

Dane's eyes bulged. "Isn't that what you've been making such a fuss about all this time? Getting things back to normal?"

"Yeah...," Blayze said, "I mean, I'm not saying I *don't* want it back, just that I've kinda grown to enjoy your ability. I haven't had much experience with actually modifying emotions, but when you learn to quieten the sensory overload, it's pretty cool being able to read people's energies toward you. It's laughably easy to work out who's bullshitting me and who's the real deal. Oh, and I haven't missed being a scrawny runt, solidly under six foot. Being a burly redheaded Viking certainly has its advantages."

"I get you." Dane scratched the back of his neck, though it didn't actually itch. "For me, I'm amazed I've enjoyed carrying around this truly awesome burden of power. There's so much I can do with only a wave of these hands. And the fact I haven't once felt the cold is quite fun. Beyond that creepy well, of course. If I'm really being honest… you know what I can't stop thinking about?"

"What's that?"

"I can't stop thinking about how easily I took my dick earlier."

He'd said it matter-of-fact on purpose, and Dane was pleased to see that Blayze hadn't flinched. There was a strangely tangible ever-present current charging itself between them that seemed to spark up whenever they got near, and that didn't stop simply because they were in the middle of the woods during the dead of night.

"It was very impressive," Blayze praised. "I remember when I first started hooking up with guys, I was convinced I was a strict top, and it took me years to get into bottoming. Not gonna lie, I will probably always prefer bottoming, but being versatile is fun too. You should try it."

"Yes, I should." Dane bit his lip and scooched his ass a couple inches over in the dirt. "For now, I want to be with you in any way that I can. Sex or no sex."

Dane was unable to hold back a broad smile, and all the permission he needed was in Blayze's eyes as he gently took hold of his face, snaked Blayze's hand to the back of his neck, and pulled him into a slow, deep kiss. The moment their lips touched, a fervor ignited and demanded more body contact, more intimacy, more reason for the monster in his pants to get hard. As much as they were in this place to find something of dire importance, there was no sense of urgency as he relished Blayze's company.

He truly was a fantastic kisser. He responded in kind and mirrored every one of Dane's actions, and they must have spent a good half hour rolling around in the dirt, absently listening to the trees groan in the wind as they grew completely and utterly absorbed in each other. Though he'd had to consciously manage their combined heat levels, Dane was having the time of his life feeding off Blayze's hyped-up energy, and when he broke from the kiss and stared down at him, eyes glazed over with lust, he nodded his head, both feeling and knowing exactly what he wanted.

When Blayze slid down his body, the sound of his pants zipper cut through the midnight air, and before Dane's cock had much of a chance to say hello to the woodlands, Blayze whimpered in delight and shoved it in his mouth.

"Fuck," Dane stated, pure and simple.

His mouth was warm and wet from all the kissing, and while he bobbed up and down, applying a purposefully hard sucking pressure on the base, then relieving most of that pressure when he came to the tip, he made sure to never break eye contact.

"You're so good at this," said Dane when Blayze laid his tongue flat against his shaft and really started going to town. Every now and then he'd give his balls a gentle tug, and as a result, Dane would happily throb inside his mouth. "Man, you've gotta teach me."

Blayze chuckled as he removed the dick from his mouth, then licked his lips. "Just gotta use your intuition." He climbed back up Dane's body so he could pepper kisses along the soft part of his neck. "It takes a real man to know how to treat a good cock. Well, that and practice. You can never get too much of that, and it's true when they say practice makes perfect. So?"

"So?" Dane looked at him blankly.

"D'you wanna practice?"

Dane nodded enthusiastically. "Yes, please. No time like the present, right? Should we do sixty-nine? Not to be greedy or anything. I'll go on top—it'll give me better access to you."

"Okay." Blayze grinned like the Cheshire cat as he swung himself around and undid his own fly.

When he finally managed to wrench his dick out of his pants, it was already harder than a diamond, and when he pulled back the foreskin and exposed the head to a convenient streak of moonlight, Dane dove down and latched his mouth on, delighted to taste a salty-sweet combination. He would've preferred to have Blayze fully naked so he could play with his thighs, but he probably didn't want to get completely covered in mud, which was fair enough.

Blayze fumbled at Dane's waist, and when he got the hint and remembered that the cock-sucking exercise went both ways, he angled his hips downward and slid his cock into the waiting mouth.

"Ugh," Dane called out to the woods.

Was there anything better than having a sexy man service your cock? Right then, Dane couldn't think so. He let the sensations take his body on a joyous journey as he tried very hard to keep his brain in this one and focus on his own task.

"Don't forget to lay your tongue flat to the shaft and guide it up with your mouth," Blayze said, voice sounding far away. "People always forget the tongue… but it's a pretty big deal when you do it right."

Taking the tip on board and using Blayze's method was made a little difficult given that the dick was the wrong way round. Ever the pragmatist, Dane was keen to perform a combination of firm shaft sucking, slow deep-throat, and soft head licking. The technique got easier when he built up some kind of rhythm to it, and he must have been doing something right, because Blayze's cock started to pulse in his mouth, and his lower body began to tremble.

"Mmprrh," he said, mouth full of dick. He took it out for a couple of seconds, and his raspy breath tore through the quiet air. "Dane, I think… if you keep going like that, I'm gonna explode."

"Then do it," Dane ordered. Then he clamped his mouth down on Blayze's cock as he shoved his own deeper into Blayze's mouth.

He closed his eyes and relished the raw pleasure he was offering Blayze. Simply the thought of sending his own looming orgasm down Blayze's throat was enough to desperately crave his in return. He felt himself throbbing in Blayze's wet mouth, and the pressure that had been slowly but surely building in his balls was mere moments from release.

"Hurgh," Dane said—his own polite way of warning that he was about to explode too.

As Blayze's convulsions came to a head, Dane welcomed the salty-sweet joy as it erupted in his mouth and trickled down his throat. As his dick began to do the same, he groaned in delight as they shared another deliciously intimate experience.

Blayze's thighs started to calm down, and as his cock softened, Dane worked the foreskin and lapped up the remainder of his treat as he removed his own from Blayze and felt him eagerly do the same.

Dane carefully rolled off him, and his dick lolled against his pants. When Blayze sighed like his soul had just left his body, they both sniggered at the star-speckled sky.

When Blayze reached his hand out and put it on Dane's stomach, Dane instinctively grasped it with his and held on to it as he rode the adrenaline comedown. He wanted to say something funny or witty to make light of the situation or perhaps even quell the abruptly intimate surge of the postorgasm moment, but as he lay there in total bliss, he couldn't find any words, and he was surprised to find that he would very much prefer to not spoil the moment if it meant he could just keep ahold of Blayze's hand.

CHAPTER SEVENTEEN

BLAYZE HAD been lulled into such a meditative trance of peace that he couldn't be sure if he'd fallen asleep or not. The stars were unusually bright, and while they weren't quite spinning, they were certainly doing a merry little dance in the wake of yet another universe-shattering orgasm. Holding on to Dane's hand was a surprisingly welcome comfort during the foreign out-of-body experience, and he wondered how long he could get away with it before it started to feel weird. They were here for a legitimate task, after all, not to have sex and revel in each other's company. And yet, right now, that was all he wanted to do.

"Can I ask you something?" Blayze's voice sounded strained and timid, so when he reluctantly let go of Dane's hand and sat up to cough, he leaned on his elbow and tried again. "I don't wanna seem like a creep or anything."

"You aren't a creep." Dane rolled his eyes and assumed a mirrored position. "Stop overthinking and shoot."

"What was it like when you were younger? With your power, I mean. We touched on mine back in the Shard, and I'm intrigued about yours. I feel like it's quite a taboo subject among mages—the whole struggle of learning about your power and what effect it has when you're told time and time again to keep it under your hat. We don't talk about it enough. Why is that?"

Dane shrugged. "People like to think they're open-minded until they're faced with hard truths. Instead of embracing the conversation in hopes that you could actually learn something of value from it, people shy away because it's uncomfortable in that moment. Then all they end up doing is to carry on bottling it up until the next person tries to chip away the wall."

"Huh," Blayze said. "That's a very wise take on it. Also, a pretty wise way of dodging the question, bud."

Dane shook his head and playfully pushed Blayze's sternum.

"Beyond the mandatory sessions assigned by the MRF, I had extensive therapy to combat the specific nature of my ability," Dane admitted. The lines on his face remained hard and stony, and he didn't seem to mind one bit about talking on the subject. "It's not like my folks treated me bad in any way... but they weren't exactly equipped with the counseling PhD required to advise somebody who can, for all intents and purposes, read minds. Talking it out with someone who did was very helpful. Cost a lot of money, mind you, though it was better than ending up in a psych ward after smacking my head against the wall when a room full of people's energies got so loud."

"That must've been tough." Blayze reached his other hand out and squeezed Dane's forearm. "Luckily for me, I didn't hear weird energy voices growing up, and the stigma behind Pyros was something I'd later find out about. Or at least, it didn't feel like that was the reason for all the crap at the time. Hindsight tells me otherwise."

"Did you have a hard time at school?" Dane asked.

"A little. Because Mexico City is so densely populated, our schools were always a mage-human mix because we didn't have the luxury of all these privatized mage-only ones. Things did get better when I came of age and traveled to wizard college, but before that, any and all bullying was done in secret, which was pretty weird in itself. You'd think being able to manipulate fire would be scary and something not to fuck with, but kids don't often think that way. When they see vulnerability, they exploit it, and it's weird because, back then when I was a nervous wreck, they were dumb enough to pick at the thing I had no control over, yet clever enough to not get caught by any human kids, teachers, or parents. Moving to New York when I turned twenty was when I really began to reinvent myself, and yeah, I'd probably do a few things differently given another chance, maybe be a little less standoffish with people who are just trying to vibe. That's the kind of thing that makes me wonder what things would be like if our kind does make some grand thing of coming out. Like, maybe in twenty years' time, nobody will bat an eyelid at mages and they can just do their thing. After how many times I've come out as gay or Pyro or a gay Pyro, I'd probably envy the ease at which people could be themselves."

"Yeah, I know, right?" Dane bobbed his head enthusiastically. "How great would it be for the next generation to not have to experience all the subtle segregation? I'm sorry you had to go through all that. It's very important to have your own identity and self-worth, and I'm glad you got there in the end. Oh, and by the way, I might be well off now, but

I didn't go to one of those private mage schools before wizard college either. Although there were a handful of students who would reveal themselves at a later date once I left, there was only one mage teacher at my school that I actually knew about—Mrs. Wendall. She was an Air Weaver who had a real fondness for Dickens, and because I'd practically eat books like I was starving, I always stayed behind in class for an extra five minutes when I got the chance so we could chat about all things mage-related. Fortunately, on the bullying front, we had a zero-tolerance policy, and because of some incidents in the past, people took it very seriously. Maybe it's a London thing, or maybe it was the luck of the draw."

Blayze lifted his free shoulder in an attempt at a shrug. "Maybe. It's hard because you don't realize what the long-term effects being put down every day has on you until later in life. The power of hindsight likes to let me know why I didn't get invited to all the parties or hang around town with the cool kids, but what can I do about it now? Regret and lament or move the fuck on? Which do you think is easier?"

When Dane got back into full sitting position, he opened his arms and waited patiently for Blayze to fall into them. The look on his face was of acceptance rather than pity, and it was almost too easy to be with him in an intimate capacity. He wondered if there was something in the air of the woods tonight. It certainly wasn't like him to break down the concrete wall simply because of some great sex, no matter how mind-blowing it had been.

"Trust me when I tell you I'm not saying this for the sake of it," Dane said softly. "You're one of the coolest people I've ever met. Growing up is a difficult thing to do no matter the circumstances. We all have our struggles coming into adulthood, but it's how you choose to deal with those struggles that makes the difference. And those people who you probably don't even know the names of by now? Imagine their faces when they see how well your business is going to do when it takes off. I wasn't bullshitting when I said your pieces are amazing, and I know I can drum up some contacts who'll request semiregular shipments. Although… I mean, why not set up shop somewhere over here? London is full to the brim of art lovers, especially if you can theme some of your work from the Victorian era. I got you, Blayze. Above anything, I want you to remember that."

"I can't just drop everything and go because…," Blayze started. When a crease pulled down his eyebrows, he absently disengaged from the hug and tried to finish that sentence. And yet he was genuinely stumped with what words he should slot in.

Why couldn't he make the hop over here? Hell, his lease was almost up, and he was living from one paycheck to the next. If he really wanted to, he could donate the pitiful amount of belongings in his apartment and never lay eyes on New York again. Was he acting like this in anger? Or was there a deeper meaning? It was like he was back in the store worrying about buying the tea lights again. Even if Dane wasn't in the picture, did there actually need to be a deeper meaning for him to feel this way? Or should he simply live in the moment and act as nature intended? He already knew he could stand to be a bit more open-minded by responding to what his body wanted in the moment. His brain could work out the rest later. Why couldn't that be the case for other things too?

"Hey," came a voice. The only reason time resumed was because Dane waved a hand in front of his face. "You okay in there, bud?"

"Yeah," Blayze muttered, staring at the dirt. "I'm good. Never usually allow myself to become this introspective. Normally when that happens, I reach for three fingers of bourbon. We don't have any of that, do we?"

"Sadly not," said Dane. "However, we do have a Dryad to confront, and I'm a little nervous about that, not gonna lie. What's say we get to it?"

Blayze tried to not to feel overwhelmed with the door he'd just taken a sledgehammer to. It was healthy to be open and honest about emotions, especially with yourself as much as others, so instead of going into meltdown mode, he was emboldened by the new options in his life once again.

It was good to have possibilities, and he didn't feel boxed in, destined to play one role anymore. It was a very welcome feeling, and as he climbed off the ground and took Dane's hand so they could head back down to the riverbed, he celebrated that feeling and elected to carry it with him, and he marveled as it began to shroud him with a curious sense of joy.

CHAPTER EIGHTEEN

"THIS IS bullshit," Blayze moaned. Dane could tell he was close to giving up, and he couldn't entirely blame him. His legs were getting tired too, and the thought of doing the entire journey back again was almost enough to call it a day and start fashioning a shelter from twigs. "We've been scanning these woods for what feels like hours," Blayze continued, "and I still don't know what we're looking for. I swear Trina might as well have asked us to look for a glass hammer."

"I know it's annoying." Dane looked back to find Blayze cross-armed, face like thunder, a minute away from uprooting the trees. "I think we're close. I don't know. Don't you feel some sort of... tugging?"

"No," Blayze said. "We did that hours ago."

Dane rolled his eyes, amused. "Not that. It's more of the ethereal sort. Like we're meant to be here, you know?"

"I don't, actually." Blayze's crankiness had taken on a different manner entirely. His shoulders were tight with tension, and there was a big vein on his forehead about to pop as he marched up to Dane. "Look, man, I've been having a pretty swell time up until now, but if you're trying to hoodwink me or something, then you're not better than the Seer, and if you think I'm gonna sta—wait a sec, what's that?"

Dane's heart skipped a beat. "What's what?"

"Over there," Blayze said dreamily, staring off into the distance like he'd been hypnotized by the moon. "You don't see that?"

"Are you screwing with me, huh? Is this your way of getting back at me or something?"

Blayze raised a finger and pointed down the riverbed. When Dane followed it, he squinted, but it was impossible to miss what he was pointing at.

Over to the east, nestled between two giant oak trees, was a doorway. At least, it very much looked like a doorway. The boughs of the tree seemed to connect to each other, forming an archway, beyond which shimmered another place. It most definitely hadn't been there before, and it was too much of a coincidence now that the moon had reached its highest point in the sky.

"Let's do this," Dane said.

Scurrying down the bank, he played an adult version of hopscotch across the stones and very nearly lost his footing on the slippery moss. When he was eventually across, he turned back to help Blayze, but despite being in the bigger body, Blayze had no trouble dancing across the stones like a graceful river nymph.

Dane put his hands on his hips and raised an eyebrow. "Showoff."

As they advanced on the gate, the difference in the light made it easy to tell that they were about to step into another realm. Where their forest was veiled in relative darkness save the glow of a shifting moon, beyond the doorway, the new set of trees were bathed a dusky haze.

Though he had plenty of misgivings, there was only one thing for it, so Dane gave Blayze an encouraging look, took hold of his hand, and led him through. It was like walking through a wall of silk, and as soon as the resistance faded, the smell of damp invaded his nostrils. The air was very close in this space, and Dane bristled as a soft breeze tickled his back.

Under the chirping of the birds, the trees seemed to whisper to themselves, telling each other about their unexpected visitors. Blayze reaffirmed the grip on Dane's hand as they navigated a seldom-trodden pathway that led directly into a sun-spattered clearing, on the far side of which stood the greatest tree he'd ever laid eyes on. The trunk stretched about fifty feet wide, with the height easily surpassing three hundred, and its beautifully interwoven roots gave way to a collection of twigs so large they broke up the sunlight into random beams. The leaves in a healthy blossom were like jade-colored shovels the size of dustbin lids, and to say it was awe-inspiring would be an understatement.

"What do we do?" Blayze whispered, apparently disinclined to disturb the eerie tranquility.

Dane shrugged. "It's gotta be this tree, right? We're not gonna get the sap over here, are we?"

Blayze screwed his face up and dropped his hand. Retrieving the dish from his pocket, he shoved it toward Dane as they proceeded to approach the base of the tree. When they got to about five feet away, a feminine, yet commanding, voice filtered through the breeze.

"Pray tell, upon what winds have two fleshlings blown my way?"

Looking around the grove, Dane tried and failed to place the origin of the voice. It seemed to be coming from both nowhere and everywhere at the same time.

"Such saplings," the voice continued to echo, "should not be left unattended."

Blayze and Dane swung round again, growing increasingly nervous. This time the voice definitely came from the tree itself. With a *creak* and a *crack*, they watched as a slender nine-foot-tall figure camouflaged with skin the very same mottled brown color as her dwelling peeled itself away from the tree. The Dryad was both reedy and sturdy, lithe yet muscular. She was naked in form and hairless besides a head of wispy brown vine curls that tickled the base of her breasts. Standing there, gawping openmouthed, Dane was positively enchanted.

"And so," she continued, "as a gracious host, I must ask—may I take your names?"

"I'm Da—"

Blayze clamped a hand down on his shoulder, startling him into silence. When he turned cautiously back to the tree spirit, he bowed his head slightly. "You may not take our names, but we will freely share. You may call me Blayze."

"Ahh," Dane said, taken aback to have almost been tripped up on such a literal play of words. He needed to be careful going forward. This magnificent fae creature had a wealth of untold power at her disposal, and he'd be damned if he was the one to put his foot in it. "And you may call me Dane. What should we call you?"

"You have not the wind nor the leaves to pronounce my name. However, for the sake of propriety and for the purposes of this conversation, you may call me Dryad."

"All right," said Dane. "So, Lady Dryad, we seek your help."

"Oh?" she said, a genuine smile of surprise curling her lips. In the next moment, the steadily growing wind turned and blew toward her, increasing in speed. "I should have known that there were ulterior motives for this unsolicited visit. Yet polite as you are, you bring with you the unmistakable smell of ash." Up until that point, her eyes had been a curious shade of blue-green, but they began to melt into the shade of autumnal leaves as the wind slowed. "My grove is precious. It will not be reduced to kindling by a descendant of those who play with fire."

"Please don't banish us, Lady Dryad," Blayze stepped in. "We aren't here to harm you. We've been sent on a quest to obtain three magical artifacts, and you hold the key to the last."

"A quest?" she said, curious. Her building rage settled as she breathed in the wind around her and stared at Blayze. "How quaint. Then pray tell, what is it you demand of me, fleshlings?"

"We require a small amount of sap from your grove, to act as a stimulant for a moon lily that will reverse the wish set upon us by a Djinn."

Dane wondered if he had deliberately omitted the fact they had swapped bodies. Probably. Even if he wasn't too clued up on the hierarchy of magical creatures, he did know that Djinns and Dryads were famous foes, and it was very clever of Blayze to play on her doubtless desire to hinder him.

"To thwart a singer of fire and flame…." She turned to the sky in contemplation. As she paused, the wind stilled entirely, and in that moment, it was as if every single tree in the woods were watching them. "That is a worthy cause indeed. Very good, fleshlings. You may claim what it is you desire and then take your leave."

"See, the thing is… I know a little something about fae," Blayze said. "And I'm pretty sure that every favor must be repaid sooner or later. I'd prefer to have the terms laid out right now, if you don't mind."

She tilted her head in appreciation and smiled slyly. "Shrewd enough, this one. Long has it been since druids visited our groves and blessed our development. Longer still since we have seen the likes of your kind. In return for granting you the final piece of your puzzle, I would have you swear to plant this seed anew." Unfurling her hand, in the center of her palm lay a golden seed no bigger than an acorn. It was smooth, round, had vines that contorted in on itself, and much like everything else in this place, was utterly and irrevocably beautiful. "It has been too many years since a new sister has awoken from slumber."

Dane turned to peer at Blayze. He looked confident enough, even if it was all an act, and he wondered what to make of Dane's jittery aura. The Dryad was very imposing, both in her stature and in her nature, and the nerves were beginning to get the better of him. He'd been feeling a steady tingling across his body for some time now, but he'd been doing his absolute best to quash it down. Carrying the weight of a power that wasn't his was starting to take its toll, and he couldn't be sure whether the fury of this mystical forest was a moment away from raining down on him. Worse still, he wasn't sure how he would respond.

"Where would we plant it?" Blayze asked.

"Somewhere at least ten thousand acres from this exact spot, somewhere productive in soil, and above all, somewhere safe."

As desperate as Dane was to ask how many other groves they had dotted up and down the country, he had the wherewithal to remain calm, speak the smallest number of words necessary, and trust in Blayze's knowledge of bargaining with this earthly phantom.

"How often would we need to tend to it?"

"I would ask that you water it but the once. From there, my sister will employ the nutrients found within the earth. It will take many years for her to achieve a territory as prosperous as this... and yet, as I did in the past and my other sisters before me, she will endure."

Blayze thought it over for a minute or so, looked at Dane, then nodded when he took the confirmation written in his eyes. Turning back to the Dryad, he held out his hand.

"We'll do it. Thank you. For both your trust and your patience."

"The thanks are all mine," the Dryad said.

When she bent down to delicately place the seed into Blayze's waiting hand, she withdrew herself slowly and gracefully, then stepped aside from her tree. Now that she was out in the open, her scale really hit home, and Dane had to crane his neck to keep his eyes on her as she opened her mouth and began to whistle a barely audible tune.

Blayze placed the seed in his pants pocket and zipped it up. Then he motioned for Dane to join him as they watched the bark of the tree split at her song. Moments later it began to willingly bleed sap, and when they stepped up to the tree, Blayze put the dish to the bark, made a trowel out of his hand, and used it to scrape some of the treacle-colored goop into the pot. When it was full to bursting, he sealed it shut, placed it in his other pocket, then made a sour face as he wiped the excess goo covering his hand back onto the tree.

Dane turned around to thank the Dryad once again, but he got a case of whiplash when he realized she was already gone. She hadn't made a sound or bent the light in any way.

"Pretty quiet for a giantess," he muttered to Blayze.

"Hah," he said absently. "Let's save the jokes for later, okay?"

As they headed for the doorway back to their world, it was probably the first time in his life that Dane was eager to trade the sunlight for darkness. Though it was an undeniably gorgeous location, there was a heaviness in the air that he couldn't seem to shake, and he wouldn't be all that sorry to leave this place.

They grabbed hold of one another's hands again, and right as they were about to step into the gate, a silken voice whispered through the trees. "Should you fail to uphold your end of the bargain, my wrath will be terrible and swift. Do not disappoint."

THE JOURNEY back to the B and B was mercifully quicker than what Dane expected, especially as the exit door from the grove had put them far closer to the edge of the woods than where they entered. Ignoring the fact that his safety trail had been for naught, it was well into the witching hour as they tiptoed the halls of the building and searched for their room with red, raw eyes.

Away from the daunting stature of the trees and inside the safety of four solid concrete walls, Dane breathed a sigh of relief. "Man, that was nuts. Why did you make a deal with her? It looked like we were about to get the sap for free."

"That's where you're wrong," Blayze said. "You never want to be in debt to fae—no matter which kind. They're tricky beings, for sure. It's terribly bad luck to be on the wrong side of one. You did well to measure your words, and overall, I'm pleased with our trade. She just wants more space for her family. Who are we to deny that?"

Dane hastened to agree. "Seems harmless enough. I think it went down fine, all things considered. I'm happy that I didn't burst into flames. I was sorely tempted, mind you. That place gave me all kinds of strange vibes. Tomorrow is going to be very interesting."

"Yeah, well, so you're aware, we're not leaving early. I'm gonna sleep for a solid twelve hours. And I'm totally not dealing with the couch tonight. Which side of the bed do you prefer?"

"Either's fine." Dane grinned as he headed to the bathroom to rinse his mouth out with some complimentary mouthwash. "Have whatever you want from the minibar," he called. "Think we've earned it."

Once his teeth were clean and his face washed, he came back to find that Blayze had tanked a miniature bottle of rum, then collapsed onto the right-hand side of the bed.

When Dane clicked the light off and climbed in the other side, the only sounds were the AC unit and Blayze's level breathing. As much as his body was dog-tired and his brain had seen enough stimuli for at least fifty dreams, Dane found himself wide-awake, staring at the ceiling.

Though he was in a near-permanent state of horniness lately, it wasn't dick he craved—neither Blayze's nor his own. It was company. Since he'd met him, Blayze had soared in his estimation for desirable companionship. At first he'd been a prissy and tight-lipped piece of work, but when Dane finally understood the reasons why he held himself apart, it had been easy to warm to him. He was softly snoring now, no doubt making good on his promise to remain unconscious for every minute of those twelve hours.

Even if Dane suddenly craved some philosophical chat to understand why vulnerability made people so endearing, the last thing he wanted to do was intrude on Blayze's well-earned rest. Instead, he carefully shuffled across the bed and wrapped his arm around Blayze's torso. Lifting his arm, Blayze accepted it instinctively, as though Dane was his missing puzzle piece, and when Dane closed his eyes with a contented smile on his face, it was a mere matter of minutes before he felt himself drifting off too.

CHAPTER NINETEEN

NOW THAT they had the third and final tool to reverse their predicament, Blayze expected a hasty departure. He'd never been much of a morning person, even if they awoke in midafternoon, but Dane's embrace was a disarming comfort, and the astonishment continued after he'd taken a shower and found room service spread across the bed.

There were squares of toast with fancy packs of butter, scones with clotted cream and jam, freshly squeezed orange juice, flakey baked croissants, and a pot of coffee that might as well have been liquid gold. Dane was different somehow too. As he stood at the foot of the continental feast and piled up his plate, the smile reached his eyes in a way it hadn't before.

"You okay?" Blayze asked.

"Never better," said Dane as he took a seat. "How long do you want to stay? We've got, what? Three days to rectify the swap until we're doomed for good? Where's the harm in staying here for another night? It'd only take a few taps on my phone."

Blayze smiled and took a sip of coffee, then tackled the mountain of food. He was touched. Clearly Dane was eager to spend more time with him, and as much as he'd have adored spending a proper day in the English countryside, strolling through luscious green fields or playing croquet or drinking tea at a grand manor house, now that he was starting to actually care about this man, the last thing he wanted to do was let him spend more money on his behalf, knowing he wouldn't be able to return the favor. The unavoidable change back was looming on the horizon, and he had to rip the Band-Aid off and find out for certain whether they had any ties beyond their circumstances. He wondered how to let him down without lying or making it sound like he was desperate to get back to the Seer.

"It's all good," Blayze said. "Not to be rude, I kinda prefer city life. New York boy at heart, remember? So, if we head back to London and you find you want to spend more time together doing something else before… you know… then I'm totally game."

Dane nodded and paused to clear his plate. He didn't look disappointed as such, but there was an unwelcome air of tension lingering around. "Sure thing," he chirped. "Whatever you say. I'll book a taxi before I hop in the shower. Sorry. I grew up around fields and cows, so whilst I'm living in the city for now, I get excited when I come back to places like this. Sometimes I forget that's not the case for everyone else."

Very deliberately, Blayze held his gaze. "You don't have to be sorry. In spite of you almost getting us tricked into fae slavery, I've had a fab time."

Usually Blayze preferred it when he was on the higher ground, especially with guys as hot as Dane. But recently he found it more rewarding to be on a level playing field. Just when he was about to articulate these thoughts, a stern voice cut through the room.

"This is an update for all of our brethren," it said.

"What the fuck?" Dane asked as he got up. "Where's that coming from?"

"The washroom, I think."

Blayze set his mug down and followed Dane in search of the voice, though he had a fair idea what they were about to face. Sure enough, when the pair of them reached the freestanding mirror next to the bathtub, staring back at them was an illusion of three MRF officials. Each was dressed in one of the best suits money could buy, but no matter how dapper the trio looked, their stony faces told a different story.

"Hear us," said the man in the middle. "Our kind has existed in secret since the dawn of time, but due to unforeseen and largely unavoidable circumstances, we are now faced with a decision. Do we spend the coming days, months, or even years performing damage control with mass memory wipes? Or do we seize this opportunity to integrate with humans in hopes of finally being seen as equals? We cannot understate the importance of this deliberation, and to prove how much we appreciate every single one of you who have been patient with us on this journey, we are asking this question directly of you. We request that you cast your vote at the end of this message, so listen well, as only one vote will be registered per mage, and you will not be able to change your mind once said vote is cast. You must either place your palm on the left-hand side of the mirror if you elect the route of memory wipes, or place your palm on the right-hand side if you elect the route of integration. Thank you.

There is no wrong choice. No matter the outcome, we will continue to thrive as a unit built on community values. We will be in touch again in due course with the results."

At some point during the relay, Blayze's jaw dropped to the floor. The gravity of what they were being asked to do was little more than a cosmic joke, but he didn't get to laugh for long because, once the image of the officials faded, the mirror bisected itself. The left-hand side had morphed into a leisurely rippling ocean, whereas the right-hand side looked like a shimmering pool of molten chocolate. And that was it. No text or other imagery or subtle manipulation in terms of coloring. The MRF genuinely wanted honest opinions.

Without so much as a single beat of hesitation, Blayze slammed his palm on the right-hand side so hard it almost toppled the wooden frame. His vote registered with a satisfying *ding*, and whatever psychic technology the mirror was employing meant it knew another mage was in the room with him, because the projection remained right where it was, awaiting Dane's vote.

The deliberation was unmistakable as it flashed across his face, and as his hand hovered in front of the mirror, there was a sour moment where Blayze was genuinely unsure what he was going to do. What was the holdup? He remembered their conversation back at the Shard where Dane had played devil's advocate and laid out the reasons why full exposure could be seen as a bad idea. But Blayze had simply assumed he was freeballing ideas and that he was unequivocally on the side of freedom. Was everything he had come to learn about this man a lie? Did Blayze even know him at all?

Suddenly, whatever was holding him back relaxed its chokehold, and with something between a giggle and a snort, Dane laid his hand flat to the right-hand side. Another audible confirmation reverberated around the room, and once the mirror went back to normal and displayed a reflection of their astounded expressions, the air around them felt charged.

Dane looked at Blayze, and Blayze stared right back, completely at a loss. Together they had set in motion something they could scarcely comprehend, and yet, as agonizing as it would be to await the results of the vote, Blayze couldn't keep the optimistic grin off of his face.

Blayze was still in a state of shock in the taxi and on the subsequent train back to London. He laughed at Dane's jokes and looked out the window when he scrolled on his phone, but for the life of him, he couldn't get his brain to slow down. To think he was anxious on the way up because of the conversation with Evangeline bordered on absurd. She was probably just as blindsided by the message as everyone else, and that previous headspace was nothing compared to the internalized pandemonium he was going through now. There was an endless reel of images flitting throughout his mind, and normally, when he had too much shit to unpack, the worms would never get back in the can if he opened it all the way. The future had never looked so uncertain, and while it was a sizeable task just to keep his composure and not fling himself out of the train emergency exit, he had to focus on the positives.

Living in another mage's body for the better part of a week and sharing his life in an exceptionally intimate way had done him a world of good. Even if they didn't end up going on lavish dates by the end of the year, the life lessons he learned from Dane—and *being* Dane—had been priceless and irreplaceable. He had to keep that in mind going forward.

The bustling streets of London were a very welcome sight, even if the smog-filled air made him sneeze three times in five minutes. As they dipped into a cute bakery to pick up some late lunch on their way to feed the plant and visit the Seer, Blayze promised himself to get out of his funk and get himself out there.

Money was important to him—that wasn't likely to go away anytime soon. Dane was a good example of somebody who had money and didn't make it the focal point of his life. Was that simply because he had it? Blayze was sure the shoe would be slightly more uncomfortable if the roles were reversed, but he wanted to make a mindful effort not to resent people for what they'd earned. All he needed to do was believe in himself and his trinket business. Once he was making a decent wage, he too could indulge in things like days out in countryside cottages and not feel guilty when other people wanted to treat him. He'd spent too long living a champagne lifestyle on a lemonade budget, and it was high time he took responsibility for shoving things on credit cards and hoping for the best.

"Hey," Dane said in the elevator, pastries under his arm while Blayze carried the coffees. "How are you holding up? You've been distant since the ride back, and I didn't want to mention anything until we were home."

Home. What an interesting word choice. Was it an accidental slip of the tongue? Or something casual yet deliberate? His brain was fried. Things didn't compute properly anymore, and it was both scary and thrilling.

"I'm fine," Blayze assured. "Just thinking some things over, is all. It's a good thing. Cathartic. I feel better for it."

"So long as you do." When the elevator pinged open, Dane spread his hands and let Blayze find the doorway first. "I had a really great time," he said as he jammed a key into the lock. "Would be fun to do it again sometime. Maybe under freer circumstances. And who knows, maybe that way of thinking isn't just a pipe dream anymore?"

"Yeah, maybe," Blayze acknowledged. Now that he was in the comfort of Dane's apartment, the dissociative mood was coming to a head, and he was about ready to get into whatever hours-long conversation it warranted. But when he tried to set the coffees down, something arguably more important caught his attention and he missed the counter entirely, triggering a steaming hot spillage all over the tiles. "Argh, fuck me sideways."

"What's up?" Dane closed the door, tossed the pastries to the side, and grabbed Blayze by his shoulders. Concern grew in his eyes. "Are you okay? I knew something was wrong, but I'm here to talk whenever you need to. You know that, right? Even if it's just something that sounds dumb... if it's bothering you, I want to hear it. You got that?"

"Yes, I promise I will, but right now it's not really the coffee I'm worried about," Blayze said.

When Dane finally paid attention to his peripheral vision and turned to face the plant dead-on, his jaw hung open as he registered that it had grown into a full-on perennial with six elegant and healthy flower heads.

"Son of a bitch." Dane shook his head and made a series of incoherent sounds. "Are you...? Did we...? Um, should we...?"

"Yep. I know, right?" Blayze wasn't sure if he was angry or happy or confused. Maybe he was all three. "Call me crazy, but I've got a sneaking suspicion we didn't actually need any of these damned relics. Trina's got some explaining to do."

CHAPTER TWENTY

AFTER EVERYTHING they had been through in the last twenty-four hours, Dane was a clusterfuck of emotions. Once he and Blayze cleared up the coffee spill, they left the assortment of pastries to gather dust as they pondered what to do next. The plant had blossomed into something truly magnificent—easily the most impressive display of organic growth Dane had ever seen—and the how of it was far from lost on him. Clearly, the two of them trusting in each other and working together had forged its path, and if they didn't actually need the sap of a Dryad's grove to complete the development of the plant, it was also very unlikely they ever needed the two previous accelerants. Now all that remained was the obvious task to go clip some petals and rush them off to the Seer and get her to brew the potion. And yet, as much as he craved to be reunited with his giant body and tiresomely overbearing power, he had to tread carefully.

Blayze had been unusually quiet on the way home, and because he had a visible guard up, his feelings were impossible to decipher. Hell, for all Dane knew, Blayze could end up holding his body hostage because he'd taken to it so much. The thought was highly improbable; he was letting his imagination run away with the fairies again, and it was time for some hard truths.

"I know I already asked," Dane said as he took up a barstool next to the plant. "So, at the risk of getting a punch in the arm for harassment, are you sure everything's all right?"

Blayze also took a perch at the counter, but he didn't answer immediately, which was likely a good thing. The automatic response would have been a lie, and he was actually learning to speak before he spoke, which was another positive—if also weird—sign. Judging by the way he stared at the plant without really seeing it, there seemed to be a full-on war going on inside his head.

"I…," he started. "I don't want this to end."

"Oh. That's it?"

"What do you mean, that's it?" Blayze turned on him. "Don't try to oversimplify this. It's anything besides simple."

"I didn't mean it like that." Dane surrendered, his hands in the air. "Of course it's not simple. Then again, I guess it could be… if we wanted it to be."

"How do you mean?"

"Who says that us getting our bodies back means we don't have to see each other anymore?"

Blayze furrowed his brow. He didn't speak for almost a minute, though not for lack of trying. His mouth kept opening and closing, and one time he even lifted a finger, then let it go when his shoulders sagged in defeat.

Dane reached out, placed a hand on his back, and silently pleaded with Blayze to look at him again. When he did, they both smiled. "See how easy it is to simply be with each other? That's not going to change when we go back to ourselves. At least, I hope it won't. Even if the skin we've been wearing this past week has been different, it's our minds that have connected, and believe it or not, I don't want to let go of that either."

"You don't?"

"No. Actually, I kinda saw it as a given, or a nonissue. I was a bit worried you were gonna say you liked my power so much you wanted to keep it."

"Hah," Blayze bellowed. "Yeah, right. As if I'd leave you to walk this earth as a grade A Fire Wielder. You've done way better than most would have, but total control takes decades of training, and you've got no idea what you're doing."

Dane sneered and elbowed his ribs. "As it turns out, I happen to agree with you. I think I have done pretty well, considering how volatile this power can be. The London Eye's still standing, right?"

"True, true." The grin on Blayze's face remained there for a while, and even when it did leave his lips, there was a cheerier aura about him. "Okay," he said as he climbed off the stool and squared his shoulders, positioning himself to pluck a couple of petals. "Enough prolonging the inevitable. Let's go get our bodies back."

IT WAS almost sundown as they sped across the city to get to the Seer, and as soon as she saw the pair gawping at her wonderful wares once again, a knowing smile spread across her face.

"Well, well," she said as she glided across the room to put the front door on the latch. "It was only last night when I began to wonder what had become of you two."

"A wild goose chase, I reckon," said Dane. "We're pretty certain, but we have to know. We didn't need any of those items you listed, did we?"

The look on her face said it all. "Back when you two first came to me, neither could stand to be within three meters of the other. Do me a favor, would you? Take a moment to look at yourselves now."

Confused, Dane looked to his side and was surprised to find Blayze standing no more than a foot away. Though they weren't touching, there was something about their collective body language. She was right. There was a tangible difference.

"Clever," Blayze said. "You might've just told us. Would have saved an awful lot of legwork on our part."

"Ah yes, because that's always worked in the past for inquisitive mages. Especially male ones at that." Trina rolled her eyes fondly, then softly laid a hand on each of their shoulders. "Rest assured, had I laid out my plans, it would have negated the intended effect. They don't call me the Wise Old Seer for nothing, and this particular Seer isn't blind to the way you look at him."

When Dane glanced at Blayze again, his temples were bulging where he was grinding his teeth, and his cheeks had flushed a curious shade of tomato. Did she mean what he thought she meant? If so, that was probably a conversation better saved for later on.

"Now then," Trina plowed ahead and kept a sly grin on her face as she reached into Blayze's right-hand coat pocket to pluck out the two moon lily petals. "That's a grand specimen, indeed. It must have flourished very well to yield growth that large. I've had a long day, and you pair have had a long week, so let's not delay further. Let us finally put things right."

CHAPTER TWENTY-ONE

THEY HUDDLED around Seer's table listening to a curious ensemble of ocean waves and a rainforest choir, and Blayze tried to quell the hammering in his chest.

Owing to Dane's candid yet welcome chat, he was less nervous about the emotional aftermath of the switch and more about the switch itself. Though they'd originally undergone it postorgasm, he distinctly remembered almost passing out when they swapped, then actually passing out when he realized what had happened. He couldn't shake the suspicion that the experience would be twice as bad in reverse.

"You boys are very lucky," Trina said as she tossed a furry sprig of some unknown herb into the aggressively bubbling pot. "I am down to my last batch of witch hazel. Somebody ought to give me a medal for the celestial miracles I have performed this week."

Dane cleared his throat. There were a few beads of sweat running down his forehead, and he was holding on to Blayze's hand on the table, apparently trying to squeeze it into a mushy, bony pulp. "I can see to it that you are adequately compensated… but could we maybe hurry this along? The smell of this brew is starting to make me feel a little sick."

"I'm only playing," said the Seer. "You keep your money. I have no need of it. And better to peg your nose. We're going to be a while."

Seeing the surprise on Dane's face, Blayze bit his tongue. This woman was doing her best to help them, and it wasn't her fault he found himself in the midst of a meltdown. He had seen a vast display of weird and wonderful abilities in his time—shapeshifting, teleportation, telekinesis, and telepathy. But he also knew of someone who had developed an understandable form of OCD because they could see bacteria with their naked eyes, and just the other week he'd met a young girl who could immediately solve every mathematical equation that fell on her ears. Even his ex could manipulate the state of foodstuffs, for crying out loud. So why was he so nervous about that ominously bubbling cauldron?

Why did it feel like the viscous vat of liquid was their combined doom rather than their salvation?

"You must remain connected at all times," Trina said after an eon. She looked pointedly at their linked hands as she fetched two glass beakers from another basket. "Do not let go, no matter what happens."

Without waiting for approval, she started to mutter something under her breath. After a moment or two, her eyes rolled around in her head and she began to quiver all over. Dane's first instinct was to move and see if she was okay, which was cute, but Blayze clamped his hand to the table and shook his head.

"Let her do her thing."

When Trina's consciousness eventually returned to their current plane, there was a lopsided smile on her face, and she crossed her arms and dug both hands into the cauldron. A loud sizzling punctured the silence, and a giant plume of smoke obscured most of her frame. The odd smell of the potion was nothing compared to the unmistakable scent of singed flesh, and when the smoke eventually dissipated, Trina yanked her hands out of the bowl and slammed the glasses on the table. The gloopy iridescent purple liquid inside wouldn't stop fizzing, and Blayze went wide-eyed when he saw the extent of damage to her forearms.

"Worry not," she soothed quietly as she fetched something else from her infinite supply of exotic commodities. This time it was an off-white balm, and as soon as she slathered it across her wounds, her skin began to visibly knit itself back together. "I will be good as new in little more than a few minutes. Quickly now, before the compound begins to regress."

Blayze turned to look at Dane. It was crunch time, and every ounce of worry was back in full force. He didn't know whether to slurp his beaker like a tequila shot or sweep it off the table and bolt out the door. When Dane met his eye, there was an echo of the same worry, and yet there was also strength. He both knew and trusted this woman, and because Blayze had taken the time to trust him, that same confidence was passed down by proxy.

"Hey, short stuff," Dane said as he palmed one of the glasses. "If this doesn't work, we'll figure something out. I got you, remember? We're in this together no matter what body we end up in."

"Okay," Blayze agreed, voice breaking as he tried to pinpoint the exact moment he'd become such an insecure sap.

Maybe things would change when they swapped, or maybe things would stay the same. Wasn't that an exciting gamble? As he swiped up his glass and raised it to his lips, he was unquestionably happier with any potential outcome now that Dane had effectively promised to be in his life in some capacity.

"Now," Trina demanded.

Blayze kept his eyes glued to Dane as he gulped the beaker. The stuff tasted like fossilized dragon eggs rolled around in city garbage, then sprinkled with arsenic for good measure. There was a very real chance that his stomach would reflexively refuse to keep it down, so he shut his eyes to suppress that urge. He imagined himself and Dane snuggled up together in bed. That put him at ease, and when there was nothing left to swallow, he patted himself on the back.

And then came the tingling. He forced open his eyes and tried to focus on the room, but it was both blurred and spinning. His skin was literally on fire. A week ago, he could've walked down the street and gone about his entire day under the very same sensation without so much as blinking. But after being without the curious little flame for so long, it was a complete shock to the system that she was coming back in full force.

"Shit," he said, "I'm burning up. It doesn't feel right."

Dane's eyes were rolling around in his head, and when he began to convulse, he was doing a very good impression of the girl from *The Exorcist*. No doubt he was getting every nearby aura poured into his brain, and even if Blayze couldn't entirely say he was sad to see them leave his own head, he suspected the toll it would take on Dane would be slightly more tolerable.

Blayze blinked back tears as the world twisted itself like a wet dishcloth. A sharp punch to the gut forced his eyes back open, and it quickly dawned on him that he was now on the left-hand side of Trina, with Dane on the right. Just like that, he was back in his own body, and the Seer looked at least a head's height taller.

Turning to look at Dane's face was a pretty surreal experience. He'd grown so accustomed to seeing his real body in what had essentially been a walking mirror, and it was bizarre to appreciate the fact he'd been hanging out with a legitimate stud muffin. Dane was busy examining Blayze with those delightfully walnut eyes, and there was a cheeky half smile on his lips. When he tore his gaze away, he stared at his hands as if they could still make fire.

"Whoa," Blayze said. He held out his hands and delighted in the knowledge that if he did want to set them alight for any reason, he could once again do so. "That was next-level. All right, panic over, I guess. Thank you so much, Trina."

For a second there, his mind had threatened to take a dark turn, because he'd been a dumbass to think Trina had any intentions beyond genuine aid. Looking at her now, exhausted and slumped in her chair, gently massaging her arms where she had been so selfless to put them at first, he wanted to reward her somehow. She didn't care for money—not that Blayze had any to give—but her deeds would not go unnoticed. Maybe she *should* get a handful of medals. In this quirky little shop tucked into a corner of London, she had done more to help mages this week than the MRF had done in years.

"How do you feel?" she asked in a soft voice. "Any light-headedness? Wooziness? Imposter syndrome?"

"None for me," Dane said as he got up from the seat so he could stretch. "In fact, I feel like a new man. My legs feel like they could run a full marathon and not grumble once."

"That'll be the ginger root," Trina said. She cast her eyes lazily over to Blayze, implicitly asking the same question.

"I'm good," he said hastily. "How are you? Seems like you could sleep for two days straight. Can we get you anything?"

Trina grinned and almost drifted off at the thought. "My place of rest isn't far from the shop. Think I will manage to get myself home and fix a mug of chamomile. Though I do wonder...." She brought a curious gaze up to Dane. "Unorthodox as it might seem, now that your ability has returned to you, should you wish to get back in the saddle, so to speak, I would be grateful if you could bestow a small gift upon me."

"Of course," Dane said, nodding his head vigorously, excited. "Anything. Though, just so you know, the effects will only last until I'm out of range. With that in mind, what sort of emotion would you like?"

The Seer hummed as she wracked her brain. She could opt for peace, glee, contentment, or even something more obscure, like love. Even if it was an artificial fabrication, love healed all wounds, and if you got it right and didn't go completely batshit in the process, its strength was incomparable. Harnessing the power of love was like a weapon in itself—and it was arguably stronger than any gift from any mage on the planet. Blayze would know. He'd been experiencing the familiar burbling of it in the pit of his stomach over the last few days, and because it had precisely nothing to do with artificial fabrication, he had yet to put a voice to those feelings because everything was still very much up in the air.

"Wonder," Trina said decisively. "I have experienced this childlike emotion only a handful of times during my existence on this plane, and I yearn to encounter it again, no matter how fleeting."

"You got it."

Blayze watched as Dane closed his eyes and focused. A small V appeared between his eyebrows as he began to wrestle with his mind, but when he did eventually grasp hold of the emotion and transfer it over, Trina breathed an audible sigh of relief and went utterly slack in her chair. A moment passed in which she hung in physical limbo, and then she promptly slid off the chair, muttering to herself on the floor in a display of unbridled joy.

"Oh shit," Blayze cried, raising himself out of his chair to bend down to her and check she hadn't swallowed her tongue or something. "Should we... uhh, do something?"

"Huh," Dane said at his side. "Maybe I shouldn't have ramped it up to one hundred, but she'll be fine. Nobody ever died from being too happy, did they? Come on, we can linger for a little while, but let's give her some privacy to enjoy herself."

"If you're sure?" Blayze asked. He was still hesitant about leaving her to her own devices when she was practically drunk or drugged up, but when the Seer showed herself to be lucid enough to flutter a small wave of goodbye, he felt considerably better. "Okay, good. Thanks again, Trina. We'll never forget what you've done for us."

As they crossed through the beaded curtain back into the shop, the Seer started to roar with infectious laughter. Grinning from ear to ear, Blayze entwined his hand with Dane's and absently perused her glittering wares as he reflected on how far they'd come.

They had been on quite the emotional roller coaster, and even if Blayze wasn't entirely sure how to handle the abundance of new self-discoveries, one thing was certain—if they accidentally swapped bodies again and he had to do it all over, he wouldn't change a damn thing.

CHAPTER TWENTY-TWO

DANE WAS back where he truly belonged, and it was nothing short of magnificent. The world outside had gone dark, and they had no need for words, because there was no question as to their destination.

Although the power of fire had been banished from his body, Dane didn't have to worry about London's brisk temperature, because there was a different breed of flame in his veins. While it seemed virtually unquenchable in the moment and was so potent it was making him all jittery, he knew the perfect way to appease it.

"You good?" Dane asked as he closed the door behind him.

Blayze moved into the room, triggering the automatic lighting. There was purpose in his eyes and a fervor in his movements as he eliminated the small amount of distance, ripped open Dane's shirt, and shoved him up against the door. Once his nipples were exposed, Blayze wasted no time latching his mouth on to one and firmly tweaking the other. With his free hand, he pawed at Dane's midriff, then began to groan in exasperation as he struggled to get his own belt out of the loops.

"Huh," Dane said, pleasantly surprised. "No preamble. I like the way you think. Here, lemme help you with that."

When Blayze drew himself back up to full height, Dane bent down and took the chance to kiss him as he undid his belt. Blayze tasted faintly of sweet peppermint mouthwash, and while his skin was soft and delicate, there was nothing gentle about the way he began to devour Dane like he'd been stranded out in the Sahara Desert for weeks on end.

As much as he had enjoyed the quirks of living inside someone else's body, now that they were back where they belonged, things felt easier. Blayze was a lot more confident in his actions, and Dane very much looked forward to seeing how that translated to the bedroom.

"Hell yeah," Dane said when Blayze stripped him of his pants and boxer shorts, then tossed them across the room.

Because he had front-row seats to watch Dane's cock get harder, he had a salacious smirk on his face, and when he undid his fly and offered up his rapidly growing bulge, Dane was unable to stand the fiery frenzy any longer. He peeled Blayze out of his bottom layers and threw them on top of his. Then he scooped him up into his arms, melded mouths, and carried him to the bedroom.

Nothing else mattered beyond the two of them, and he accidentally bumped them into the doorframe.

"Moron," Blayze laughed. "Fuck, man, I need you so bad. I need *us* so bad."

But when they eventually made it to the bed, Blayze detached himself a bit sooner than Dane would have liked. When he started rooting through one of the bottom drawers, it threatened to kill the mood because his emotions began to bounce all over the place. First it was horny, then needy, now strangely sentimental. What was going on in that head of his?

"I bought these in that store on the way to Oxfordshire." Blayze showed him a small collection of fuchsia-colored tea lights. "We were so busy I forgot all about them. I wouldn't mind lighting them now, if that's cool."

Dane nodded and watched as Blayze set three of them on the bedside table, ignited his pinky finger, and lit each of them individually. Almost immediately, a delicate rose scent wafted through the room, and when Blayze got rid of his shirt, jumped onto the bed, and started gently playing with his cock, his energy went back into horny mode and brought the mood right back up.

Dane did away with his final layer of clothing and joined Blayze on the bed. He stayed on his knees, not sure which act of pleasure would befit the occasion. Now that this gorgeous hunk of a man had opened him up to being versatile, there were many options. He wanted to ride the final wave together, that much was certain, but what was the best way to get there?

"Eat my ass." Blayze effectively decided for him. "I know you've been hungry for it."

"Oh, you know it," Dane said, and he licked his lips when Blayze turned around, arched his back, and presented himself to him.

Even though Blayze was a self-confessed hygiene queen, Dane loved that there was some fuzz on his peaches. He grabbed hold of them, spread the gift so willingly offered, and exposed Blayze's tight pink hole.

"Wow," he said, caught in a moment of awe. "What a beautiful sight."

He could probably sit there for hours watching it twitch in anticipation, but because Blayze was obviously keen for some carnal pleasure, Dane laid his tongue flat and gave a decisive stroke. It was met with a deep and extensive sigh, which was high praise, and when Blayze backed up onto Dane's face, he took that as encouragement, and he licked stronger and faster.

"Work it," Blayze moaned into the pillow, hips swinging. "Oh yeah, man, you work that hole."

Dane was happy to do exactly that, and he was encouraged by the lust-driven voice inside his head as he fully embraced Blayze's scorching hot aura of desire. Letting go of his cheeks, Dane buried his tongue into Blayze's ass and started tickling his balls, jerking him hard and fast.

When Blayze's thighs started to quiver, it was a testament to how much he wanted a shared experience, because he pried Dane's hands off his junk and turned around to pull him down to his level for another sensuous kiss. This time around it was sloppier and much more careless, and yet that added to the excitement. When Dane decided that he too wanted his ass played with, he gave Blayze's forehead a kiss, then mimicked his position from before and let him have at it.

"Whoa," Dane moaned as he closed his eyes and basked in the divine, sensitive sensation. He'd never get over the fact that such a small action could provide such an acute and incredible feeling, and given how much he wanted to be with Blayze for the long haul, there was no reason why they couldn't make it a daily ritual.

If Dane had been hungry before, Blayze was practically starving. He would score top marks in an ass-eating championship, and after only a few minutes, Dane could feel himself leaking onto the duvet. The temptation to give it a few hard tugs was definitely there, but he resisted in the name of fairness.

"Got any toys?" Blayze wondered. "Call me crazy, but I'm sensing that we're both wanting something up there right about now. How's about we share that experience?"

"Good idea," Dane said. "There's a few in the top drawer."

Blayze gave Dane's ass an eager slap and a squeeze and then got down from the bed and rummaged through the top drawer of his nightstand. When he got a good look at the collection, the disbelief on his face was priceless.

"A few, you say?" Blayze laughed. "Hun, there's more dildos and plugs in here than the Adam & Eve headquarters. I thought you didn't bottom?"

Dane shook his head and rolled his eyes. "I don't... though I do get horny all on my lonesome, so I always end up ordering bigger sizes, then wimp out last-minute. Um, in terms of what I can actually take, the small veiny blue one is good. Might I suggest the twisted black dragon for yourself?"

When Blayze found the one he was talking about, his jaw almost detached from his face. Narrowing his eyes to slits, he smacked the rubber toy on Dane's ass. "Are you serious right now? Look at the size of this thing! You could knock someone out with this. No freaking chance." He tossed it back in the drawer, heard it ca-*thunk*, and then searched again. This time he came out with a humble flesh-colored plug that was a few sizes larger than the blue one.

Knowing what was looming, Dane put his face down to the covers, instinctively arched his back deeper, then shivered all over as he listened to Blayze fetch the lube and warm up the rubber by practicing his hand-job technique.

"Are you ready?" he asked, voice suddenly husky. "I'll go as slow or as fast as you want."

"Thank you." Dane measured his breathing and heart rate as Blayze breached the ring ever so gently.

Given that he hadn't taken more than a couple fingers in years, getting filled up would be weird to say the least. But it was a mind-over-matter thing. That's what he kept telling himself like a mantra, because that's how it had been when he'd taken his own dick in Blayze's body. He had wanted it bad then, and it was a good sign that he wanted it equally as much, if not more so, now.

As the toy explored deeper and deeper, the fiery heat in his ass made him instinctively clench against the rubber. Mercifully, because the fire raging in his bones was starting to dampen somewhat, it was considerably easy to relinquish resistance. The sensation was so obvious and acute that his head swam with all sorts of devious images, and yet they brought forward a stark realization. He wanted Blayze. No, he *needed* Blayze, in more ways than one. Sure, they'd screwed a handful of times now, but this time was different. Blayze could have dashed to the airport as soon as they left the shop, and Dane had half expected him to do exactly that. Even after he lingered, he could also have hidden his emotions and played a drawn-out game of hard to get. There was a time when he'd have seen someone like Blayze doing that, because on the face of it, he came off like a gold digger. That was the furthest thing from the case, however. He'd been open and forthcoming about how much their time together had meant, and because he recognized another lost soul, they were drawn together like magnets.

Ever since they met, Dane had been noticeably worried about coming off as the clingy one, but he'd felt something powerful and hadn't wanted to let go of that rare sense of belonging. He owed it to Blayze to return the favor of directness, and now that they weren't forced to spend time with each other because of a bizarre case of ill-advised wishing, they were free to explore their coupling by natural means. Dane had strong hopes for their future, and he couldn't wait to see what it had in store for them.

He was a hot and sweaty ball of raw sexual energy, and Blayze was radiating like a furnace. With an expert amount of technique and coaxing, he enabled Dane to take the plug all the way down to the hilt.

"Fuck... that feels amazing," he said, practically drooling. The widening of his hole and the fullness of the object inside was so apparent and so intimate, and he couldn't hide the wide grin curving his lips as he rotated around to find Blayze already bent back over. "Looks like it's your turn."

He grabbed the dildo he'd selected and mirrored Blayze's warm-up method, making sure to properly acclimate before he took the plunge. Because Dane was so worked up and eager to press on, the hardest part of toying him was finding a balance of pace that worked for both of them. It very much helped that Blayze had undergone considerably more practice in the past, and with only a couple of stop-starts, a boatload of carnal grunting, and lots of affectionate squeezing, it wasn't long at all before the plug stretched out Blayze's hole, and given how his much his hips were swaying, it seemed more than happy to welcome its new reality.

"Damn," Dane announced. "Great job. That looks right at home in there. How's it feel?"

"Incredible," Blayze said dreamily. When he turned back around and got back on his knees to match positions, his eyes were glazed with lust, and there was a poignant moment where they simply appreciated each other. Then they collapsed onto each other's mouths again. "Fuck, Dane," Blayze said between breaths. "I'm so horny right now. Really gotta cum. Are you close?"

The halted words might as well have been Mozart to Dane's ears.

"I sure am," he moaned.

They grabbed hold of each other's dicks, and it took little more than ten hard strokes for the all-too-familiar pressure to build in Dane's groin. The plug was quietly working its magic, massaging his prostate, sending wave after wave of tender and blissful agony. Kneeling on the bed, making out with the hot-headed and gregarious American hunk, knowing he also had a big fat plug up his ass.... Dane had never known intimacy like it. Being with him in this capacity was easy, and when he pictured himself and Blayze spending countless nights exploring each other's bodies, finding new ways to turn each other on and make each other's cocks spit out creamy wads of joy... it was enough to send him over the edge.

"Oh, Blayze—I'm gonna bust," Dane cried as he reached for the stars, then kept on reaching until he located a supernova in a private pocket of their universe. When he heard Blayze roar at the ceiling, losing himself on their combined journey to euphoria, the apartment vanished as Dane latched his mouth on to him again.

This time, the kiss was different. No longer did they feel like two separate people connected by circumstance. They had been through an extraordinary journey together, and in spite of some tricky obstacles, had managed to come out on top and stronger. As he felt his lips work their own unique breed of magic, Dane's memory was cast back to the first time he met Blayze in the bar. He remembered as clear as day how his anxiety wouldn't even let him talk to him—let alone think about touching him. But after everything they had been through, he was no longer scared to act on his need for physical affection. The fear of rejection had been flung out the window, and he finally felt comfortable enough to run his hands through Blayze's hair, trace lines on his back, and even squeeze him into a cuddle.

"Wow," Dane said as he collapsed onto the bed.

The comforter was practically soaked with their sweet release, but as long as he was here in this moment with this precious man, the mattress could have been made of nails and it would still be the perfect place to relish their postorgasm bliss.

"Dude," Blayze said simply. His chest was rising and falling as rapidly as Dane's. "That was...."

"I know, right?" Slowly, so as not to ruin the moment, Dane turned to face Blayze and found him watching him through dreamy, glazed-over eyes. "Sex shouldn't be this good, should it? Like, am I allowed to say that?"

Blayze carefully reached out a hand and stroked the side of Dane's beard. "It's good because *we're* good. We click like that, don't you think?"

Dane agreed. He also recognized that this was a good opportunity to make good on the promise he'd made himself. It would be too easy to back out, awkwardly go make two cups of tea, then be on their separate ways, but he wanted this. Wanted them. Had done since they first screwed around. It was crunch time, and he needed to be bold, be courageous, and throw the idea of rejection right out of the window, because there was no way that was their fate.

"Look, Blayze, I've gotta be honest with you. Oh no, it's nothing bad, this is a good thing, trust me. When I first met you in the bar, I thought you were a piece of work. You seemed like the type of guy who could do no wrong, who thinks the sun shines out of your squeaky-clean ass."

"Are you sure this is a good thing?" Blayze asked, eyebrow cocked.

"Yes." Dane smiled. "I want to confess that I was the one who was wrong. You aren't self-centered or arrogant, and you know what? Even though it was one hell of an adjustment period, I'm glad we made that stupid wish to swap bodies. It taught me that A, I can be a little quick to judge. B, my ability isn't half as bad as I sometimes make it out to be. And C, I should be more open to the idea of finding someone, especially when they probably and—not gonna lie here—very hopefully want me back."

Blayze took half a minute to digest and process Dane's words, and it was clear that he was thinking awfully hard about his response.

"I can relate with pretty much all of that. You and I are a lot more similar than I first thought too. Here I thought I was imposing on this God-tier Viking Brit who had the looks, the money, but not the smarts. Turns out you've got all of that in droves and then some. Your heart is almost as big as your dick, and right now, I'm pretty happy with that. Was it easy dealing with what we had to deal with? Hell no. Would I do it again? Hell maybe. Whatever the case, I'm grateful we got to make memories that no one will ever truly understand. It's more personal that way, and yeah, if you hadn't guessed by now, I'm pretty freaking keen on you. Think Trina made it pretty obvious, didn't she?"

Dane guffawed at the memory. "Yeah, she really did that. Also, I don't care what she makes of it, I'll be sending her more witch hazel than she can make haybales with."

"Good idea," Blayze laughed. "That woman needs knighting for what she's done for our community. For us."

"Agreed. And hey, I know it's been a lot like work since you flew over the pond, and I'm sorry for that. In all honesty, I don't know how things are gonna play out between us. Who can say if we end up getting together and meeting each other's family? Maybe we'll rent out a rooftop apartment in Spain? Or maybe we fuck one more time, then you're out that door? Unlikely, but still. What I do know is that I'm happy and willing to try, and I'd be honored if you gave me the chance to pick up where we left on that tour of London."

"Interesting," Blayze said, always equipped with a disarming smile at a moment's notice. "I said those things in anger before. It wasn't really work when it was helping you out. I enjoyed spending time with you, and I guess I didn't want to do things apart from you so soon. Also, you know what? After all we've been through, I think we could both do with a vacation. Though, what's say we make a deal to calm down on all the wishing, yeah?"

Dane kissed Blayze on the tip of his nose, wrapped an arm around his torso, and held him tight. "Sure thing, my salty-sweet American Pyro. You've got yourself a deal."

EPILOGUE

IT HAD been four months since Blayze first set foot on English soil, and as long as the visa extension remained up to date, he had no plans to leave. The results of the MRF vote were a staggering 94 percent in favor of integration, and for better or for worse, mages were gradually making themselves known in every corner of the world. When it eventually became public knowledge that they were only the tip of the iceberg and that a whole other subsection of other supernatural entities also walked the Earth, humanity changed very quickly.

To say they were tumultuous times was like saying wishes were easy to reverse. Technological and medical advances began to soar, and people were quick to view each other in a completely different light. There was ample religious discreditation, political upheaval, and even antimage rallies around the world, but the loudest voices rarely represented the majority, and Dane and Blayze were happy to find overwhelming support. There was a place in the world for them after all, and despite a very tangible minefield of concern, mages began to view themselves differently too, and there was a collective exhale of breath that the community had been holding for millennia. In the right circles, mages were celebrated, revered, and even idolized like celebrities. Some people even worshipped some of the grade As like modern-day deities, though such reverence was vehemently dismissed by the wielders. With time, that particular band of extremists would no doubt settle down.

Despite having issued a formal statement and making a handful of televised appearances, the MRF was uncharacteristically quiet. Since their prime directive of keeping mage life a secret was no longer relevant, they would probably be disbanded, or at the very least reformed. Overall, it was exciting to wonder what the world would look like in a few years' time.

Their tenth date marked a turning point, and when Dane and Blayze officially became a couple, they headed to Glastonbury for a celebratory festival. Letting loose and getting back to basics by wrapping themselves in each other's company was nothing short of revolutionary, and on the way back home, they found a suitable spot to plant the seed for the new

Dryad grove. Blayze often wondered whether the existence of Dryads would eventually become known too, but seeing as the doorway would never be revealed to any beings without magical talents, it seemed like unnecessary information to offer up.

Once his abilities became known to the wider world, Dane worried he'd face instant dismissal from his security job, but when the company learned that he could dampen incidents in the blink of an eye, they were quick to triple his pay. When his streaming community learned of his gift, his subscription count grew by the thousands, and he took a great deal of ironic pleasure when three of SciCo's technicians begged to moderate his chat.

Although he was the biggest proponent for change, Blayze was hesitant to formally make the jump. The treatment of Elementals had been getting better over the years, and he was gradually coming to understand that there wasn't a target on his back just because he was a Pyro. But some things were easier said than done. Decades of conditioning was hard to shake, and it was almost too good to believe that everlasting peace could be achieved. A little caution wasn't unwise, and someday soon he'd be able to admit to everyone who he was, but owing to Dane's word-of-mouth promise, he was inundated with Etsy orders. For the time being, he was happy to work through the backlog and keep himself busy. People liked to have pretty things lying around their house to act as a constant while society outside changed with every passing day. Maybe they'd toss them in the trash when they found out who they were made by and how… or maybe some things weren't meant to be controlled, and nature would simply take its course like it had done to get them to where they were in the first place.

The very fabric of civilization was being unraveled and rewoven, and that was no small thing. Yet through it all, between navigating the labyrinth of uncertainty on their doorstep as well as the ups and downs of a freshly budding relationship, Dane and Blayze were content to watch everything unfurl from the comfort of their apartment. They made a point every day to be careful what they wished for, grateful they had CharmD each other by chance, safe in the knowledge that their blessed life together was being carefully watched over by the ever-flourishing moon lily they had so tenderly nurtured.

Keep reading for an excerpt from
Book Three of the CharmD Saga
Soulspawn
by Sebastian Black!

CHAPTER ONE

THE LINE at Lenny's was exceptionally long, and Henry bounced on the balls of his feet as he waited to place his order, eager to press on with the morning. It was Wednesday already, and there was still a ton of work to do before the upcoming presentation at SciCo Enterprises. Program checks, sound synch, renewing asset licenses, hiring a mage beta tester. Balls. Had it really slipped his mind to find one of those? He had to make that a priority. Though he didn't plan for them to be his proprietary market, gamers could be ruthless sons of bitches, especially when they're horned up and looking for love. Too often a buggy or poorly executed title would be dropped like a sack of shit. If that was Henry's fate, all the blood, sweat, and tears would've been for nothing.

No. That wasn't going to happen. Everything had to be flawless.

Henry stepped forward a few feet in the queue and pinched his nose. He'd been working on overdrive to get everything done, so it wasn't the first time he wished he had an extra set of hands. Unfortunately, that was one of the drawbacks of working in a small team. Evelyn was a dab hand at coding, and Kell gave great results in the sound department from his remote office in Singapore. It would probably disrupt momentum if they were to employ anyone else, and their wallet would take a sizeable hit… but the finish line seemed to be getting farther with each passing day, and Henry had morphed into a zombie running on autopilot. Just that morning he almost slipped getting out of the shower, and he could've sworn his cleaning robot actually laughed at him. Damned AI was growing more lifelike by the day.

Once his brainchild was out into the world, Henry planned to book a vacation somewhere exotic yet cool, spacious yet private—save maybe for a handful of burly leather daddies. That was a reward worth working for.

"Next customer, please," came the dulcet trill of the automated merchant.

As he stepped up to the booth, Henry's likeness was captured on the camera above the vendor. He scanned his wristwatch, registered the beginning part of the transaction, and spent a moment fixing his hair while the projection kicked in.

What kind of a day would it be? Sweet or savory? Both? Whatever the case, he'd better not forget to buy something for Evelyn again, or she might follow through with her promise to glitter-bomb his filing cabinet.

"Two cappuccinos," Henry told the ever-joyful mascot, Lenny the Lemur. "One chocolate croissant, uhh, a plain croissant, and two cheese twists."

Keeping the disconcerting smile on its face, the disconcerting Madagascan Lemur blinked in and out of existence as it processed his order. "I am sorry, did you say *strawberry croissant*?"

Henry blinked slowly and cringed at the way the modular voice tried to imitate his tone. "No. One chocolate, one plain."

"I am sorry, did you say *almond croissant*?"

"No, I did not." Henry breathed through his teeth, starting to get impatient. Whether the bot didn't understand his faintly foreign twang or because it was a rusty old piece of garbage was beside the point. Everyone around him was managing to get their orders in just fine. "For the love of all that's holy. Listen to me, Lenny, I'm not speaking Cantonese or anything here."

Before the words had barely left his lips, he realized the facepalm of a mistake.

"Xuǎnzé yuèyǔ. Huānyíng lái dào Lenny's," the automated voice said in perfect Cantonese. "Jīntiān wǒmen néng wéi nín tígōng shénme fúwù?"

Henry rolled his eyes to the ceiling. This was one of the few downsides to advanced speech recognition—the wrong word here or there and you suddenly found yourself being spoken to in five different languages you never had the chance to learn.

"Speak to me in English," he stated, careful to enunciate every syllable before the automated server could continue further.

"English has been selected," began the annoyingly adorable Holo-Lemur. "Welcome to Len—"

"—two coffees and two cheese twists," Henry cut in. "And I would very much like one *plain* croissant and one *chocolate* croissant. Got it?"

"I am sorry," Lenny said, holding out an index finger, pausing for dramatic effect. "It appears we are all out of croissants."

Henry was at a loss and huffed a deep sigh. The jarring mishap had only served to waste both of their time, and his stomach had gone from a gentle purr to a steady growl. When he saw the guy next to him pull two steaming golden croissants from the pass, Henry saw red.

"Argh, fuck it!" Henry shouted and promptly threw a punch at the lemur's face. Being a hologram, the punch of course simply went straight through, and the only thing his fist connected with was an artisanal brick wall. And it hurt. Bad.

"Ow," he said, snatching back a throbbing hand. The pain was blinding, and in a rare sense of real-world stimulation, a bunch of other customers within earshot had taken their gaze away from their cells to gawk at him.

When a guy in uniform came through a side door, Henry felt his cheeks flush with shame. Especially when that person turned out to be the cute guy with the leaf-green eyes and outrageously chiseled jawline who he'd spotted a few times here and there over the last few months.

"Everything okay, sir?" the guy asked, a slight smile curving his lips when he read the situation.

His name tag read Elijah, and his jet-black beard and moustache were as expertly trimmed as ever. Today the medusa ball resting in his cupid's bow was a pleasing rose gold shade, and despite not being too clued up with the piercings or tattoo world, Henry had always thought it was a pretty striking detail that played with the boundaries of his archetypal twinkish profile.

"All good," Henry lied, nursing his hand.

"Here," said Elijah, holding out his palm. "Lemme help with that."

Confused, Henry watched as Elijah cast a furtive glance around the café, wanting for some reason to make sure everybody's heads were back in their cells before he clasped his hand over Henry's.

"Hey there," Henry said, trying to pull back against a surprisingly firm grip. He was a moment away from causing another scene, but then he felt a pleasant warmth running through the skin of his hand, his bones started to creak, and all of his knuckles gave a satisfying *crack*, and before he knew it, the pain was gone.

"Oh," Henry said when he pulled back his hand, inspected it, and realized what had just happened. Most healer mages worked in the medical sector, not coffee houses. Still, he was mighty grateful, and for some reason, it elevated "cute guy's" status to "really helpful hot guy."

"Well, thanks for that. Real kind of you."

"Don't mention it," Elijah said, seeming to put emphasis on really meaning it. "Though please don't smash up any of the computers in the future, all right? They might be old, but they're still expensive."

Nodding in a half daze, Henry watched as the mage went back through the side door and left him with the selectively hearing lemur.

"Just... give me two coffees," Henry surrendered. "Surprise me with the rest."

"Okay," Lenny the Lemur chirped. Then he disappeared and got to work. In thirty seconds flat, Henry's food was ready to collect in the tray below, and because it was a lot more than what he usually ordered, it came prepackaged in a brown paper bag. "Have a productive day!"

"Sure," Henry said absently. He held his wrist up to the scanner, and as soon as he heard the credit deduction beep, he grabbed his coffees and pastries and hustled out of the café, trying hard to get his brain back on track.

While it was barely midmorning, the heat outside was already sweltering. Paris had once been famous for magnificent architecture, vivacious culture-driven communities, and first-class gastronomy. Regardless of how many of those things remained true, priorities had shifted in recent years, and these days it was little more than an overcrowded sweatfest, largely aided by the fact they were now the current world leaders in genetic engineering, which inherently made them the go-to place for biohacking.

Mercifully, because Henry didn't often care to venture outside of his work bubble, everything was in walking distance, and he never had to endure the travesty that had once been public shuttles. But it left him at the mercy of walking on the street, and because he was busy ruminating about the fact the guy that he'd had his eye on these last few months was a fully fledged mage—maybe even grade A—he almost spilled coffee on other pedestrians on three separate occasions. In fairness, it was mostly their fault, seeing as they had their eyes glued to holo goggles or had android companions in tow.

When he finally got inside the shelter of commercial block 174B, the short and solitary elevator ride up to the office was very welcome, and the aircon that greeted him on the sixth floor was nothing short of divine intervention.

When he paced over to his team's quadrant, Evelyn jumped up from her desk, practically salivating.

"Took your time," she said, glowering at him through mandarin-colored contacts. She liked to alternate them, depending on whatever matched the latest shade of her coiffed mohawk, and this week it was a pleasing tangerine. "Whatcha got in the bag? I'm freakin' starved."

Henry rolled his eyes, passed her over a coffee, and put the goods on the desk. "Lucky dip today, I'm afraid. Had a fist fight with Lenny."

"Another one?" Evelyn said, shaking her head. "I don't get you sometimes. If Lenny's janky bot servers keep glitching, why do you keep giving them your money? There's a storefront every two paces itching for trade. Why not step out of the box sometimes?"

Henry shrugged. "Their coffee is ass, but they have good pastries. And there's a cute guy who works there who, *by the way*, just happened to magically heal my hand after I injured it."

"Are you serious?" Evelyn's eyes bulged. "What's a healer mage doing in a coffee shop, of all places?"

"I know, right? I thought the same thing. Maybe he's doing some feel-good community service to 'give back' after spending a terribly long year filming his autobiography."

Evelyn chuckled. "Yeah, maybe."

"Also," Henry said, still vexed. "I don't wanna be that guy again, but would it kill people to look where they're going? Unless I missed the memo, I don't think the government plans to widen the sidewalks anytime soon. How is humanity supposed to thrive when they insist on dragging along their ever-loyal mech pets? It's creepy and weird."

"Tchh," she dismissed as she rooted through the bag and made an assortment of faces at its contents. After her eyebrows shot up, she snatched out a sugared jelly donut and practically crammed it down her throat. "You're only saying that because you don't have one. People get lonely sometimes. Mm-hmm, that *is* good. Merci beaucoup. And anyways, it's been like this for how many years now? I don't know why you're still surprised."

"Like… I know Parisians aren't typically famous for their charm, and yet why does it feel like everyone I run into has some kind of stick up their ass?"

"I can think of a few things. First, the housing crisis, likely owing to the insane rise in population, which wasn't helped by the tidal wave of immigration during all the civil wars. Not that I've got my tinfoil hat on or anything, but it can't be coincidence that a string of those happened soon after a bunch of mages came out with supernatural abilities. Also, it turns out the ice caps aren't just melting, they're being metaphorically blowtorched, oh, and the cherry on the cake is a global record level of inflation. Shall I continue?"

"Nah, you're good." Henry sat down at his desk. "You know what I love about you, Ev? You always manage to put such a cheerful spin on things."

She sneered and settled back down to her infrared keyboard with a cheese twist lodged between her teeth. Even if she had become something of a cynic lately, she was hands-down the best coder in the province, and Henry couldn't think of anyone he'd rather have at his side for the final push.

"Well, let's get to it, shall we?" he said as he logged into the SENSr mainframe. "We've got a long day ahead of us."

"FUCKNUGGETS." HENRY gulped the last of his lunchtime bourbon, then pinched his nose to alleviate the oncoming headache. "That's the fourth one to turn us down today. Is every mage on the planet so highly strung? We've gotta get something sorted ASAP."

"Agreed." Evelyn threw down her fork and motioned at her screen to juggle another set of profiles on the public mage registry. The number of faces didn't look good. "Half of this bunch are guaranteed to be busy, seeing as they're so high profile. See this guy here? The one with the pompous-looking eighties side part? He's a grade B Shifter—he'll be making more money in Vegas than what we could ever offer him."

Henry deliberated pouring another drink, then decided against it when he almost knocked over the bottle. As the director of SENSr, he had always believed in fair pay for fair work, and even if he was a clear station above Evelyn, he was glad she never sniped at him about occasionally drinking on the job. Everyone on the project was growing more and more stressed the closer the deadline came, and despite doing a grand job when her head was in the game, she'd been known to have a glass of wine or two to prevent herself becoming a mindless coding machine.

"Money shouldn't be an object." He frowned. "Not if we actually want to take the world by storm. I've told finance at SciCo a thousand times that they need to quit being so stingy. I'm the one who's invested five hundred thousand euros—which, by the way, is pretty much every penny I've ever owned. What's another loan when we're all gonna be sharing millions?"

"But money *is* an object, dude. Though it's a generous one, our budget is tight. We've already sunk every extra penny we got from SciCo into extensive R & D, coding, hardware, and basic marketing. This last step should be the easiest, and I'm half tempted to say screw it, let's skip it. Though if we do, I'm certain something will come back to bite us on the ass. It's hella frustrating that we're getting cockblocked by a bunch of people who were forced into stardom simply because they were lucky enough to wield spells. Seriously, what are we going to do if we can't find anyone?"

"We'll find someone," Henry insisted. "We have to. Maybe we could put up another ad in the beta forums?"

"Are you kidding?" Evelyn asked. "Don't you remember what happened last time? Oh, that's right, I was the one who dealt with all the cleanup from about five hundred fraudulent call-ins from people foaming at the mouth for any kind of work. If you wanna kill time sifting through all that bullshit, be my guest."

"Mm-hmm," Henry said. He did recall how much of a pain in the ass it was to purge and block so many contacts from their system. And each time he did so, he was effectively reducing future sales before the product even went live. "Well, I guess we gotta keep at this and hope we stumble across a mage who doesn't live every day basking in the limelight."

"Yeah, good luck with that," Evelyn huffed and retreated back to her pasta salad.

With a flick of his wrist, Henry enlarged the next profile. The power to amp people's emotions wouldn't be much good, even if the remarkably redheaded Brit was sexy enough that they could simply slap his image on the poster and watch the sales roll in. Next was a tight-lipped Telepath from Mexico, but it would be years before they could think about implementing the sort of tech to properly utilize such a Gift, so in the trash she went.

"What about this one?" Evelyn pointed toward the bottom of the screen, where the face of a handsome olive-skinned man was highlighted by a background of orange flames.

"A Pyro?" Henry scoffed. "Last thing we need is someone burning the building down. Ah, what about him?" The last profile among the list was a timid-looking guy with leaf-green eyes and chestnut curls, but judging by his set of credentials, there wasn't a hugely positive outlook. "He's got, what's this? Biomancy? Never heard of that. Probably about as useless as the rest."

A snort at his side suggested his ignorance was amusing. "It relates to biology," said Evelyn. "Means he can alter the state of plant life, heal flesh wounds, and if I'm remembering correctly, it also includes the ability to age and de-age himself, as well as others. Depends on the grade."

"Modifying plant life? Whoa, that's pretty cool. Would give us some really valuable and actionable data for sure. Why didn't we know about this before? He's damn fine too. You know I appreciate some eye candy in the workplace. Uhh, wait a second...."

As he peered closer at the screen, it took Henry far too long to understand why the name Elijah rang a faraway bell, why his face was starting to look more familiar by the second, and why his heart had started to drum an erratic beat in his chest.

It was the healer mage from the café. There was no doubt about it. He even had the same distinctive medusa piercing, though in the tidy little headshot it was a striking shade of lemon yellow.

"Whoa, Evelyn," Henry said. "This is the guy who healed my hand earlier. Why didn't I recognize him sooner? I think my brain is finally melting. Ergh, who cares? It looks like we might have found our mage after all. Let's make him an offer he can't refuse."

As soon as he discovered the romance genre, SEBASTIAN BLACK was hooked. From Rowling to Tolkien, from E. L. James to Stephanie Meyer, meaningful bonds can be found in the most unlikely genres. Though Sci-Fi and Fantasy are Black's top picks, they can't be without romance. Daring heroes and compelling heroines are what make fiction come alive, and when he began his writing career, "balls to the walls" quickly became his mantra. All writing should be tackled fearlessly. You can create a gourmet meal from the measliest of ingredients and seasonings, but you can't do much with a blank page!

Oathsworn

Can love set a
mage free?

Sebastian Black

CharmD
Saga

Book One of the CharmD Saga

Former chef Jasper Wight has been magically ensnared in his apartment for over three months. Cabin fever doesn't begin to cover it. All he can do to pass the time is indulge in his hobby—painting portraits of his neighbors. But once a handsome new man moves into a swanky nearby penthouse, Jasper is no longer content merely to watch. Following his gut, he reaches out through astral projection….

Finn Anderson is the CEO of a food app funded by his parents, but he struggles to believe in the dream. When a mysterious someone starts leaving messages on his mirror, he learns the world holds more possibilities than he ever imagined.

When a chance encounter brings Finn to Jasper's door, the pair are soon as enamored with each other as Finn is of the magic he's just discovering. But navigating a relationship that spans two worlds is only the tip of the iceberg. They still have to figure out how to free Jasper from his apartment, how to make Finn's business into a success, and whether an outsider can be trusted with the secrets of the magical world.

www.dreamspinnerpress.com

Soulspawn

He was supposed to test the
dating simulator—not get
stuck in it....

Sebastian Black

CharmD
Saga

Book Three of the CharmD Saga

It's 2043, and software engineer Henry Bell is on the verge of a breakthrough. His virtual-reality dating simulator, Unity, is finally ready for beta testing. All he needs now is the right mage for the job.

Biomancer Elijah Johnstone is broke, his air conditioner has just given up the ghost, and it's too hot to sleep. When Henry makes him a cash offer to try out his magic in Unity's 3D landscape, he jumps at the chance, tries a simple spell… and ends up stuck in the computer simulation.

Trapped in a world of Henry's design, Elijah must rely on Henry not only for human interaction, but for his lifeline to reality. They're not supposed to be on a real date, but they need to free Elijah and save the program Henry has bet his future on. The thing is, once they perfect the program and pull Elijah out, Henry won't need him anymore. After all, how can a love forged in a virtual world possibly be real?

www.dreamspinnerpress.com